The Rules of Dreaming

For Paula —
With love —
Brian

Also by Bruce Hartman:

Perfectly Healthy Man Drops Dead

The Rules of Dreaming

a tale by

Bruce Hartman

Swallow Tail Press

Published by Swallow Tail Press,

Philadelphia, PA, USA

swallowtailpress.com

ISBN-13: 978-0-9889181-0-8

ISBN-10: 0988918102

Cover design by Kit Foster

Translation from *Die Elixiere des Teufels* by the author.

"... it came to me that what we call dream and hallucination might be the symbolic perception of the hidden thread that runs through our life and binds it together in all its domains, and nevertheless that the man who with that perception believes he has gained the power to break the thread and take it in along with the dark power that rules over us, must be regarded as lost."

E.T.A. Hoffmann, *The Devil's Elixirs* (1815)

Setting and Time

EGDON, NEW YORK, 1999. A rural town about two hours northwest of New York City. Home of the Palmer Institute, a prestigious private psychiatric hospital.

Characters

HUNTER MORGAN — A 21-year-old schizophrenic who has resided at the Palmer Institute for the past seven years.

ANTONIA MORGAN — Hunter's twin sister, also schizophrenic and a resident of the Institute.

MARIA MORGAN — The twins' mother, an opera singer who hanged herself seven years earlier.

AVERY MORGAN — The twins' father, a wealthy local landowner and manuscript collector.

SUSAN MORGAN — Avery Morgan's young second wife.

DR. NED HOFFMANN —The twins' physician at the Institute, recently graduated from his psychiatric residency.

NICOLE P. — A 28-year-old graduate student in literature who recently experienced a psychotic episode and was admitted to the Institute, where she is a patient of Dr. Hoffmann's.

DR. MILES PALMER —A world-famous psychiatrist, the founder and Director of the Palmer Institute.

DR. PETER BARTOLLI — Dr. Palmer's half-brother, also a psychiatrist. Formerly at the Institute, now in private practice.

OLYMPIA — Dr. Bartolli's daughter. A dancer and performance therapy artist.

MISS FRANCINE WHIPPLE —Librarian at the small local public library. DUBIN — A blackmailer.

MRS. PATERSON — A nurse at the Institute, formerly employed by the Morgan family.

DR. JEFFREY GOTTLIEB — Staff psychiatrist and Associate Director at the Institute.

JULIETTA —Receptionist at the Institute.

FRANK LYNCH — Former local police chief, now retired.

DR. KLEIN — Chief of Psychiatry at a small community hospital about fifty miles north of Egdon.

I. Olympia

All right, Dr. Klein, you can turn that thing on now. I'm ready to tell my story. But first you have to understand, I'm not who you think I am.

Okay. We're listening.

Late last summer, after less than two months at the Palmer Institute, I witnessed an extraordinary performance. One of my patients, Hunter Morgan (that was not his real name), sat down at the piano in the patient lounge and started playing like a virtuoso. Hunter was a twenty-one year old schizophrenic who had lived in the Institute for the past seven years, and as far as anyone could remember he'd never touched the piano before. The piece he played was classical music—that was about all I could tell—and it sounded fiendishly difficult, a whirlwind of chords and notes strung together in a jarring rhythm that seemed the perfect analog of a mind spinning out of control. He continued playing for about ten minutes and then suddenly stopped in the middle of an intense climactic passage. Without acknowledging his audience—which consisted of his sister Antonia, his nurse Mrs. Paterson, a few other patients and myself—he stood up from the piano and ran out of the room.

Since I was new at the Institute, the impact of this performance was lost on me at first. I assumed that Hunter had been studying the piano from an early age. The nurse, Mrs. Paterson, gave no sign that what she had just witnessed was the least bit unusual, and as for Antonia, Hunter's twin sister—she was also a victim of schizophrenia and I knew better than to expect a reaction from her. It wasn't until later that afternoon, when I reviewed Hunter's chart and questioned Mrs. Paterson specifically about the piano playing, that I realized how uncanny this incident really was.

"You mean he's never played the piano before?" We were standing by the nurse's station on the second floor, where Mrs. Paterson prepared the twins' afternoon medications.

"Not that I know of," she said, looking away.

"You were with the family before the twins came to live here, weren't you?"

"Yes I was."

"Didn't he play the piano then?"

"Not that I know of." Mrs. Paterson was a wiry black woman of about sixty, with flat dark eyes that never gave away a secret. She picked up her tray and started toward Antonia's room. "It's time for Antonia's asthma medication."

I followed her down the hall and cornered her in front of Antonia's door. "Their mother was an opera singer, wasn't she? She must have taught Hunter to play the piano."

Mrs. Paterson's forehead was glowing with sweat. "Dr. Hoffmann," she said, lowering her   voice. "I've been with the twins since they were two years old. Neither of them ever had any piano lessons."

"But their mother—"

"She used to sing with them and that's all."

"But then after they came in here Hunter must have had lessons."

"If so, it must have been in the middle of the night. Now let me do my work. I don't have time to talk about this any more."

Hunter Morgan and his twin sister Antonia had been admitted to the Institute seven years earlier, at the age of fourteen, a week after their mother hanged herself on a light fixture in her rehearsal studio. Neither had ever ventured anywhere close to reality again. They were the only children of Maria Morgan, the opera singer, and Avery Phelps Morgan, scion of a wealthy local family who now had three younger children with his second wife Susan. This had been explained to me by Dr. Miles Palmer, the Institute's Director, who supervised the twins' care and treatment for seven years without any real success. Hunter suffered from auditory hallucinations, disorganized speech and constantly shifting multiple personalities. Antonia's illness was almost a mirror image of her brother's. While Hunter talked—which was almost constantly— Antonia was silent. When Hunter unleashed an outburst of incoherent, violent imagery, Antonia was all sweetness and light. And when the rest of us had given up trying to decipher his meaningless sound and fury, Antonia would be hanging on every word as if she alone could make sense of it.

I was fascinated by them. Even though it was my first real job, I was determined to accomplish what Dr. Palmer and the others who practiced at the Institute had been unable to do: to break through the wall of schizophrenia and connect with Hunter and Antonia, to bring their world back into ours. It was a presumptuous goal for an otherwise modest thirty-year-old—my name is Ned Hoffmann, by the way—who had just finished his psychiatric residency. My background and upbringing were conventional: born and raised in the suburbs of New York, father in the construction business, mother always wanted me to be a doctor; and no one who knew me could understand why I'd chosen psychiatry when I could have been a cardiologist or even a urologist like my Uncle Art. I was at a loss to explain it, except to say that as soon as I began my residency at the state hospital I knew I'd made the right choice. Like any doctor, I cared passionately about people and wanted to help them. I certainly have my faults—more than I realized, as will become apparent—

but cynicism is not among them. If anything I'd say I'm a little naive, particularly about myself, a little too shy and introspective to put my good intentions into effect. At the state hospital I soon realized that most of my patients were beyond help. The most I could hope for was to understand them. But wasn't that enough? To walk with the patients through the dark side, seeing their world as they saw it, feeling it as they felt it—wasn't that the most valuable gift anyone could give them? And at the famous Palmer Institute, with its small patient population and superior resources, I could go even farther, maybe even leading a few of them back towards the light.

It was a dangerous path—far more dangerous than I imagined—and I must have been incredibly naive not to be aware of its dangers. But naive and presumptuous as I was, after two months at the Institute I felt that I could do something for the Morgan twins that no one else had been able to do. Personally I was lonely, living by myself in the Institute's residential wing, even a little depressed. The only woman I ever talked to, other than mental patients and aging nurses, was a twenty-four-year-old tart named Julietta who sat at the receptionist's desk filing her nails when she wasn't sneaking off to one of the empty bedrooms with one of the physicians. I sympathized with the patients, possibly a little more than I should have. In any event I set my goal at rescuing the twins from the parallel universe of schizophrenia where they had been doomed to spend their lives. And so that afternoon when Hunter Morgan sat down at the piano and gave his astonishing performance, I knew I wouldn't rest until I understood where that music had come from.

Since Dr. Palmer was in San Francisco for a professional meeting, the only colleague I could talk to about Hunter's piano playing was Dr. Jeffrey Gottlieb, the Associate Director. Approaching him was never an appealing prospect. He was an ungainly little wretch who never seemed to do anything right and usually found someone else to blame for his misfortunes. If you asked him a question, he would squint at you from beneath his beetle brows and tilt his balding head ever so slightly in case his words and tone of voice failed to convey the right level of disdain. As a psychiatrist he was a cynical subscriber to the dope-'em-up school. But he was the Associate Director and I was the new kid on the block, and in Dr. Palmer's absence I felt I had to tell someone about Hunter's extraordinary behavior. Predictably, Gottlieb was not impressed and his advice was more medication.

"If he's acting out like that, you've got to titrate his dosages upwards. Whatever he's taking, give him more of it."

"But he's already taking about twice the recommended dosages."

"What's the alternative, Hoffmann? Piano lessons? This is medicine we're practicing, not occupational therapy. Raise his dosages."

I hesitated, and Gottlieb treated me to one of his dreaded let-me-give-you-some-friendly-advice looks. He stepped closer and probably would have put one of his paws on my shoulder if he'd been able to reach that high. "At this Institute," he said, "we follow the physiological model of illness and treatment. We don't believe in Freud, Jung, aroma therapy, spiritualism or any other form of quackery."

"I know that."

"It hasn't always been that way. When this place was founded, psychiatry was still in the Middle Ages and Miles's brother did everything he could to keep it there."

"I know all about Miles's brother," I said.

"Peter Bartolli. They're half brothers, actually."

"I've heard all this before." In fact Gottlieb was the one I'd heard it from, three or four times. I started to walk away.

"Bartolli's a complete quack," Gottlieb continued, following me down the hall, "and he'd like nothing better than to wheedle his way back in here."

The nurse, Mrs. Paterson, called me from the end of the hall. "Dr. Hoffmann?"

"I have to see one of my patients," I said, trying to escape.

Gottlieb grabbed my elbow. "Just a word of advice: you don't want to be labeled a heretic—"

"A heretic?"

"And you don't want to be perceived as neutral in the rivalry between Miles and his brother. This is Cain versus Abel and there's no upside being in the middle of it. Raise the dosages."

"Thanks, Jeff," I said, hurrying away. "Thanks for the advice." I was offended by Gottlieb's portrayal of Dr. Palmer, and although I wouldn't have admitted it, I didn't share Gottlieb's disdain for Freud and Jung and some of the other innovators he dismissed as quacks. Wasn't it possible that Hunter's piano playing represented the first step in a therapeutic encounter with the unconscious? Wasn't that something we ought to encourage rather than artificially suppress?

Imagining that I knew all the answers, I shook off Gottlieb like an annoying insect and paid no attention to his advice. Instead, as if going out of my way to defy him, I decided to lower the dosages of Hunter's medications.

At that time there was another patient, Nicole P., who had been requiring most of my attention. Nicole was twenty-eight years old and a graduate student in literature at a prestigious university in New York City. She had checked in to the Institute two weeks earlier with symptoms of anxiety and disorientation. Her natural cheerfulness, she told me, had been overtaken by a sense of impending doom and the fear that she was on the brink of going crazy. Still her green eyes sparkled with humor and intelligence. She spoke English with a lilting accent she said was Irish, though she was quick to add that she'd been educated in England, where she took a first in modern languages at Oxford. Recently she'd gone through a painful breakup with a boyfriend named Richard who had abused her and then begged her not to leave him, but most of her anxiety seemed to stem from her inability to find a topic for her dissertation.

Nicole was nimble and petite and very pretty. No, I take that back—"pretty" doesn't come close to doing her justice. She was one of the most beautiful women I had ever seen, with cascading red hair and a bold, astonished look in her eyes that made her seem at once wild and angelic. But since my profession has liberated society from all of its taboos save one—that a psychiatrist shall not fall in love with his patient—all I could do was listen sympathetically as she pulled herself back together and prepared to return to her studies. I put her on appropriate medications and she began to make progress immediately.

As it happened, Nicole had been in the lounge when Hunter sat down to play the piano. Later that same afternoon I met with her for the last therapy session before her discharge, which was scheduled to occur in a couple of days. She and I had spent a good deal of time together, talking of subjects that people usually reserve for their closest relationships. We were both young and unattached, lonely and frustrated with the challenges of making our way in the world. I wanted her to find me as fascinating as I found her, but of course that was impossible. My job was to expose her deepest secrets while acknowledging none of my own, to elucidate the rules of her troubled dreams while concealing those inner demons that were just beginning to make their presence known in my life.

When she sat down in front of my desk that morning, she looked as beautiful and vulnerable as ever. And she had the same anxious spark in her eyes that I had seen the night she was admitted. "Nicole," I said after a few preliminaries, "you've done very well here. Do you feel that you're ready to go back to the University?"

"Of course," she smiled. "Everyone's mad in my department. They'll scarcely notice."

I smiled back, glad to see that she was able to defuse her anxiety with humor. "I'm glad it's been a positive experience for you."

"It gave me some space, some time to think. And the people here have been wonderful."

"Our staff does a great job."

"I was thinking of the other patients, actually."

"The patients?"

"You know I'm quite fond of Hunter and Antonia."

"Of course," I nodded. "Hunter and Antonia." I shouldn't have been surprised, but I was. Nicole had spent most of her time during the past two weeks with the twins. I had assumed that she was humoring them.

"I mean," she went on, animated by the warmth of her feelings toward the twins, "obviously they're both very special and have their own unique ways of dealing with the world, but there's something that shines through, isn't there?"

"Yes, there certainly is."

"Hunter talks to me all the time and I feel that the two of us have become quite close, even though"—she made a face—"well, you know..."

It was easy to finish her thought. "Even though you can't understand a word he says."

"The words I can understand. But it's as if there's been a completely different meaning assigned to each one."

I stood up to adjust the window shade. The windows in my office reach to the ceiling and on a late summer afternoon the sunlight can be blinding. Nicole receded into darkness as I lowered the shade, and a thin blade of sunlight slashed across the dust and seemed to cut her in half at the waist. "It's possible," I said, "that there's a chronic chemical imbalance in the part of his brain that processes language. So far we haven't figured out a way to fix it."

"You make him sound like a malfunctioning robot."

"No, a malfunctioning human."

"But this isn't a malfunction. It's something he's doing on purpose."

"On purpose? What do you mean?"

She leaned forward, and the blade of sunlight swung upwards to cut across her throat. "Where I grew up in the west of Ireland—about as far away from Dublin as you can go without getting in a boat—English is still thought of as the devil's tongue. There are people in my family who deliberately use the wrong English word just to throw the Devil off their track."

"You think Hunter's doing something like that?"

"I don't know. Sometimes he looks at me with a fear in his eyes that seems to come from somewhere beyond the merely human. Couldn't he be trying to keep the Devil off his track?"

I knew I had to tread carefully. Listening to patients, there often comes a time when you realize that metaphorical language is being used literally. "Do you believe in the Devil?" I asked.

A sudden breeze jostled the window shade and the blade of sunlight flashed across her face. She didn't flinch or blink but gazed back at me with a solemnity that took me completely by surprise. "Something like that," she said. "Only human."

We sat in silence for what seemed like several minutes while I tried to make sense of what she had said. And then the clock chimed the hour, signaling that our session was over. She shook my hand and thanked me warmly for everything I had done for her, and then she hurried toward the door, saying that she'd look forward to seeing me again the next week at our scheduled follow up visit.

"Nicole," I said, "did you hear Hunter playing the piano this afternoon?"

"Yes I did." She stopped in the doorway, framed in the shadows that darkened the adjoining hall. "It was impressive, wasn't it?"

"Impressive isn't the word, when you realize that he's never had a lesson or even touched a piano before."

Her smile faded. "That's uncanny."

"Do you know much about music?"

"I learned to play the piano at school. The teacher was a nun who used to rap my knuckles every time I made a mistake."

"Do you know what piece of music he was playing?"

"I think I've heard it before. One of the German Romantics, I think, maybe Schumann."

She started through the door, but just before she disappeared into the shadows she turned back around and her eyes caught a sparkle of the afternoon light. "He went mad, you know."

"Who went mad?"

"Robert Schumann.   The composer.   Died in an insane asylum."

2

"A detective without a client," Susan Morgan said. "Isn't there a word for that?"

Dubin stood facing her in the shade beside the stone barn as she struggled to keep her golden retriever from knocking him down. He was a slender man with quick dark eyes and a delicate moustache. Most women found him irresistible, but Susan Morgan—she was much younger than he'd expected, a tawny blonde with freckled cheeks and a wide, skeptical smile—glared back at him with amused contempt. Dubin never argued with people who thought they were more important than he was. He was thirty-nine years old and his goal was to retire at forty. In the meantime he wanted people to know that he was a fair man, a man who could be trusted. And he wanted them to know that he was very good at what he did.

The Morgans lived in a classic country mansion surrounded by cypresses and boxwood hedges, with a long tree-lined driveway and a handsome stone barn standing to one side. Dubin had parked on the gravel next to the barn and followed a shady path back to the house along a row of hosta in late-summer bloom. From somewhere in back came the sound of children and barking dogs. He wondered who would answer the door. A butler or a maid? Not likely. Even rich people don't have servants anymore. They have children, and the children have servants—in this case a pretty Scandinavian au pair with a pierced nose who opened the door clutching a squirming toddler under her arm. She greeted him with a smile and led him into a small room off the foyer that looked like a miniature museum. The walls were hung with original documents signed by the likes of Millard Fillmore and William Howard Taft. Not that Avery Morgan couldn't afford Washington and Lincoln—but to display them might have attracted too much attention from the wrong kind of people. People like Dubin, in fact. They might try to take advantage of you.

Avery Morgan was well over six feet tall but he had a high chirping voice that seemed out of place in a man his size. His hair was gray and the whites of his eyes were the color of a bloody mary. "Sorry to keep you waiting," he said as they shook hands. "Is something the matter? Please sit down."

Dubin lowered himself into an uncomfortable chair. "This will come as a shock," he said, "but I think your wife may have been murdered."

"Susan? She's in the garden."

"No, I'm sorry. Your first wife. The opera singer."

Morgan frowned and lowered his voice. "My first wife committed suicide. She had been very depressed."

"Was there a note?"

He squinted at Dubin suspiciously. "Didn't you say you were from the police?"

"No."

"But you said you were a detective."

"That's right. I am a detective."

Morgan shifted in his chair as he tried to grasp where the meeting was taking him. "Mr. Dubin"—he chose his words carefully—"I don't know who you are or exactly why you're here, but if you have some information I'd like to hear it. Have you found evidence that Maria was murdered?"

"Let's just say I have more than a hunch."

"When a terrible thing like that happens," Morgan said, his eyes darting toward the door, "you want to know the truth, of course. But you can't keep stirring up the past in hopes of finding an explanation for something that probably doesn't have an explanation in the first place."

"I understand."

"Unless some specific information comes to light. Do you have something specific?"

"Not right now," Dubin said. "But I'm looking."

"Good. Let me know if you find anything."

A little girl ran into the room and climbed on Morgan's lap. He set her down gently and rose to his feet. "I'm going to have to ask you to excuse me."

Morgan had three children with his second wife. Dubin had caught a glimpse of the two from his first marriage the evening before, watching a strange dance performance on the lawn behind the Palmer Institute. The twins Hunter and Antonia—how old were they now? Twenty? Twenty-one? They sat with the other patients in sedated rows on a terrace beneath the Institute's looming silhouette while Dubin watched through the fence at the edge of the woods. There was something dark, almost subterranean about the Institute, as if its steeply gabled roof and its Victorian turrets had just emerged from underground, tangled in a net of vines.

Dubin rolled the scene over in his mind as he navigated through Morgan's musty hedges back to his car. The smell of boxwood—that was one of the drawbacks of his line of work. What money smells like when it's been in the same place too long.

A suntanned woman in a jogging suit flounced out from behind a huge cypress and stood in his path. "I heard you talking to my husband," she said with a proprietary smile. "I'm Susan Morgan."

"My name's Dubin," he said.

"Do you have a first name?"

"Not really."

"Are you from the police?"

"No. I try to avoid the police."

She paused to pet an enormous golden retriever who had lumbered up beside her like the village idiot. Panting and drooling, the dog tried to climb into her lap even though she was standing. Then the dog noticed Dubin and lurched toward him, but she caught it by the collar and pulled it back.

"Who are you, then?" she asked.

"I'm a detective."

"A private detective? Who's your client?"

"I don't have one yet."

She stared at him for a moment and then broke into a low, conspiratorial laugh. "A detective without a client. Isn't there a word for that?"

Dubin tried his most winning smile. "Unemployed?"

"No," she said, returning his smile. "I think it's called a blackmailer."

Today the only people who spend their lives in places like the Palmer Institute are the criminally insane and the very rich. I didn't need to be told that the Morgan twins fell into the latter category. Their father, Avery Phelps Morgan, whose money goes back at least as far as the Big Bang, had put them there to please his young second wife Susan, who objected to their presence at home. Frankly the Institute's almost medieval atmosphere—with its masonry walls, its mazelike corridors and its lack of natural light— was less conducive to good mental hygiene than to a lifetime of seclusion. To his credit, Avery Morgan visited often, spending more each year on his children's care and treatment than more fortunate parents spend on summer camps and Ivy League educations. The day after Hunter's amazing piano performance, Avery Morgan arrived just before noon and spent a few minutes conferring with Jeff Gottlieb, who was officiating in Dr. Palmer's absence. Then he stepped into the cavernous patient lounge where I sat with Antonia and the nurse, Mrs. Paterson, while Hunter, wearing headphones, watched Kenneth Branagh's film version of *Hamlet* for the three or four hundredth time. The lounge—which contained the piano, a TV and video player, a stereo system and other electronic gear—served also as the patient library, with floor to ceiling shelves housing a vast collection of books and videos that Hunter spent most of his time devouring in the dim light. This is not something I would have recommended. It fed Hunter's tendency to try on fictional personalities instead of finding his own—one day he'd be the Terminator, the next day Cool Hand Luke. On that particular day he was Hamlet, the melancholy Prince of Denmark, and like Hamlet he was not overjoyed to see his father.

"Good morning!" chirped Avery Morgan. He was a tall but uninspiring man of about fifty who always tried to sound cheerful, though he usually succeeded only in being condescending. He wore a pair of gabardine slacks, an expensive golf shirt and the kind of deep tan that only a rich man can afford. He took a seat on one of the wicker chairs across from Hunter and Antonia and smiled at them hopefully.

"Good morning," I said, glancing at the others to signal that I expected them also to respond. Mrs. Paterson nodded curtly and looked away. Antonia smiled as she always did but said nothing; she was in the middle of one of her asthma attacks, which gave her silence a breathless, expressive quality, as if she was overcome with longing or exasperation. Only Hunter seemed to be considering a thoughtful reply. He paused the movie and eyed his father suspiciously.

"Smile and smile," he said. "Smile and smile. Sweet bells jangled in a nutshell though it have no toys, smile and smile, kiss and kiss..." He continued in this vein for several minutes, stringing random words together as if they meant something. Antonia nodded fervently as if in complete agreement with her brother's meaningless babble.

Morgan responded as usual to their nonsense by smothering it with nonsense of his own. "I hope you're both doing well," he interrupted. "Your mother and I"—he always referred to Susan as their mother, though she never paid them the least attention—"are going down to Washington today to visit Uncle Graham and Aunt Ingrid. Do you remember Uncle Graham and Aunt Ingrid? They're very nice people and they have a very nice house just outside Washington, with a huge swimming pool and a big fuzzy dog named Ralph...." This is the way he spoke to them—as if they were six years old instead of in their early twenties—and frankly I had a hard time telling which was more demented, the father or the children.

But that morning there was a desperate edge to his condescension. His color was high, his eyes were bloodshot, and he seemed out of breath even before he started his breathless monologue. When he finally stopped talking he pulled a handkerchief from his pocket and wiped the sweat from his balding forehead. "Hot as the devil in here, isn't it?"

"Remorseless, treacherous, lecherous," Hunter said.

Morgan stood up and asked me nervously, "When is Dr. Palmer coming back?"

"He should be back by Friday."

I rose to leave and Morgan followed me out of the dimly-lighted lounge. "Say, Dr. Hoffmann"—he lowered his voice—"has anything unusual been going on? With the twins, I mean."

Something was wrong, but I didn't know what it was. I had sensed an air of malaise, even menace, in the past few days, as if something monstrous had happened or was about to happen. I was careful not to mention Hunter's piano playing. "Nothing really. I think Hunter's a little tired this morning. You're right—it's very hot in here. I think the air conditioning needs adjustment."

He squinted at me skeptically. "All right then. I'll talk to Dr. Palmer on Friday."

That night Hunter sat down to play the piano for the second time. It sounded like the same frenetic piece he'd played before, though I couldn't be sure. Again, after about ten minutes he suddenly broke off playing and rushed out of the lounge without a backward glance. From the next room I could see Nicole sitting beside the piano, recording the performance on a portable cassette recorder. When it was over she applauded with the rest of the audience, kissed Antonia good night and left the room with her tape recorder.

It was Nicole's last night at the Institute. Why had she taped the music? Was it just a keepsake, or did she have some other purpose in mind? I stopped at the office on the way back to my room and checked the schedule to find out when I would be seeing her again.

I spent the rest of the week anxiously awaiting Dr. Palmer's return from San Francisco. Not that I was worried or upset by the prospect of his return, but listening to the paranoid Gottlieb had set my mind on edge. What would he say about my decision to reduce the dosages of Hunter's medications? I knew he would question me closely. Miles Palmer had been one of the leaders of the movement that finally succeeded in consigning Freudianism and similar theories to the dustbin of history, and he was committed to the view that human behavior is ultimately a biological phenomenon. But this, in my opinion, does not mean that every patient should be dosed with an escalating regimen of chemical agents whose effects are still poorly understood. I felt confident that even if Dr. Palmer disagreed with my ideas, he would do so in a way that wouldn't jeopardize our relationship. He was a compassionate physician, a fair-minded boss and altogether the most generous spirit I had encountered in the psychiatric field. Since I did not consider myself guilty of "heresy," as Gottlieb had foolishly suggested, I had nothing to fear from his reaction. I could only assume that when he returned we would have a rational discussion of the pros and cons of reducing the dosages. And in the meantime there were some issues in my own life that I had to deal with.

3

Dubin's investigation had begun by chance, as such things almost always did. One steamy afternoon in August, cruising the shady back roads in his BMW convertible, he discovered an area where a steep barrier of hills had unaccountably turned the tide of suburban sprawl. Here they still had woods and fields, brooks and ponds, family farms and secluded estates—it was amazing to think that such a place could still exist a little more than two hours from New York—and before long he found himself in a quaint little town he'd never heard of. It was called Egdon and it had no gas stations, no bars, no fast food—in fact, none of the emblems of modern life other than a famous psychiatric institute—but it did have a small public library housed in a tiny brick building on one end of the main street. In that library he came under close inspection by the town librarian. Her name, as he later learned, was Miss Francine Whipple and she was 68 years old. Miss Whipple ran the library singlehandedly, with assistance two afternoons a week from a high school student whose alphabetical skills remained open to question. She wore sensible shoes with laces and flat heels, a cardigan sweater even on the warmest days, and a pair of no-nonsense trifocals through which she could simultaneously read the mail, keep an eye on the door, and shoot piercing glances all the way across the room in her lifelong struggle against whisperers, misfilers and book defacers.

"What brings you to the library this afternoon?" Miss Whipple inquired as Dubin stood leafing through the local newspaper.

"Research," he answered without thinking.

"Are you a writer?"

"Yes. I'm a kind of journalist."

"Now let me guess." She peered at Dubin over the tops of her trifocals, as if in the suspicion that none of their refractions would reveal the truth about him. "Do you write about politics?"

"Not really," he smiled. "I'm primarily interested in unsolved crimes."

"True Crime," she nodded. "My favorite category." She pointed to a crowded shelf along the wall. "It's an excellent collection."

Her tone of voice told him that she was referring to the True Crime section, and that he ignored it at his peril. "Oh, I'm sure it is," he assured her. "It's just that—well, those stories have already been told. I'm always on the lookout for something new."

She smiled knowingly. "Some unsolved crime that everyone seems to have forgotten?"

"Exactly." There was something in her manner that told him he'd better start paying attention. "Do you know of any?"

"I've lived in this town all my life," she said. "I know a few things."

"Give me an example."

"Well"—she looked around to make sure no one else was listening—"I don't know if it's an unsolved crime or not. At the time they said it was a suicide. But you know, it was Maria Morgan, the opera singer. Seven years ago, she was found dead in her studio out on the Warwick road. She was about to make her Metropolitan Opera debut and one day as she was practicing, she just suddenly couldn't take the pressure anymore—that's what they said, anyway—and she hanged herself. With her two children in the house."

"When did you say this was? Seven years ago?"

"That's right." She rifled through a stack of papers on her desk and pulled out a manila folder that held a sheaf of yellowed newspaper clippings. "Maybe you'd like to read these. They tell the whole story."

Dubin sat down at an isolated table and read the clippings over and over again. He liked what he read. Maria Morgan's death had everything he looked for in a new project. A glamorous woman with everything to live for, a violent, unexplained death, an aroma of official ineptitude or corruption—and rich people running for cover in a dozen different directions. But wasn't the story too old and cold to be of any value? Dubin had already decided to get out of the business, even if sometimes it gave him the illusion of bringing justice to a corrupt world. In his kind of detective work he wasn't hindered by Miranda warnings, rules of evidence or statutes of limitation; he oppressed only the rich, never the weak and downtrodden. His was the underside of the law, the shadow side that remained invisible in a world where everything had its price. But the official side—the world of real detectives who carried badges and could put you away for the rest of your life— seemed to be closing in. One more case was all he had time for and all he really needed before he could retire. "What are you doing with these old newspaper clippings right in the middle of your desk?" he asked the librarian.

"Let's just say I have my reasons."

"Such as?"

"We librarians have our ethics, just as you journalists do. You protect your sources and we protect our borrowers."

"Fair enough."   Dubin liked Miss Whipple, and her stubbornness made him like her more. "It said in the obituary that Maria Morgan was survived by her husband and two children. Are they still around?"

"The husband is Avery Morgan. I'm sure you've heard of him"—Dubin had not—"and the children, well, I guess you could say they're still in the area."

"What do you mean?"

"Well"—she lowered her voice—"they've been in the Palmer Institute ever since their mother died. They're in their early twenties now."

Dubin had heard of the Palmer Institute. "Is that around here?"

"Right down the road."

"Can you tell me how to get there?"

Following her directions, Dubin wove his way through a maze of shady back roads to a secluded spot behind the Palmer Institute where he could park without being seen. He followed a path through the woods to the Institute's rear fence, which offered a surprisingly intimate view of the terrace behind the ivy-entangled building. Even more surprisingly, there was another spectator—a small, wiry man of about fifty—who had already concealed himself behind the fence and stood peering at the terrace. The man had a delicate, almost aristocratic appearance: he wore a light blazer and a yellow shirt open at the neck, and a pair of shiny black shoes that looked completely out of place in the woods. His nose was long and beaklike, and he had a pointed chin and a high forehead enclosed by unruly tufts of gray hair, but his most remarkable features were his wide, deep-set eyes, which seemed ready to absorb the whole world into their dark uncertainties. There was something otherworldly about him that made Dubin wonder which side of the fence he belonged on.

It was almost dusk and the Institute's grim façade was enveloped in mist, a silhouette looming ominously against the faded sky. Hanging Chinese lanterns glowed on the terrace, where a group of heavily sedated patients sat watching a strange performance. Two young people, about the age of Maria Morgan's schizophrenic children, sat between a striking redhead and an elderly nurse, while on the lawn a young blond woman in a blue ballet dress leaped from side to side, waving her arms in a pantomime of emotions that Dubin hoped he would never experience. The man standing beside Dubin at the fence mirrored the dancer's performance in a series of facial tics and small, precise hand gestures, as if he were directing her movements with invisible wires.

"What's going on?" Dubin asked him.

"Performance therapy," he muttered, as if the answer should have been obvious.

"Do you know Hunter Morgan?"

For the first time the man turned toward Dubin, drawing him into his cavernous eyes. "Why do you ask?" He spoke with the trace of an accent.

"I've heard he's a patient here."

The man hesitated. "That's Hunter Morgan on the terrace. His twin sister Antonia is sitting beside him."

"Who's the dancer?" Dubin asked. He expected to hear that she was one of the more seriously disturbed inmates.

"That's... Dr. Palmer's niece."

"You're kidding."

"Not at all. She works here."

As he drove home that night, Dubin asked himself whether he really wanted to stick his nose under this tent. He smelled money, but there were a number of less pleasant smells mixed in. Death, of course, and insanity, and a rich family's nasty secrets. He had nothing invested; he could walk away and never think about this town again. But he was haunted by the image of the schizophrenic twins on the terrace, staring into the darkness as the mist wrapped itself around them under the chill shadow of the Institute's gabled roof. They had their secrets and he had his. Was their captivity something he should even attempt to unravel?

Now he stood in the morning shadows outside Avery Morgan's house trading barbs with his wife. She had just accused Dubin of being a blackmailer and he was taking his time denying it. In the shade beside the stone barn he watched the morning breeze jostle a lock of tawny hair across her forehead.

"I'm in the information business," he said. "I just gather what's out there and let my client decide how it should be used. Or not used."

"And if you don't have a client?"

"Then I keep looking until I find one."

"What information do you have?"

"Not very much so far."

"And my husband?"

"He said to keep my eyes open but he didn't really sign up as a client. That means I have to keep looking."

Susan Morgan was attractive in an unattractive way, with her cold eyes and her hard cheeks and her low, masculine voice. "Come with me," she said.

He followed her into the stone barn, past a row of horse stalls and through a narrow doorway into a small apartment that was evidently used as an office.

"How much will you need?"   She took a checkbook out of a drawer and sat down on the couch to write him a check. The desk was cluttered with books and papers.

"Five thousand ought to do it for now. Plus expenses."

"Oh," she said. "Do blackmailers have expenses?"

"I have a client now. That makes me a detective."

She smiled as she stood up. "All right, start detecting. But I want to know everything you do, before anybody else does— especially my husband.   And when I say enough is enough, you go away. Is that a deal?"

"It's a deal."

She followed him out of the apartment and opened another door that led up a dusty flight of stairs. "Don't charge me extra for this."

They climbed the stairs to an open room with a skylight that covered the barn's entire upper level. The air smelled like mice and the sparse furnishings were draped with sheets. "Maria Morgan's studio. Just the way she left it."

"Mind if I look around?"

"Not now. Maybe on your next visit."

In another moment they were back in the driveway.   The golden retriever, in a friendly gesture, jumped up on Dubin and spattered him with mud from head to foot. Susan pulled the dog off, laughing at Dubin's distress. She laughed more as he squinted into his car's side mirror and tried to shake the mud out of his wavy dark hair.

He retreated into his car. "Thanks for the check," he said. "I'll give you a call in a couple days."

Susan had stopped laughing but there was still a mischievous gleam in her eyes. "You know, Dubin," she said, "you really ought to give up blackmail and become a detective."

"Why?"

"You look exactly like Edgar Allan Poe."

By the time I finished my psychiatric residency, I imagined that I knew everything I needed to know about human beings and their mental pathologies. For that reason I must have been particularly vulnerable to the most insidious of those pathologies, the madness of love. In the space of a few months I became obsessed with three women—an artist, an ingénue, and a nymphomaniac—each of whom brought me a step closer to ruin. The name of the first one (not her real name, of course) was Olympia.

Olympia was Miles Palmer's niece, the daughter of Peter Bartolli, and she was a beautiful, exotic creature—at least that was how she appeared to me through the lens of my infatuation: tall and statuesque, long limbed and graceful, with almond eyes and a platinum complexion that made her look like a visitor from another world. Her mother was a Russian ballet dancer, the onetime wife of Peter Bartolli who had raised her singlehandedly after the mother waltzed off with another man. At that time Bartolli was Associate Director of the Institute, and Olympia spent her childhood in this strange environment surrounded by wealthy psychotics and the doctors who humored them. As a result she took on the coloration of both groups: she was kind and generous but incredibly self-centered, driven by emotion but at the same time devious and manipulative, intellectually accomplished but given to crackpot notions. Some who knew her thought she should have stayed on as a patient.

I'll never forget the first time I saw Olympia. She had come to the Institute to conduct one of her "Performance Therapy" sessions. Dr. Palmer was away at a professional meeting—it was the night before Hunter Morgan's first piano performance—and my nemesis Dr. Jeffrey Gottlieb was in charge. Personally, I never approved of these events; it seemed to me that they nudged the patients in the wrong direction, away from reality instead of towards it. But Dr. Palmer had maintained a close relationship with Olympia even after her father's ouster—she'd grown up there, he said, and she'd always be welcome—and his generous attitude meant that periodically she would show up for one of these extravaganzas. Sometimes she danced, sometimes she put on a little play, and sometimes (without Dr. Palmer's knowledge or approval, I'm sure) she lectured the uncomprehending patients about New Age spirituality, homeopathic medicine, and various other fads that were close to her heart. She even had a room where she could sleep overnight when she visited the Institute.

On this particular occasion she had choreographed a kind of ballet that required an audience of patients and staff to sit on the terrace while she cavorted around on the lawn behind the Institute. I had spent the afternoon attending to some personal business, and when I returned I caught a glimpse of Olympia through one of the upstairs windows. She drifted through the evening mist in a blue ballet dress, waving her willowy arms gracefully, sometimes violently, as she acted out some ghostly drama. As dancing it probably left something to be desired, but in terms of raw passion and beauty I had never experienced anything like it. And when at the climactic moment she raised her eyes to meet mine, and held them there for a long moment, I wanted to rush outside and embrace this beautiful phantom before she disappeared into the night. But then she did a strange thing: the music stopped and she whirled onto the terrace toward Hunter and Antonia, who sat between Mrs. Paterson and Nicole, and she bent over to kiss each of the twins on the forehead. And then without looking at anyone else she put her hands together and slowly slipped back into the shadows like a feather floating away on the wind.

Olympia's room, as it happened, was in the residential wing just around the corner from mine. Most of the residential wing had been blocked off for years; my room and Olympia's were the only ones still in use. That night, after I made sure all the patients were safely in bed, I waited in the dimly-lighted hall to see if I could catch a glimpse of Olympia. When she appeared I pretended to be fumbling with my keys, but on her way past me she smiled archly, as if she took it as a token of the power she exercised over men, women, children, animals—indeed all living things and probably more than a few inanimate objects—that they would forever be fascinated with her and her movements.

"Good night," she murmured as she unlocked her door.

"Good night," I said. "I enjoyed your performance."

She stared back at me uncomprehendingly. "It wasn't intended to be enjoyed, exactly. It's a type of therapy."

"Oh, I know that," I stammered. "And quite honestly I'm fascinated by its therapeutic possibilities. For the patients it's therapy, but for those of us on the other side—therapists rather than patients, I mean—it can be very beautiful."

"Is there really an 'other side'?" she asked. "Isn't therapy really just another way of learning to experience the world?"

And with another enigmatic smile she slipped into her room. I spent a restless night dreaming about Olympia and her almond eyes. I imagined myself falling in love with her—basking in her smile, entranced by her words, thrilling to her gentle laughter as she strolled beside me or danced with me on a moonlight cruise. We sipped wine in sidewalk cafes and coffee in bohemian bistros; we splashed in the Caribbean and cycled through the South of France. Hesitant, even tongue-tied at first, we gradually opened our hearts to each other, confiding all our hopes and dreams. I bought her a bouquet of long-stemmed roses, comforted her when she was sick, paced the floor despairingly when she stayed away. It was a montage of every hackneyed image of the intoxicating whirl of love that Hollywood ever put on the big screen, and when I woke up I was sure that it was all true, every frame and flicker of it.

That was an illusion, of course, which quickly wore off as I rolled out of bed and staggered into the shower. I don't know if I ever really fell in love with Olympia, and I doubt if she ever loved me, but I'll never forget that dream and the sensation it left me with. I should have recognized it for what it was—a token of my deteriorating mental health—but some illusions are too precious to do without, even when you know they are illusions. The sensation, even the false sensation, of being in love with Olympia was an experience I did not want to forget.

The next morning I made the mistake of asking Gottlieb what he knew about Olympia. "Oh, what a wacko!" he laughed. "Just like her father. Did you see her cavorting around on the lawn last night? The patients must be wondering what they're doing in here if she's allowed on the streets."

"I don't know. I thought her dance was very beautiful."

"Has she told you about her past life regressions? She will, if you give her a chance. She used to be a temple prostitute in the court of Cleopatra." He laughed uproariously.

"She seems nice enough to me."

"She is very nice. Her basic problem is that she grew up surrounded by crazy people, with her father and Miles Palmer vying for her affections. For those two everything has to be a competition, if not a fight to the death, and they spoiled her rotten."

Gottlieb was taking a little too much glee in bursting my bubble. When I started to walk away he called after me. "Hoffmann," he said, lowering his voice. "You wouldn't want to make the mistake of getting involved with that girl. I considered that when I first met her too." He shook his head. "Bad idea."

I smiled and nodded as if I appreciated his advice, but kept walking. Getting into a conversation with Gottlieb was always a mistake, especially on the subject of women. He was balding, bug-eyed and overweight, and he had a wife and two kids. Yet for some reason he seemed to think of himself as God's gift to women.

Everybody knew he was sleeping with Julietta, the voluptuous receptionist who didn't need a past life regression to look like a prostitute. I tried to picture the two of them together, and it made me feel a little sick. Julietta flirted with me sometimes as I passed her desk, stopping me to ask some pointless question as she tilted forward in her low-cut dress. If I kept going she'd call my name in her low, sensuous voice; if I turned around she'd slide her tongue over her lips in a pantomime of desperate love. One day Gottlieb walked into the reception area just as I began to respond: she giggled, and he warned me off with a proprietary smirk. Then I remembered what he'd said about Olympia—how he'd considered getting "involved" with her when he first arrived at the Institute. That must have been seven or eight years ago, when she was still a teenager. I felt like going back and telling Gottlieb that Olympia would never have considered going out with a creature like him, even for a minute, even when she was seventeen years old, and that if I ever even heard of him putting one of his smelly hands on a young girl I would....

But I had to stop fantasizing and start my afternoon rounds with the patients. In those days I still didn't understand how things fit together at the Institute. That afternoon Hunter Morgan would sit down to play the piano for the first time. Only much later would I begin to grasp the connection between that strange performance and Olympia's of the night before.

Nicole had mixed feelings about going home after two weeks at the Institute. She occupied a dingy garret in a dark rambling house that had been converted to apartments, overseen by a nosy landlady named Mrs. Gruber who owned several cats but never seemed to feed them. Nicole's entrance was through a side door that led up a musty staircase to her apartment. The familiar clutter was there, just as she'd left it, even the dirty dishes in the sink. There was comfort in that, she told herself. Getting back to normal, all the little routines of life—that would put her mind in the right groove.

Washing the dishes, taking out the trash—what a smell!—cleaning the toilet, vacuuming the rug. All that would distract her from the bigger issues. And there were even more urgent concerns: she was famished and everything in the refrigerator was sprouting black spots and patches of hair. Anything in the cupboards? Half a box of stale cookies, a can of chicken noodle soup. Barely enough to take her through what promised to be a long night. Maybe this wasn't such a bright idea, renting an apartment so far out of the city. After the breakup with Richard, she'd thought the rural setting would help settle her mind, help her focus on her work. And what did she end up with, besides commuting on the bus two or three days a week? A smelly apartment, a nosy landlady, and two weeks in the loony bin. In fact the apartment was beyond smelly; it was frighteningly isolated—at the top of a dark winding staircase used only by feral cats—and positively gothic in its gloom, with shadows so deep she had never actually looked into some of the corners. The kind of place where a woman could be murdered in her bed and none of the neighbors would notice or care.

One bright spot: the computer was still on, waiting faithfully for her return. The screen was blank but all she had to do was touch the space bar and a magic technicolor world rose up before her. Out of habit she opened her "Things To Do" folder. Most of it was out of date now—unminded reminders, dead deadlines, pointless appointments. With one sweep of the mouse she consigned the entire contents of the folder to the trash bin. It was a grand feeling, having nothing to do, but it was short lived. Now the computer stared at her with a gaze blank and pitiless as the sun. Tentatively she started typing:

Bread, milk, eggs, corn flakes.
Pick up dry cleaning.
Find a thesis topic.
Keep from going crazy.

This won't do, she thought. How am I going to keep from going crazy if I have to think of a thesis topic? Let's put that one on top and keep it there. Thing To Do Numero Uno: Keep from going crazy. Easier said than done—especially when you might already be crazy. No, Dr. Hoffmann said you're definitely not there yet. No reason to think you ever will be. So there's still hope, even if you do have to think of a thesis topic that will satisfy the Dead White Males who run the Critical Studies department.

She heated the can of soup and dipped the stale cookies in it one at a time. Not bad. When she finished that she boiled some water for a cup of tea, which she would have to drink black since the milk in the fridge was sour. Now what? There was the mail—when she came in she'd tripped over a pile of mail that had been stuffed under the door. Bills she couldn't pay and catalogs full of clothes she couldn't afford. Too depressing to think about. She sipped her tea and wondered what to do next.

Thing To Do Numero Uno: Keep from going crazy. But how? Much as she liked Dr. Hoffmann, she wanted to accomplish that particular Thing To Do in her own way, without any help from the pharmaceutical industry. She reached in her purse and found the pills he'd given her, and without thinking very much about it she ran into the bathroom and flushed them down the toilet.

Now, she thought, I'm on my own.

4

Miss Francine Whipple could hardly contain her excitement when she spoke with Dubin in the library that afternoon. It had been four days since his surveillance of the Palmer Institute, and his account of what he'd seen stirred her imagination as nothing in the True Crime section had ever done. She was brimming with theories, speculations and even a few facts about the Morgan twins and the Institute. And Dubin—with Susan Morgan's $5,000 check in his pocket—found a new interest in what she had to say. "I need to find out all I can about Maria Morgan's death," he told her.

"Writing one of your articles?"

"Thinking about one."

"Well, you can come in and talk to me about it whenever you want." She glanced around furtively and lowered her voice. "I just hope I'm not a suspect."

"A suspect?"

"I knew Maria Morgan better than most people. Doesn't that make me a suspect?"

Dubin shrugged gallantly. "If you insist."

"Did I tell you she was rehearsing *The Tales of Hoffmann* at the time she died? Under the direction of Casimir Ostrovsky at the Met. She used to come in here and tell me about the production, knowing how much I love opera, especially that one. They were changing the plot around, if you can believe that." She started digging through the pile of papers on her desk. "I might have some more clippings somewhere. Or be able to find them for you."

"For me or your other borrower?" Dubin smiled. "I'm a little jealous."

"Let's not talk about that."

"Is it the police?"

"No, it's not the police. Do you think I'd consider them a borrower?"

"They might still be interested."

"Not since Frank Lynch retired."

Frank Lynch. Dubin remembered that name. He was the cop quoted in the newspaper articles. "He said there was no doubt it was suicide."

"Yes," she agreed. "That's what he said in the newspaper. But privately he had his doubts, I can tell you that."

"Where is he now?"

"Retired a couple of years ago. He lives somewhere down at the Jersey shore, I think."

The door flew open and a slight young woman with reddish blond hair fluttered inside. There was something almost angelic about the way she beamed at Miss Whipple with her emerald eyes. "Hello," she said to the librarian.

"Hello, Nicole. How are you?"

The young woman seemed a little embarrassed as she hurried past the desk. "I'm just fine, thank you," she said with a slight lilting accent. "Where's the music section?"

"All the way in back."

Miss Whipple waited until the young woman was out of sight, then leaned closer to Dubin and whispered: "Just got out."

"Just got out of what?"

"The Institute. She checked herself in a couple of weeks ago. This is the first I've seen her since."

Dubin gestured quizzically, not wanting to be overheard.

"Very sweet girl but she seems to live in her own world."

"I see."

"She's a graduate student," Miss Whipple nodded, as if that explained all.

The young woman stepped back with a music CD called *Piano Music of Robert Schumann*, which she checked out at the desk. Then she smiled at Miss Whipple in her ethereal way and flitted out of the library.

Dubin followed her with narrowing eyes. "If she was in the Institute, she might know something about the Morgan twins. Where does she live?"

"Right here in the village. Commutes in to the university three days a week."

He headed for the door. "I'll see you in a day or two."

"You're wasting your time following her," the librarian called after him. "She doesn't know anything about it."

Olympia remained at the Institute for the rest of the week. The day after her ballet on the lawn, I was preoccupied with Hunter's first encounter with the piano and Nicole's final therapy session. On a couple of occasions I noticed Olympia gliding down a corridor and I felt a bashful thrill when she flashed her smile in my direction. I remembered my dream, of course, and the precious illusion that I was in love with her. By the light of day that idea seemed absurdly improbable—but so did Hunter's piano playing, Gottlieb's cynicism, Julietta's lasciviousness, Antonia's ethereal innocence, and so many other features of everyday life at the Institute. As it turned out my own grip on reality was weakening. Like my patients I had emotions that were secret even from myself, lurking in the shadows like demons in a medieval woodcut; it was only a matter of time before they would start to intrude on my life.

At night on my way to bed I stole a glance at Olympia's door and wondered whether she was in her room. Then on Wednesday evening she gave another performance therapy session, this time in the patient lounge. The presentation was altogether different from the last one, and Olympia came across as less vivacious and self-assured, even somewhat bored and guarded, until the moment when Hunter suddenly sat down at the piano. Once he started playing—it was the same piece he'd played on the two earlier occasions—her face lit up and she started spinning around the room as if she were in a trance.

Then came the inevitable moment when Hunter stopped short in that jarring climactic passage and fled back to his room. Olympia faltered, almost fell, then gestured to me—I had been watching in alarm from the back of the lounge. "I'd better call it a night," she said, forcing a smile. "This was very good. I'll see you all again next time."

It was clear that I had been chosen to escort her to her room. I took her arm and we stepped slowly away from the lounge while the orderlies ushered the patients to their beds.

"Are you OK?" I asked.

"I'm fine," she said, catching her breath. "Just a little surprised, that's all."

Looking back at that moment, I can see that it was a turning point, the first step in a misadventure I could not have foreseen and am embarrassed to relate. I called it the madness of love, and madness it may have been. But it was only a dream of love.

There was no one else in the residential wing, and when we reached her door she pulled me inside. As the door closed behind us I found myself folded in her willowy embrace. Without saying a word, we stood for a long time kissing and caressing each other as our clothes gradually slipped to the floor. It was a warm, still night and her skin felt soft and moist. I kissed her face, her neck, her breasts, all the way down to her magnificent thighs, and then we tangoed naked across the room and fell on her bed. A cool breeze wafted in through the half-open window as she stretched herself back and I rolled on top of her. The curtains were open slightly but that didn't matter—outside there was nothing but darkness and the mechanical chattering of insects. We started gently, almost tentatively, as if we were trying something new, but then quickly our hearts began to pound and they continued to pound until we had both cried out in that closeness that has no equal in this world. Yet through it all, mingled with my tenderness for Olympia, there was a sense of detachment and unreality that I will confess I often feel in such moments. Although I know this is happening to me, I am also aware of myself as being apart from it, watching as if in a dream.   And what I saw in the dim light frightened me—an Olympia entirely given up to the motions of love like a perfect machine whose movements are directed solely to the task it is designed to perform.   And there was such a wild energy inside her—an acceleration so intense that it seemed to propel her beyond her limits—that I was afraid she would break apart before we were done.

The first words out of her mouth astonished me.   "I want to introduce you to my father."

We were lying on our backs gasping for breath as the sweat melted off our fevered bodies.   "Your father?" I cried.   "What made you think of that?"

She laughed and started kissing and caressing me again, and once again her feverish energy overpowered us both.   Before long our hearts and our bodies were pounding with a whirling beat that reminded me—in my detachment—of that demonic music Hunter had discovered in the piano.   But this time when we had finished I felt guilty and ashamed, as if I had crept into a patient's bed, and all I could think about was Hunter Morgan and his piano music and the fact that in two more days Dr. Palmer would return to the Institute.

Nicole knew she was drinking too much coffee when she couldn't concentrate long enough to worry about whether she was drinking too much coffee.   In the morning she'd bring home a 20-ounce Colombian from the little convenience store around the corner. That was breakfast.   Lunch was another 20-ouncer—absolutely necessary if she was going to make any progress on finding a thesis topic.   By four o'clock, still no progress in that department but a deepening sense of restlessness and frenzy.   The apartment was like an inferno and every once in a while she thought she could hear someone creeping up and down the stairs.   Probably—hopefully—

one of the landlady's cats. She skittered to the window and peered down through the cypress trees that surrounded the house. Nothing unusual there, just a black BMW parked in the shade across the street and a man in sunglasses who turned away when she looked out. She yanked on her running shoes and fled outside—by the time she hit the sidewalk the BMW and its driver were gone—and endured three miles of sweat before it was time for another stop at the coffee shop. Standing in line behind her—where had she seen that guy before? No matter: 20 more ounces of coffee, please. You can always reheat it in the microwave.

By eight o'clock when she took the first bite of her frozen pizza she was wired as tight as a mandolin. Tapping her foot. Drumming her fingers on the table. Racing her eyes distractedly around the gloomy apartment. Her home, she realized, looked like the set for a 1950s horror movie: peeling wallpaper, cobwebs in the corners, stalactites dripping from the rotten plaster ceiling—everything but Vincent Price and the organ music. Instead of organ music, she had the bone-grating sound of animals (she hoped they weren't rats) scurrying around behind the walls. Suddenly she remembered Thing To Do Numero Uno: Keep from going crazy. Not so easy when you're living in a tomb and you have an appointment with your advisor on Monday. And you still don't have a thesis topic. Go with what you know best, he'd told her: Modern languages. French and German literature. Semiotics, whatever that was (at what point in her graduate career were they going to tell her what semiotics actually was?), close reading of texts—"You took a first at Oxford, didn't you?" And here she sat on the bed in her cluttered apartment, having wasted a fine afternoon watching soap operas, ready to plunge into an evening of idiotic sitcoms. Better make sure the door is bolted.

Somewhere in the middle of a beer commercial, the days and nights of exhaustion finally caught up with her and she slipped into a violent sleep. It lasted a little over an hour but the dreams that gripped her seemed to span decades, hurling her back and forth between one end of her life and the other. It was all there: her childhood in the west of Ireland, boarding school in Sligo, the years at Oxford and Munich and now in America, packing her bags and walking out on Richard as he sat sobbing in his underwear on their only comfortable chair, and in the middle of it all her dead brother at the bottom of the cliff looking straight up at her with his swollen mouth and his two black eyes, bruised and broken, hungry water swirling beneath him. She woke up gasping and flailing her arms as if she were being shoved into an alien world, holding her eyes closed as she struggled to pull the dream's final images into waking consciousness: It wasn't her brother at all or her mother or father but Dr. Ned Hoffmann, pursuing her through a shadowy mountain landscape—and cursing her, when she leapt over a cliff to escape him, with the unmistakable howl of madness.

The howl was what woke her up. It was really the neighbors' beagle mimicking a fire siren that wailed in the distance. The animals in the walls were scrambling madly in every direction, as if they too were trying to escape. Nicole looked at the clock—it was midnight—and killed the TV with her remote control. Then she turned off the lights and tried to go back to sleep. In the darkness the room still throbbed with the echo of her dreams. The image of Dr. Hoffmann howling after her through the shadows—could that be from drinking too much coffee? Be careful. You could lie here all night and go crazy. Better check the lock on the door. A cat (she assumed it was a cat) scurried away and down the stairs.

She remembered the CD she'd found at the library: *Piano Music of Robert Schumann*, performed by Alicia de Larrocha. Maybe that would help her sleep. She stuck the CD in her portable disk player, pulled on the headphones and lay back on her pillow. The music was Romantic, as she remembered from her school days, but it sounded strange to her ears: one minute chromatic and expressive, the next minute jagged and jittery, relentless, breathless, like a puppet in perpetual motion. Easy to see why poor Schumann went mad. Then suddenly there it was—the piece Hunter Morgan had played by heart without ever having touched a piano before. At least she thought that's what she was hearing. She stopped the CD and rummaged through her purse for the cassette she had recorded of Hunter's playing. When she found it she plugged it into her Walkman and sat up on the bed with the disk player wired to one ear and the Walkman to the other. Yes, the music was the same. What was it? According to the liner notes it was a piece called Kreisleriana:

> Kreisleriana, Op. 16. Completed in 1838, this series of episodic sketches was inspired by the eccentric fictional musician Johannes Kreisler, a character in various tales by the German Romantic writer E.T.A. Hoffmann (1776-1822).

"Hoffmann," Nicole muttered, springing off the bed. She threw herself into her desk chair and touched a key on the computer. The screen flared into action and she typed her way furiously into the very core of the internet. "Déjà vu, déjà vu, déjà vu," she said as the screens flashed by. "All over again."

After fifteen minutes she reached for her coffee mug and found it empty. Déjà bu. She laughed out loud at her own joke and turned back to the keyboard. Forget the coffee. With or without caffeine, it was going to be a long night.

5

Dr. Palmer returned from San Francisco on Friday, though I didn't have a chance to speak with him until Saturday morning. By that time Gottlieb had given him a characteristically poisonous account of everything that happened while he was gone, including the surprising piano performances and my decision to lower Hunter's dosages. So naturally I spent most of a sleepless night rehearsing what I would say in my defense. I don't know why I felt so apprehensive. My relationship with Miles Palmer had always been cordial, though of course when we were talking about a patient I deferred to his advice. Yes, he was touchy on the subject of Peter Bartolli and his daughter Olympia, but at the time I wasn't aware of any connection between that subject and my reduction of Hunter's dosages. And so I was prepared to stand my ground.

Later I came to understand that the Peter Bartolli issue colored everything that happened at the Institute. When I began my work there I'd been surprised—and more than a little disappointed—to learn that Dr. Bartolli was no longer in the picture. Though I never mentioned it to anyone, I felt a secret kinship with Bartolli, owing to an incident that occurred while I was in my third year of medical school. My interest in psychiatry had been first aroused when the two brothers came to the campus and put on a mock debate with the provocative title, 'Has the brain lost its mind?'

This eagerly awaited event left a deep impression on me. The auditorium was filled to overflowing with anxious medical students, drowsy residents and combative faculty members. The speakers arrived late, and after a few preliminaries the Chair of Psychiatry introduced them to enthusiastic applause. Though they were brothers, they could hardly have looked less alike. Miles Palmer was tall and athletic, handsome in a distinguished, gray-haired way, his every movement projecting solidity and authority. Peter Bartolli looked like a character from a fairy tale—almost gnomelike in appearance, with exaggerated features and dark, deep-set eyes that never seemed to look in one direction for more than a fleeting moment. By the time they spoke at my medical school, the Palmer Institute was famous but psychiatry itself had become schizophrenic, hopelessly at war with itself over the question of whether traditional approaches to therapy could hold their place in a world dominated by drugs and biological models of behavior. "There's been a revolution in the past twenty years," Miles Palmer declared, towering over the podium authoritatively. "A revolution in our understanding of the brain and what used to be called 'mental illness.'"

"And like most revolutions," Bartolli interrupted, crouching behind his lectern to peer impishly up at Palmer, "this one has left its share of mangled victims in the streets." He flashed a wide grin at the audience. "I'm only his half brother," he said, "in case you were wondering why I'm so short."

We all laughed, nervously, uncomfortably. None of us was prepared for Bartolli's strange appearance or the irreverent tone he seemed to be setting. "You talk about the brain," he went on, turning again to face his brother, "but what I'd like to know is, whatever happened to the mind? Isn't that what we ought to be concerned about?"

"What you call the mind," Dr. Palmer scoffed, "is merely the brain as seen from the inside out."

"And what you call the brain is merely the physical mechanism the mind has evolved to perpetuate itself."

More nervous laughter from the groundlings, myself included. Could this impudent creature be the famous Peter Bartolli? we asked ourselves. What was he trying to prove?

Crouched behind his lectern, he gave us his answer in a hoarse aside: "I'm here to play the id to my brother's super-ego!"

Palmer cut off the laughter with a dismissive wave of his hand. "If there were such a thing as an id," he told the audience, "I could think of no one better qualified to play it than my brother."

They continued in this vein for nearly an hour, and it was the most exciting hour of my medical education. Of course it was all an act, a dramatization of the struggle tearing at the heart of psychiatry—or so I assumed at the time. Not until later, when I'd finished my residency and signed on for a full-time job at the Palmer Institute, did I realize that the hostility I'd witnessed between the brothers was not only real but of mythic proportions. "The mind, unlike the brain, is infinite!" Bartolli had shouted in an impassioned moment toward the end of the debate. And after the presentation had ended, he leaped back on the stage and had the last word. "I leave you with a challenge," he told the medical students. "No matter where your career takes you, remember that the human psyche must be viewed with the naked eye. Not through a telescope from light years away, nor through a microscope that can focus only on synapses and neuroreceptors. You have to look at it from a human distance, the distance between one person and another. And that's the hardest part of this profession. To enter it, you must be a scientist—but to succeed, you must be a human being."

Now this unlikely champion of humanism was gone from the Institute, even before I'd been able to meet him, his place as Associate Director usurped by the egregious Gottlieb, and here I stood in Miles Palmer's office trying to explain why I had lowered Hunter Morgan's dosages based on the way he played the piano. Of course there was more to it than that: the current dosages were much higher than recommended, and the piano playing might have represented Hunter's attempt to break through his drug-induced isolation and wrestle with some long-forgotten part of his unconscious. As always, Dr. Palmer was courteous and respectful. He did not pull rank. Instead he listened attentively and explained why he disagreed with my approach. He seemed fascinated by my account of Olympia's strange dance on the lawn and asked repeatedly whether I thought it was linked to Hunter's piano playing, which had begun the next afternoon.

"It's possible," I allowed. "Although it wasn't the same music. I don't know what she was dancing to, but it wasn't piano music. It sounded like a whole orchestra."

"With singing? Was it an opera?"

"I don't know. Possibly. I don't know much about opera."

"No, neither do I. I don't care for it, do you?"

"No. I never did."

Dr. Palmer offered me a seat and we both sat down, he behind his enormous desk and I in the deep leather wing chair that was usually reserved for wealthy donors and relatives of patients. "You see," he explained, "Olympia is my niece—she has my eyes, have you ever noticed? And, I like to think, a little of my intellect and common sense, at least more than she could have inherited from my brother. She practically grew up here, and I've tried to care for her and make her feel welcome even after Peter's departure. In my opinion, the more time she spends here and away from him, the better off she'll be."

He stared as if expecting me to agree, but I turned away uncomfortably. "I don't know your brother."

"Peter's a strange bird," Dr. Palmer said, shaking his head. "I love him, of course, as a brother. But he's done a horrible job of bringing up Olympia—there's something missing in her, something essential that's not quite there. And as if to compensate for that, he's infected her with all his New Age nonsense—aromatherapy, past life regression, performance therapy. It's all a bad joke. But I hope I can be a good influence on her, and you can too, Ned. Please show an interest in her, if you can."

"Sure," I nodded. "I'll try to do what I can."

On the subject of reducing the twins' medications, Dr. Palmer was less tolerant. In his view, there was no scientific or ethical basis for the "humanistic" approach his brother advocated. I admitted I was troubled by the shift from psychotherapy to chemical intervention because of what it implied for the human spirit.

"You start out in psychiatry because you want to help people discover their unique individuality," he said with an understanding smile. "But the longer you practice, the more you wonder whether anyone, yourself included, has any unique individuality to discover."

"I can't accept that kind of psychological determinism."

"Of course you can, or you wouldn't be a psychiatrist. The whole premise of psychiatry is that you can influence causes and effects."

"Shouldn't we at least acknowledge the power of the unconscious?" I realized that I was challenging him, and it gave me an unexpected thrill. "Instead of making the patient wrestle with his demons, aren't we just helping him avoid them? Aren't all these medications just another form of repression?"

Dr. Palmer forced a smile and leaned toward me with his head tilted in an imitation of fatherly indulgence. "You're a mechanic, not a priest, Ned. Try to keep that in mind." In a habitual gesture of control, he stood up and waited for me to do the same. "But forget about lowering those dosages. Put them back up where they were."

Despite the frankness of our discussion, there was something I couldn't bring myself to say to Dr. Palmer about Hunter and Antonia. Everyone at the Institute referred to them as "schizophrenic" because that was the official diagnosis, carried forward on their charts over a seven year period. But in fact their illnesses bore almost no resemblance to classic schizophrenia or any other recognized form of mental disturbance. Whatever they had, it was unrecognizable, unique, defying classification. This troubled me because it went against all my training and experience up to that time. Patients, I'd been taught, can always be diagnosed—that is, categorized—because they're not like you and me. They are not normal, healthy individuals with unique personalities that can express themselves in an infinite number of ways. They have illnesses with certain symptoms; there are only a limited number of possibilities. In other words, even if the rest of us are unique, mental patients are not. But here were Hunter and Antonia, who defied medical classification. The lexicon of modern medicine was useless in the face of their individuality. The only thing you could say about them was that they were crazy. Mad. That's what they were, I told myself privately: Mad.

And yet I did not agree with Dr. Palmer's insistence that their medications be kept at such extreme levels. That was only cutting them off from themselves and their demons. But I lacked the courage to defy him and order that the dosages be reduced. In any case, as we realized when it was too late, Hunter found a way to do that for himself.

Dubin sat at the bar sipping a Grey Goose martini at the end of a long, empty day. It was the kind of day he liked. He still had Susan Morgan's $5,000 check in his wallet and he wouldn't start spending it until he'd earned it. If he never found anything worth paying for, he'd return her money. If the case played out as he hoped it would, he might earn enough to retire on. In the meantime he had to live. Did blackmailers have expenses? she'd wanted to know. Of course they have expenses. They have expenses no one else can imagine, and a couple of Grey Goose martinis at the end of a long empty day is the least of them. Not the kind of expenses most men have: wives, kids, mortgages and the like—Dubin had learned that the hard way. Sandy, his ex-wife, stood by him through scandal and investigation, scapegoating, breakdown and recovery, on the unspoken assumption that when all was said and done he would be his old self again. That could never be, he told her the day he brought home his first fee as a blackmailer, an incredible $50,000 from a wealthy aficionado of kiddie porn. She left him the next day. It was ironic: Sandy always wanted a nice apartment with a balcony and trees and an outdoor pool and now that was exactly where he lived. She coveted a sports car and now he drove a BMW convertible that one of his clients had given him in lieu of a fee. Were there expenses? Of course but they had been paid in advance. The sense of betrayal, the complicity, the realization that exposing evil will not make it disappear—they were already entered on the ledger and they could never be recovered or written off.

Everyone knew him in the bar, and they knew enough about him not to talk to him. He liked the mute TV screens, the secondhand smoke, the subdued frenzy of the place. Familiar faces—some smooth, some wrinkled, all of them as gray as the goose in his martini. They all had their success stories, their tragedies, their farces. Nobody cared. The bartenders, the regulars, the cocktail waitresses—they knew who he was, but they didn't care. Just the way he liked it. Nothing to hide and nothing to declare.

He took a sip of his martini and wondered why Susan Morgan had given him a check for $5,000. Not blackmail exactly, though she was very astute in sensing his purpose—he had no information, only suspicion, and her instruction had been to keep looking, not go away. If Avery Morgan was a wife-killer, she would naturally want to know it. And maybe she intended to blackmail Morgan herself with the information she got from Dubin; it would make for an interesting divorce. In that case Dubin was a bargain. He could never extract as much money from Susan Morgan as she could squeeze out of her husband.

The barflies were working themselves into a lather about something on the TV. A new scandal involving the President. New accusations, new denials, new outpourings of contrived emotion. Dubin looked away from the screen and concentrated on his martini, which was unfortunately nearing its end. The news didn't interest him anymore. Back when he was a reporter, he'd follow every detail of every scandal, every crime, every political twist and turn, trying to calculate how he could contribute to the hysteria. Now he listened only to the sports and the weather, and even those he found wearily predictable. But he was sympathetic to the President and his mistresses and co-conspirators. He knew what it was like to have a secret, lots of secrets, to dread their exposure but never really to expect it. The dull panic that hits you when it finally happens. A sense of déjà vu, the perverse satisfaction of justice. If someone had blackmailed him, he wondered, would he have paid? They say it never works for long, but how do they know? It might have worked for him.

The next morning Dubin arrived at the library shortly after Miss Whipple had sat down at her desk to sort the mail. At the end of his last visit, disregarding her stern advice, he'd followed the red-haired graduate student she called Nicole to a rambling old house a few blocks away, where she lived in an attic apartment, and since then he'd kept her in his sights, wondering how much she could tell him about the Morgan twins. She was a fascinating creature, ethereal and elusive, who darted in and out at all hours to purchase enormous quantities of coffee and little else. Apparently she never slept, or if she did it was during the day when Dubin had other business to attend to. At the moment he needed to do some research on Avery Morgan and the library was as good a place to start as any. The few people in town he had asked about Avery Morgan seemed anxious to avoid saying anything about him. All he knew about Morgan, beyond his official biography—Exeter, Princeton, and a list of country clubs so exclusive that no one but their members have ever heard of them—were the bloodshot eyes, the chirping voice and the museum of obscure presidents. This last point was probably the most telling: the man was a collector. Dubin had known a few rich collectors and they're an odd breed. Possessive, secretive, proud—and utterly obsessed with their hobby. And some men collect wives the way others collect statues or figurines.

"How's the research going?" Miss Whipple asked.

"Slowly but surely." Dubin had taken a seat on a hard wooden chair facing a hard wooden table across from the librarian's desk.

"I was just thinking about the collecting angle. The Morgans collect autograph materials, don't they?"

"Well," Miss Whipple said warily, "he does."

"Avery Morgan?"

She nodded.   "He's been collecting autographs and manuscripts all his life. Still comes in here now and then to look at the auction records."

"Auction records? Where do you keep them?"

"And dealer catalogs, when he doesn't get them in the mail." She pointed to a shelf in the reference section. "They're right over there."

Dubin spent half an hour flipping through *American Book Prices Current*, the published records of prices realized at major auction houses for rare books and manuscripts. He went back seven years, before the date of Maria Morgan's death and worked forward from there, browsing randomly through the pages, trying to put himself in the mindset of Avery Morgan pursuing his hobby on the eve of his wife's death and in the years that followed. Nothing noteworthy struck his eye and he was about to give up when he turned to the dealer catalogs that were filed on the shelf beside the auction records. In one of the more recent catalogs, just over a year old, he found an item that echoed in his mind. It had been circled with a felt-tip pen.

"What was the opera Maria Morgan was rehearsing when she died?" he called to the librarian.

"*The Tales of Hoffmann*."

"Who wrote it?"

"Offenbach."

"He wrote the story?"

"No, he wrote the music. I don't know who wrote the story."

There it was, circled in red, in Catalogue 97 of Stephen Witz & Son, 987 Madison Avenue, New York, specializing in rare literary and musical autograph material. Item number 263:

> OFFENBACH, JACQUES. Autograph letter signed. 28 August 1880. The last letter written by Offenbach to his friend Albert Wolff before the composer's death on 5 October 1880. Offenbach complains about the machinations of his wife, accusing her of destroying his life's work by "vandalizing" the score of *Les Contes d'Hoffmann* as it neared completion. In the delirium of his last illness, Offenbach insists that he has duped his wife by hiding the real manuscript, which he has arranged to be delivered to Wolff after his death. Very good condition. $12,000.

Dubin was tempted to rip the page out of the catalog and slip it into his pocket, but since Miss Whipple was watching he walked to the xerox machine and invested a dime making a copy.

"Did you find something interesting?" she asked, appearing beside him.

"Why is this item circled?"

"Vandalism, as far as I'm concerned. If I only knew who did it—"

"Was it Avery Morgan? Did he look at this catalog?"

"If I ever catch him writing in the books—"

Dubin had the sensation that at last he'd found something tangible that could lead him in the right direction. "I need to find out more about *The Tales of Hoffmann*."

"The Music section is all the way in the back."

"No. The information I need is more specific. When I was here before, didn't you mention the name of the director Maria Morgan was working with?"

Miss Whipple peered at him cautiously over the tops of her trifocals. "I might have," she said. "It was Casimir Ostrovsky."

"Do you know where I can find him?"

6

Nicole had been scheduled for a series of follow-up visits at weekly intervals after her discharge from the Institute. In my growing obsession with Olympia I had almost forgotten about Nicole, but that Wednesday afternoon I was delighted to notice her name in my appointment calendar.

"Dr. Hoffmann?" She slipped into my office, a little embarrassed to be there, which I took as a good sign. By her own account she was adjusting well, taking her medications, and planning to continue in graduate school. A few panic attacks, occasional disorientation, but no new psychotic episodes. She'd gotten over the breakup with the boyfriend and had no interest in dwelling on it. Her main preoccupation was with her frustrating search for a dissertation topic. "That's not something I can help you with," I said without thinking.

Her eyes darted away. "Maybe you can. Maybe you're part of it somehow."

We sat in silence for a few seconds.

"Is there something you want to tell me?" I finally asked.

"Yes. It's about Hunter's piano playing. I found out what it was."

"What it was?"

She was looking right at me now. "You know, what music he was playing. Don't you think that's important?"

"Sure. It could be very important. Although—"

"He's been playing a piece by Robert Schumann. Just as I thought. I got a CD from the library and the piece is on it. It's called Kreisleriana."

"Kreisleriana," I repeated, stalling for time. "That's a strange name."

"There's an even stranger story behind it."

"Go ahead."

"Kreisleriana is named after a fictional character called Johannes Kreisler, who's an eccentric musician in some stories by Hoffmann."

I was startled to hear my own name. "Hoffmann?"

"Not you," she laughed. "E.T.A. Hoffmann. German Romantic writer from the first part of the nineteenth century."

"Never heard of him."

"Most people haven't. But when Schumann was a young man—which was a few years after Hoffmann's death—Hoffmann was what today we'd call a cult figure."

"A Hoffmann cult?" The idea made me smile.

"He was an incredibly influential writer. He influenced Poe, Dumas, Dostoevsky. Offenbach even composed an opera about him—*The Tales of Hoffmann*—which I'm not familiar with. Do you know it?"

"I've been hearing about it all my life," I frowned. That opera, or at least its name—which was all I knew about it—was a sore point with me. Every teacher I'd ever had had taunted me with it at one time or another. "Because of my name. And maybe for that reason I've studiously avoided knowing anything about it. To be quite honest, I have no use for opera as an art form. It's totally stupid as far as I'm concerned."

"I know what you mean. Well, anyway, Hoffmann was a peculiar blend of Prussian bureaucrat and bohemian artistic genius. He made his living as a judge, and on his nights off he sat in the local tavern drinking wine and writing these crazy, fantastical stories that became enormously popular after his death."

I thought it was time to bring this digression back around to its starting point. "What does all this have to do with Hunter Morgan?"

"I'm getting to that," she said. "Hoffmann believed, quite literally, that there's a 'spirit world' that parallels this one, populated by demons and sprites who represent pure spirit uncontaminated by the corruption of the material world."

"But wasn't that just a metaphor for something?"

"No, that's what's so hard for us to grasp. To Hoffmann the spirit world wasn't just a metaphor—it was the real thing, more real than anything else we ordinarily experience—and he believed that the creative artist had to do everything possible to go there. Through music, dreams, alcohol, drugs—and if all else failed, madness."

I was beginning to see the connection. "He sounds like a character out of the 1960s."

She nodded. "Hoffmann was Jack Kerouac and Timothy Leary and Jim Morrison all rolled into one. But at heart he was a bourgeois functionary. He was never able to rise above the commonplace and make the leap into the spirit world."

This was starting to make me uncomfortable. "Now bring me back to earth. Why are we talking about this?"

"Because Hunter's been playing this music by Schumann that was inspired by Hoffmann's stories, remember?"

"Right."

"Schumann accepted the artistic ideology that Hoffmann had never been able to put into practice. And he worked at it so hard that he actually became what Hoffmann only wrote about."

"Didn't you say he went mad?"

"Absolutely stark raving mad. Institutionalized—in a much worse place than this—for the last two years of his life."

"Are you suggesting—"

"As a follower of Hoffmann, Schumann concluded that in order to be an artistic genius you have to enter the spirit world and stay there. You can't leave to go to law school or medical school or take a government job. You have to get crazy and stay crazy. And that's exactly what Schumann did."

I stood up and looked at my watch. "This is all very interesting," I said curtly, "but it will have to wait until next time. I have another appointment."

"But what are you going to do in the meantime? Obviously Hunter's trying to tell you something."

"As you are."

"What do you mean?"

"We'll have to discuss that next time. Are you planning to come next week?"

She stood up, glaring. "But this isn't about me!" she protested. "I told you all this because it's about Hunter."

"Of course it's about Hunter."

"You're just humoring me, aren't you? You think I just made all this up."

"No, absolutely not. I just don't know what to make of it. We can talk about it again next week."

After Nicole went home—I didn't really have another appointment—I sat at my desk in the gathering darkness, mulling over the bizarre tale she had just told me. Was this a story about Hunter, as she claimed—or was it really about Nicole herself? In either case, the fact that it involved a writer named "Hoffmann" could not be a mere coincidence. And clearly it was no accident that this "Hoffmann" was described as a "bourgeois functionary" who could never rise above the commonplace. Assuming the story was really about Hunter, what was Hunter trying to tell me with his piano playing? That he inhabited a spirit world apart from the one most of us regard as reality? That much was obvious. But surely it went farther than that. Wasn't he saying that I—after all, I was the "Hoffmann" of the piece—was somehow responsible for his insanity? That like Schumann he had taken on the madness I projected and made it real? Or was Nicole saying this about my relationship to her? Merely to ask such questions was to demonstrate their absurdity. It was clear that Nicole's "research" had little or nothing to do with Hunter but was an elaborate fantasy of her own.

I suspected a disguised form of transference. Transference is a phenomenon in which the patient transfers a repressed emotional conflict—often of a sexual nature—onto the therapist. In this case Nicole made it appear that she was focused on Hunter, but her emphasis on "Hoffmann" and his almost supernatural power to influence events pointed in another direction. It pointed at me.

Dubin rose early on Thursday and worked out at the gym between six and seven. Over breakfast he avoided reading the *USA Today* some misguided soul had started leaving on his doorstep—as a recovering news junkie, he never allowed himself to be exposed to the news media before five in the afternoon—and when he climbed into the BMW to begin his day's work he deftly manipulated the radio buttons with the same end in mind. Thursday was collection day, the most satisfying day of the week, when his clients paid for their misdeeds. He insisted on personal delivery, usually in cash, in suburban venues of his own choosing: convenience stores, gas stations, even banks—in fact he preferred banks, where armed guards and surveillance cameras were assigned to protect him from any recurrence of antisocial behavior. The clients were sullen, bitter, contemptuous, the meetings hurried and impersonal with a dash of weary familiarity, like illicit sex or banking itself. On days like this, when he sensed that he was being watched, he conducted business with a Zen-like simplicity. Nothing was said that could be transmitted through a wire.

Having completed his collections, he decided to take a quick drive into the city, as if such a thing were possible—in fact the traffic beyond the Lincoln Tunnel was worse than usual, an impenetrable Middle Eastern bazaar of taxicabs and desperate throngs, locked in deadly combat for every square inch between Eleventh Avenue and Grand Central Station. Angry, agonized faces on cab drivers and pedestrians alike. He crawled uptown, then over to Madison, and at last his luck turned. He found what he was looking for, even found a parking garage with an hourly rate that was less than a lawyer's.

It was upstairs in a posh building that housed an art gallery on the ground floor. Stephen Witz & Son, Inc. Rare books and manuscripts. The man who grudgingly unlocked the door—after checking Dubin's skin color to make sure he wasn't there to rob him—was fortyish, tidy-looking and smug. Undoubtedly Witz *fils*, if a Witz at all.

"Can I help you?"

Dubin decided not to waste his time with pointless preliminaries. He reached in his pocket and pulled out the wrinkled page from the dealer's catalog he'd photocopied at the library and stuck it under Witz's skeptical nose.

"Is this still available?"

"The Offenbach letter? Heavens, no! That was sold months ago."

"Did you get your price for it?"

The son of Witz chuckled shrewdly. "We always get our price. In this case, we could have asked a lot more. There was someone who really wanted it."

"You wouldn't happen to have a photocopy, would you?"

"A photocopy of the letter? I couldn't show it to you, even if I had one. There is such a thing as ethics, you know."

"What's ethics got to do with it?"

The dealer's patience for Dubin's gaucherie was wearing thin. "When people buy a manuscript," he sniffed, "part of what they're buying—sometimes most of what they're buying—is exclusivity. You wouldn't pay these prices in order to have photocopies floating all over the place, would you?"

"What if I told you I know where the manuscript is and could get it for you?"

"What manuscript?"

"The manuscript score of *The Tales of Hoffmann* that Offenbach is referring to in the letter."

Witz pretended to laugh as he watched Dubin carefully. "You mean the one he claims to be hiding from his wife, who he thinks is trying to kill him? I mean, really, wasn't that all a paranoid delusion?"

"I don't know. Was it?"

"Do you have the manuscript?"

"I didn't say that."

"You know where it is?"

"That's what I said."

"In that case, I'd say I'm interested."

Dubin folded his photocopy slowly and put it back in his pocket. "You have a buyer?"

"I might have one."

"Probably the same one who bought the letter. But this deal would have to be handled very discreetly. Not through a catalog."

The dealer nodded in acquiescence. "No, very discreetly. That will suit my client fine."

Dubin picked up one of the dealer's business cards from the counter and stuck it in his pocket, as if he was impatient to leave. "We're talking a lot of money. Well into six figures."

"I realize that."

"My commission is fifteen percent."

Witz winced. "That's a bit rich."

"That's exactly what I intend to be when I've sold it."

"Excuse me?"

"A bit rich." Dubin turned around and headed for the door.

"Did I get your name?" the dealer called after him.

"I'll give you a call."

Day and night, at the library, on the internet, commuting in and out of the city to the university, Nicole devoted herself to her researches into every nook and cranny of nineteenth century literature, with an emphasis on fantasy and the supernatural: Mary Shelley, Monk Lewis, E.T.A. Hoffmann, Edgar Allan Poe. She was under enormous pressure to select a thesis topic, but she was convinced that if she could understand Hunter Morgan's playing of

Kreisleriana and what it signified, her own problems would fall into place. She spent as much time with Hunter and Antonia as possible and kept them abreast of her findings, though neither was capable of adding any useful insights or even of showing any understanding of what she was trying to do. Nicole listened to all of Schumann's piano music, read most of Hoffmann's tales, and after two weeks, on the eve of a desperate meeting with her thesis advisor at which she was expecting to be asked to leave the program, she hit pay dirt.

Miss Whipple had recommended a battered old book from the Classics section, the sole volume remaining from a complete set of the writings of Alexandre Dumas, author of *The Count of Monte Cristo*. This volume contained a short novel entitled *La Femme au Colliers de Velour*—"The Woman With the Velvet Necklace"—and its protagonist was none other than E.T.A. Hoffmann. Nicole read the novel twice in growing astonishment. The Hoffmann in this story is an aspiring artist who leaves his fiancée—a musician's daughter named Antonia—and journeys to Paris during the darkest days of the Reign of Terror. There he falls in love with a ballerina who is really an automaton under the control of a mysterious doctor. One night he finds the ballerina in a daze beneath the guillotine and brings her to his hotel where she seems to revive. They dance wildly, but he is haunted by the fear that she is not really alive—and in the morning, when the doctor removes her velvet necklace, her head rolls off onto the floor.

All the characteristic themes and elements of Hoffmann's tales were there—a sinister doctor, an eccentric musician with a daughter named Antonia, a ballerina who may or may not be an automaton. Madness, hypnosis, love at first sight. Unexplainable synchronicities. Drunkenness, madness, and the suggestion (after the doctor rescues Hoffmann from the guillotine) that much of the preceding narrative was the raving of a madman.

"It's as if Hoffmann has come full circle," Nicole thought, "to become a character in his own nightmare world."

Dubin had been sitting in his car outside Nicole's apartment house since his return from the city. He knew she was there because he'd watched her jog around the corner in her running clothes and let herself in through the side door that led up to her garret. Dusk had fallen but no lights had come on in the apartment. Had she gone straight to bed? Dubin slipped out of his car and strolled around the building, peering upward as if to glimpse the rising moon. He could see the bluish glow of a computer screen in one of the windows. Pushing the side door open, he crept up the dark staircase to her door. He knew exactly what he was going to do. When he knocked, he could hear the floor creaking inside as she edged warily toward the door. Then suddenly the door flew open and she stood facing him in wide-eyed amazement.

From that moment nothing happened the way he had planned or expected.

"Edgar Allan Poe!" she exclaimed. "I knew it was only a matter of time before you'd come knocking on my door!"

7

"Edgar Allan Poe?"

Dubin stood frozen in the doorway staring back at Nicole as if she'd caught him in the middle of some unspeakable crime.

"Just joking," Nicole smiled, her emerald eyes twinkling in the dim light. "Hasn't anyone ever told you that you look like Edgar Allan Poe?"

"Yes, actually, someone has," he stammered, trying to smile. "But why did you expect Poe to show up at your door?"

"It's a long story," she laughed. "I'm sorry. What can I do for you?"

"My name is Dubin and I—"

"*Dubin*!" She said the name as if it were French, with the accent on the second syllable. "That's perfect! Are you a detective?"

"Yes, as a matter of fact, I am."

"And tell me, are you working with the *préfecture du police?*"

"The police? No, I despise the police."

"Ah! You despise the police! Just as I'd expect!"

Dubin grimaced. "Would you mind telling me what's going on?"

"I'm sorry! You poor man! Please come in."

Nicole led him through the dimly-lit apartment to the cluttered kitchen table, where she offered him a seat. "Don't mind me at all. I've been going stir crazy up here trying to think of a topic for my dissertation and I have Edgar Allan Poe and Alexandre Dumas and E.T.A. Hoffmann on the brain. Can I get you some tea?"

He smiled and hesitantly sat down while she poured two mugs of tea from a ceramic tea pot. "You arrived at a perfect time," she said, perching on the chair across from him. "I just had a brilliant inspiration for my thesis topic. I even have a title: Authors as Characters, Characters as Authors: The Semiotics of Authorship in Literary Romance. Isn't that fantastic?"

"Yes," he said. "That sounds fantastic."

"It's about writers appearing as characters in other writers' fictional works, where they meet characters from their own stories who were based on people they knew in real life, only now they're characters in somebody's else's story, not their own, and—well, you can see how convoluted it gets and why I could imagine that you were Edgar Allan Poe knocking on my door and why sometimes I feel like I'm going crazy."

"Sure."

"And you probably know," she added, "that I actually am a little crazy, don't you? Or used to be. You must work for the Institute."

"The Palmer Institute? No, I have no connection with the Institute."

"Oh. Then why have you been following me around?"

Dubin shifted uncomfortably in his chair. "You've noticed, then?"

She nodded, keeping her eyes locked on his. "It's been fairly obvious. The Seven Eleven. The laundromat. Sitting out there in your BMW. I thought you must be working for Dr. Hoffmann."

"Dr. Hoffmann?" The name surprised him, but he tried not to show it. "Not at all. It's an investigation into something that happened a long time ago. Something that has nothing to do with you."

She seemed confused, even a little alarmed. "Then why are you here?"

"I'm afraid I can't tell you about the investigation. But I was hoping I could ask you a few questions."

"OK." She glanced around nervously. "But I hope it won't take too long. I was working."

"No problem," Dubin smiled. "It'll just take a few minutes. What I wanted to ask you about is the Morgan twins. Hunter and

Antonia. Did you meet them while you were staying at the Institute?"

"Sure. They were my best friends."

"Then they're fairly normal?"

Nicole grinned as if the question was a joke. "Antonia never speaks—she hasn't said a word in years, according to Dr. Hoffmann. Though sometimes she sings quite beautifully when she thinks no one is listening."

"And Hunter?"

"Hunter tries on a different identity every day, as casually as other people change their socks. And he never stops talking. They all think he's talking gibberish, but most of what he says is quotations from Shakespeare or something else he's watched on a video."

"Do the doctors know that?"

"I tried to tell Dr. Hoffmann," she laughed, "but he thought I was crazy. They think Hunter has a memory disturbance. He can't remember the most basic facts about himself, like what he was doing yesterday, so how could he memorize the works of Shakespeare from watching videos?"

"That's a good question."

"What the doctors don't seem to appreciate is that for Hunter it's not a matter of memory. The reason he can't remember what he was doing yesterday is that he was a different person yesterday, or any number of different people. So it's hardly fair to expect him to remember, is it? I mean, would it be fair to ask you to remember what I was doing yesterday?"

"No, I see what—"

"If you weren't stalking me, that is." She frowned at Dubin with mock indignation. "Admittedly that's a special case."

"Right."

"And lately Hunter has started playing the piano. Schumann's Kreisleriana."

"From memory?"

"No one has any idea where it came from."

Dubin sensed that he was finally getting somewhere. "And what about their father? Avery Morgan. Have you met him?"

"Sure. He comes to see his kids every day. Sort of a squeaky, ungainly man. But he's very nice, actually. Seems to really care about them."

Nicole picked up her teapot and carried it back to the stove. "I think our time is up," she said. "I have to get back to work."

"Just one last question?"

She smiled indulgently, as if she had been humoring Dubin and not the other way around. "All right. A short one."

"Do you know who Maria Morgan was?"

"She was Hunter and Antonia's mother. She committed suicide a long time ago."

"Did you ever hear anyone talking about her? Or the way she died?"

"No. They wouldn't talk about anything like that with the patients."

Dubin hesitated in the doorway before retreating down the dark stairs. Nicole looked small and beautiful and somehow heroic in her cluttered apartment. He said good-bye, he thanked her for her time, but there was still one thing he needed to ask before he left. "Why would Dr. Hoffmann arrange for someone to follow you around and spy on you?"

"I don't know," she sighed. "I guess I'm a little paranoid."

Living at the Institute, ironically, was taking its toll on my mental health. The isolated setting, the hushed, padded corridors, the inexorable routine of endless days and boring nights (punctuated by my obsessive encounters with Olympia), and in general the atmosphere of suspension and futility that permeated the place—all of these, week after week, made it difficult for me to maintain a sense of reality. Add the cynicism of the staff and the hopelessness of the patients—in spite of the chemical warfare that was designed to obliterate it, you could read the despair in their toneless voices and their empty eyes—and I can only say it's a wonder I was able to avoid psychological contagion as long as I did. Like all psychiatrists, I had undergone extensive psychotherapy as part of my training, and I'd learned some things about myself that I preferred not to think about. In fact my therapist, Dr. Neuberger, had recommended that I continue seeing him even after I finished my residency, but of course that was impossible now that I was living at the Institute. There must have been something in the dark, asphyxiating atmosphere of that place that triggered a recurrence of the symptoms Dr. Neuberger had been so concerned about. I wish I could have stepped back and looked at myself with the practiced eye I focused on my patients.

The first sign of trouble was a sense of foreboding, a malaise of impending evil and shame. Around the beginning of October, I had my first nightmare. It was after one of those marathon sessions with Olympia, though I doubt if she noticed—she'd dropped almost instantaneously from orgiastic excitement into a deep sleep. Exhausted but still aroused, I listened to the rhythm of her mechanical breathing and imagined myself climbing an endless series of numbered steps that rose through a dark tower. At the top of the steps I came to a door, which looked like one of the doors at the Institute. It was the door to the twins' nurse's—Mrs. Paterson's—room. I knocked politely and when there was no answer I quietly opened the door and stepped inside. Mrs. Paterson was lying on top of her bed, fully clothed even though it was the middle of the night. With the back of my hand I touched her forehead and it felt cold. I picked up her wrist and tried to take her pulse, but she had no pulse. She was dead. There was an empty bottle of pills and a glass of water on the night table.

Then I did something I am ashamed to relate. I wish I could say that the person in the dream wasn't really me. But the first rule of dreaming—and there are many of them, as I've come to realize—is that in a dream you're always yourself. No excuses are possible. Even if you dream that you're someone else, or you say to yourself, 'I'm only dreaming,' you're really you and you're really doing what you seem to be doing. And what did I do? When I was sure the nurse was dead, I pulled the nylon belt out of my bathrobe and tied a noose on one end. I slipped the noose around her neck, lifted her over my shoulders and carried her into the bathroom. Then I wrapped the other end of the cord around the light fixture and tightened it until her feet were dangling a few inches above the floor. I tied the cord to the light fixture and waited until the body had stopped swaying.

There was a mirror in the bathroom. It was behind me, on the door to the medicine cabinet. I knew the mirror was there and before I left the room I glanced over my shoulder, the way I used to do when I was a teenager, just to see what I looked like when I struck a certain pose. Ned Hoffmann, I'd say. This is what Ned Hoffmann looks like. But the person I saw in the mirror—just for a flash before the image jolted me awake—was Hunter Morgan.

I lay sweating beside Olympia on the narrow bed, my heart pounding. I was afraid to move. I couldn't hear Olympia breathing, just the ticking of a clock—and my own screaming thoughts. Why did I do that to Mrs. Paterson? Had anyone been watching? Don't tell anyone, whatever you do, even Olympia— especially Olympia. I rolled over and tried to go back to sleep, and when I closed my eyes I saw the body dangling from the light fixture. Only now it didn't look like Mrs. Paterson—it looked like Maria Morgan.

It was only a dream, I told myself. And it wasn't even me.

The morning after that first nightmare, I made a point of being especially friendly to Mrs. Paterson in the dining room. As usual she sat with Hunter and Antonia, sipping her coffee and helping them concentrate on their breakfasts. She suddenly seemed small and vulnerable, and when I remembered my dream I felt small and vulnerable too. Mrs. Paterson smiled when she noticed me staring at their table, and I smiled back as amiably as I could. But I avoided her eyes and when I passed a mirror on my way back upstairs I looked away, for fear of seeing the image of Hunter I'd seen in the mirror in my dream.

Late one night Olympia and I were snuggling in her bed, talking about the progress of Hunter's therapy. "Have you considered doing a past life regression?" she asked, quite seriously.

"A what?" I knew what she meant but I wanted to express my skepticism as forcefully as possible.

"A past life regression," she repeated, sitting up to face me. "You hypnotize the patient and take them back to a prior life, where you can find the source of their bad karma. My father does it all the time."

Peter Bartolli. No wonder Dr. Palmer had warned me about him. "Sorry," I said. "I'm not a witch doctor."

"My Dad thinks it's the only way you're going to find the explanation for Hunter's piano playing."

"What do you mean? He played the piano in a past life?"

"He keeps playing a piece by somebody named Schumann, right?"

"So I'm told."

"Well, maybe Hunter was Schumann. Or maybe part of him was Schumann, or somebody else who played Schumann's works."

"The possibilities are endless."

Irony was lost on Olympia. "They are," she nodded. "That's why you've really got to do the regression. You said yourself the piano playing could be the key to Hunter's psychosis."

"I don't believe in reincarnation."

"Metempsychosis," she said, correcting me. "Technically, what we're talking about isn't reincarnation. It's metempsychosis. It's Greek; from the Greek. M-E-T-E-M-P-S..."

"It's definitely a psychosis."

"It's not a psychosis. It's the transmigration of souls, and it's completely normal."

I stopped her chatter with a kiss, followed by a passionate embrace that carried both of us quickly away from the impasse we had reached in our conversation. I loved her in spite of her nutty ideas, or maybe even because of them. She pulled off my shirt, and I gently removed hers. She ran her lips down my neck and across my breast, and I covered her body with kisses. I felt a stirring inside me that brought my lips back to hers. She pulled away, rolling on top of me. "About that past life regression," she purred, stroking my breast. "Won't you do it? Won't you do it for me?"

At that moment she was every woman who ever lived, and I was every man. Naturally I agreed.

8

Dubin's phone rang as he was stepping out of the shower. It was Susan Morgan and she didn't bother to introduce herself. "Avery's gone to Washington for the day," she said with an air of authority. "Can you come over about ten o'clock?"

"At ten o'clock I'm still sobering up from the night before."

"Then get good and sober and come over at eleven."

The Morgan estate looked the same, only quieter. No kids, no au pair. Even the golden retriever seemed to have taken the day off. Susan came out to greet him, wearing a white tennis dress that displayed her legs to good advantage and a sun visor that kept her cold eyes in the shadows. He followed her into the barn where they had talked before. She led him into the little furnished apartment in the back and invited him to sit down at an oak kitchen table.

"I just made some coffee," she said. "Would you like a cup?"

"That sounds like a great idea."

She set two coffee mugs on the table and sat down across from him, watching him spoon sugar into his coffee.

"Well," she said, as if she was disappointed that he didn't have more to say. "Have you got anything?"

"Only this." He pulled her $5,000 check from his shirt pocket and pushed it across the table.

"No," she smiled, pushing it back to him. "I mean have you found anything?"

"Only this check," he repeated, returning her smile. "It's the closest thing I have to a smoking gun."

She gazed at him in ironic incomprehension.

He said, "I don't know whether to tear it up or put it in my safe."

"Why don't you just cash it?"

"I haven't earned it."

"That's very ethical of you."

"I know."

"Considering your line of work."

Dubin nodded, as if agreeing with her skepticism. He folded the check and put it back in his pocket. "The question is why did you give it to me? I didn't have any information to sell. I still don't. Until you called this morning I thought it might have been to make me go away. But that wasn't it either, was it?"

She shook her head. "I knew it would cost more than that to make you go away. In the meantime maybe I wanted to see what you could come up with."

"So you could use it against your husband?"

"It's like insurance. You buy it hoping you'll never need it."

They sat quietly for a few minutes sipping their coffee. She fixed her gray eyes on Dubin, smiling girlishly as if to say that she wasn't as cynical as she seemed. He stood up in an attempt to change the subject. "Could I take another look at that upstairs studio?"

"Sure."

Climbing the stairs behind her, he kept her muscular thighs at eye level and she seemed to be doing her best to make them worthy of his attention. Once through the door at the top of the stairs she stepped to one side like a weary real estate agent waiting for a client to make up his mind. Dubin's earlier tour of the studio had been quick and impressionistic. Now he took his time and went from one end of the long room to the other making careful mental notes of everything he saw. He examined each of the portraits, prints, and posters that lined the walls—one poster that grabbed his attention, from the Salzburg Marionette Theater, depicted an array of haunted, bug-eyed marionettes that all looked strangely alike. Beneath the dusty sheets that lay draped over the furniture he found an upright piano, a music stand, a high wooden stool, a CD player and an old record player with a turntable on a wobbly platform with half a dozen boxed sets of long-playing records—Offenbach's *Tales of Hoffmann*, Tchaikowsky's *The Nutcracker*, Delibes's *Coppélia*—filed on the shelves below. And on the wall there were more shelves containing more records, tapes and CDs, and dozens of dusty books, many of them in German or French.

Susan waited by the door, looking bored and ironic.

"Are you an opera lover?" he asked her as he pawed through the books looking for a title he had heard of.

"Only if you include soap operas."

Dubin laughed. "Everything here is Hoffmann. Hoffmann this, Hoffmann that. Who the hell was Hoffmann anyway? Was he a composer?"

"A writer, I think."

"She must have been obsessed with him."

Susan nodded in agreement. "Maria's method of preparing a role was to get obsessed with whatever opera she was rehearsing. She'd surround herself with books, pictures, music, whatever she could find that took her into the role. 'Get obsessed and stay obsessed,' she used to say. I guess it worked."

Dubin thought of the Stephen Witz catalog he'd found at the library—in which someone, less than a year ago, had circled the Offenbach letter about *The Tales of Hoffmann*—and wondered if Maria Morgan's obsession had somehow outlived her. "So you knew her then?"

"Sure I knew her. I lived here. I was the babysitter."

Dubin was taken aback. "You were the babysitter for the schizophrenic twins?"

"They weren't schizophrenic then," she said, "or if they were I didn't know it. Maria told me they had learning disabilities. Mrs. Paterson was the one who really took care of them and gave them their medications. I was just an extra hand, mostly for when they were traveling. Mrs. Paterson doesn't like to travel."

"Did your husband buy an autograph letter by Offenbach within the past year?"

"Fortunately he doesn't include me in his collecting mania."

"You don't know whether he bought the Offenbach letter?"

"What Offenbach letter?"

Dubin stood peering out the small gable window that looked over the duck pond behind the barn. "There's something about all this that doesn't make sense to me."

Susan watched him expectantly.

"Here's Maria Morgan," he said, turning toward her. "Talented, still young, headed for a glamorous, exciting future. What was she doing here?"

"What do you mean?"

He hesitated. "I don't know if I can say this without being offensive."

"Oh," she said, looking away. "You mean Avery."

He nodded.

She raised her eyes to meet his. "You mean, what would a woman like that be doing with Avery?"

"Forget it. I'm sorry I opened my mouth." He wanted to escape downstairs, out of this dusty mausoleum and back into the world of the living. He stepped toward the door, but she stood in his way.

"She probably felt the same way I do," Susan said.

Dubin said nothing.

"It's a mistake to marry someone who's that much older than yourself." Her eyes were still gray but they were no longer cold, no longer bored or cynical. Vulnerability spread across her face like the freckles she carried from childhood. Dubin smiled, hesitated, then slipped around her and headed down the stairs. She brushed his hand as he passed.

At the bottom of the stairs she was blushing. "Would you like more coffee?"

"I didn't realize you were the babysitter," Dubin said as he stirred a spoonful of sugar into his coffee.

She sat on the edge of the bed, looking past him. "I know what you're thinking. It's what everybody thought—that Avery and I were already an item before Maria died and then we just waited a year and got married. But that wasn't it at all. It was so innocent and stupid."

"You were young."

"I still am."

"Sorry."

She stood up and rinsed the coffee maker in the sink. "Seven years and three kids later it all seems pretty long ago."

"You felt sorry for him."

"I did then. But I don't feel that sorry now. Not for him, at least."

Back outside the barn, her innocence and vulnerability seemed as quaint as last season's fashions. "Avery's very upset," she told Dubin, fixing him in her gray eyes. "He knows you're a blackmailer—he's done some research about you—and he thinks you've got him in your sights."

"He could be right about that."

"He says you used to be a journalist."

"He is right about that."

"What happened?"

Dubin opened the door to his car and climbed inside. "It was one of those scandals a few years back. News stories written by reporters who weren't anywhere near the scene of the action, that type of thing. I wasn't the main attraction and I was only guilty of cutting a few corners here and there, but I got sucked in along with everybody else and when I got spat back out I didn't have a job or a future."

"So." She was trying to be polite. "It was time for a career change."

"Not really. When you write for a paper, ninety percent of what you write never gets printed. Why? Could be lack of verification, lack of space, lack of interest. Or it could be that whoever the story was written about wanted to make sure it never saw the light of day. Maybe that person made a gift to the editor or a well-timed political contribution to the candidate of his choice. And maybe that's why you were researching the story in the first place."

"Wow."

"You can call me a blackmailer if you want to," Dubin smiled. "I like to think of myself as pursuing journalism by other means."

Before he drove away, he asked Susan one last question. "Why is Avery so worried about me?"

She raised her eyebrows in a sly reference to what had almost happened in the barn.

"I mean, what does he think I have on him?"

"He says he's afraid you'll make up evidence that's not really there."

"Some people—the cops, for instance—might do that. But I wouldn't, and he'd know that if he'd done his homework."

"You're an honorable blackmailer, then."

"There's nothing honorable about me. But I work on my own terms, and they're very specific. To attract my attention you have to be very rich, rich enough to buy your own justice. And to be liable for my fee, you have to be guilty beyond a reasonable doubt."

"Your fee?" she laughed. "I love that."

"That's how I think of it."

"You took my check."

"Yes, but I still haven't cashed it."

"I guess that's a good sign."

"Yes," he admitted. "It means that anything can still happen."

Shortly before noon on the day scheduled for Nicole's next follow-up visit, I happened to glance out the window near the nurse's station on the second floor and saw Nicole walking up to the main entrance below. She wore a white sun dress and sandals, and with her red hair burning in the midday sun she looked like an angel on a mission of mercy. Since it was two hours before her appointment, I assumed that she would be having lunch with Hunter and Antonia. This was something she often did—just the day before, I'd caught a glimpse of her following the twins into the dining room—and I could only speculate about its significance. In our last session, I recalled, she had related her fantasies about Robert Schumann and his quest for madness in the "spirit world" imagined by a German Romantic writer named Hoffmann (who may or may not have ever existed; I made a mental note to look him up), and I assumed that today she planned to start where she'd left off, with some more literary nonsense fueled by her fantasies about me.

After a few minutes I found myself drifting down to the dining room, where I purchased my usual lunch (a chicken salad sandwich on wheat toast), and without being observed I found a seat behind a canvas screen that partitioned the patients' dining room from the employee lounge. On the other side of this screen sat Nicole, Hunter, Antonia, and Mrs. Paterson, and without any particular effort I was able to overhear every word they said. Hunter's conversation was the usual indecipherable gibberish, and Antonia of course said nothing beyond an occasional asthmatic sigh. But Nicole and Mrs. Paterson were in the middle of an animated discussion, which I soon realized was about me and my relationship with Olympia.

"He goes to her room every night," Mrs. Paterson was saying, "when he thinks everyone's gone to bed—"

"Does he spend the night there?" Nicole asked.

"I don't know, honey. To tell you the truth, I never hung around long enough to find that out."

"Then what—"

"But oh, Lord, the noises that come out of that room!"

"Oh my God. Noises?"

"Uh-huh. Some nights she keeps the whole building awake."

I wanted to push my fist through the canvas screen and cram my chicken salad sandwich down Mrs. Paterson's throat. Instead I coughed conspicuously and she lowered her voice, which I immediately regretted. Now all I could hear were murmuring and short bursts of laughter and I couldn't be sure who they were coming from.

Jeff Gottlieb stumbled up to my table carrying a plastic tray laden with pizza and french fries and lemon meringue pie. "Mind if I join you?" Without waiting for an answer, he deposited himself across from me and filled his mouth with pizza.

Suddenly Mrs. Paterson's voice came through the screen loud and clear. "They've been fighting over her like a plaything all her life," she was saying. "The same way they used to fight over her mother."

"Olympia," Gottlieb nodded salaciously.

"You ever notice her eyes? I bet that took some doing." Mrs. Paterson's voice dropped back to a murmur and Gottlieb added his own clarification.

"Olympia's got Miles Palmer's eyes," he said between slurps of his coffee.

"So what?"

"What do you think? She got them from her uncle?" Gottlieb leered at me with lewd amusement as I squirmed in my seat.

"There's something strange about that girl," Mrs. Paterson went on. "If you ask me, she's just a kewpie doll, just a hollow little thing that looks pretty on the outside but's got a big hole in the middle. You hear what I'm saying?"

Gottlieb was laughing so hard that the coffee was dribbling down his chin. "Is that right, Hoffmann?" he sputtered, a little too loudly. "Is Olympia just a pretty doll with a hole in the middle? You ought to know! Ha ha ha ha!"

I was so angry I bolted up from the table and hurried away without even picking up my tray or clearing away my trash. Behind me I could hear laughter—women's laughter, not just Gottlieb's— but I didn't dare look back to find out whether they were laughing at me. At any rate I couldn't have looked back if I tried: I had been stopped in my tracks by a sudden, blinding headache that seized my temples like a pair of tongs hoisting a block of ice to the ceiling. When the attack subsided I found myself standing in the kitchen surrounded by cooks and dishwashers who, by the looks on their faces, must have wondered if I was one of the patients. I introduced myself officiously and they turned back to their work. Glancing around the kitchen, I noticed a paring knife lying on a counter, with a short wooden handle and a sharp three-inch blade. When no one was looking I wrapped the knife in a linen napkin and stuck it into the pocket of my suit jacket.

Then I hurried back upstairs. I had to be ready for Nicole's therapy session at two o'clock.

By the time Nicole tapped on the door of my office I had recovered from my migraine attack and my humiliation and anger in the dining room. I straightened my desk and lowered the window shades, wondering whether she would say anything about what had happened. Eavesdropping is never dignified, but I was prepared to defend my behavior, if necessary, as a adjunct to her therapy.

"I just had lunch with Hunter and Antonia," she said blandly.

I pretended to be surprised. "Really? What did you talk about?"

"Oh, the usual nonsense. You know how it is, talking to that pair."

I decided to play along with her. "Have you noticed any change in Hunter lately?"

She shook her head. "Not really. It's disappointing, isn't it? I thought Hunter's piano playing was some kind of breakthrough that would lead somewhere."

"It still might. We haven't exhausted all the available techniques."

Nicole looked back at me curiously. "What do you have in mind?"

"Well," I hesitated—I knew I shouldn't be discussing Hunter's case with another patient, but Nicole's interest in his recovery was a healthy sign and I wanted to encourage it—"Olympia suggested that we do a past life regression, using hypnosis."

"You can't be serious!"

Her skeptical tone caught me off guard. Wasn't this the woman who, just a week before, had been lecturing me about the "spirit world"? I still had deep misgivings about hypnosis and past life regression, but I realized that bringing them into the conversation had been a lucky stroke. Through these topics I could probe into thoughts and fantasies that Nicole might otherwise have been afraid to discuss.

"Oh, I know what you're thinking," I said. "At first I thought the idea sounded kooky—you know how Olympia is—but she gave me a list of books to read on past life regression and I'm almost ready to try it. Apparently her father—Dr. Bartolli, who used to work here and is very well acquainted with this technique—thinks Hunter would make an ideal candidate."

Nicole seemed incredulous and strangely agitated. "Isn't this reincarnation you're talking about? The transmigration of souls?"

"Not necessarily. It could be a psychological phenomenon. A person could imagine himself living in some distant age and construct an entire past life based on some book or movie he's forgotten all about."

She lowered her eyes and turned away as if she were looking for an escape route.

"What are you thinking?" I asked.

"I don't believe in reincarnation," she said quietly, turning back to face me, "but I guess I've been coming to believe in something similar. Not the transmigration of souls but the transmigration of ideas."

I waited patiently for her to continue.

"It's part of the thinking I've been doing for my thesis. I think it was prompted by the research I mentioned last time on the connection between Schumann and Hoffmann."

I reached for a pencil so I could jot down some notes. Nicole was pulling me into uncharted waters and I wanted to be able to remember how I got there.

"Ideas are like seed crystals," she went on. "A writer like Hoffmann could create ideas that spread out and infect thousands of other personalities. And then someone like Schumann—"

A little shiver ran down my spine. "Why did you say 'infect?'"

"Because it could be like a crystal—something clear and bright and beautiful—or it could be something more insidious and evil, like a virus that has to migrate from one human to another in order to survive. So Hoffmann could become Schumann who could become Offenbach who could become—I don't know—Dostoevsky? Nietzsche? Joyce?"

I pretended to scribble some more notes as the full impact of Nicole's theory hit home. In my career I had encountered many delusions, but never anything so elaborate, so well thought out, so thoroughly mad as this. It's a common belief among psychotics that some distant person or force is sending messages aimed at controlling their mind and actions, to the point where many schizophrenics will claim that their voices are controlled by demons or computer chips. But this was the first time I'd ever heard this delusion articulated as a general theory of culture. Nicole's illness, I realized, was far more serious than I had imagined. I stood up to signal that our session was over. "Well, that will give us a lot to think about for next time."

And then she turned the tables on me. "Are you still dating Olympia?"

"Olympia?" I stammered. I wanted to say: We're not dating; we're just friends. But Mrs. Paterson had just told Nicole that I spent every night in Olympia's room. "We see each other sometimes."

"I'm happy for you."

"You don't like her, do you?"

"She seems very nice. But I wonder... whether she's good for you."

Suddenly I understood. It was the transference I'd detected at our last session. Nicole had fallen in love with me and now she was jealous of Olympia. "Maybe we can talk about that next time. But try to remember"—I forced a smile—"this is supposed to be about you, not me."

"I'm not jealous," Nicole said, returning my smile, "if that's what you're thinking." She stood up to face me. "It's just that— you're going to think I'm stark raving mad when I say this—it's just that Olympia seems to be carrying the Hoffmann virus and she's drawing you into her world. So this is going to be about you. And there's nothing either of us can do about it."

9

Miss Whipple had a secret that she'd kept to herself for seven years. She and Maria Morgan had never exactly been friends, but they shared the kind of intimacy that exists between a librarian and her borrower. She knew what books the opera singer read, how long it took her to read them, and how she felt about them, and that was more than many of her so-called friends knew about her. They moved in different circles, of course, but at the library they talked about books and opera, which both of them were passionate about. Shortly before she died, Maria Morgan checked some materials out of the library—a few books and some sound recordings. In those days they still circulated long-playing records, and on her last visit to the library Maria Morgan had gone home with a full-length recording of *The Tales of Hoffmann*, the Ansermet version of *The Nutcracker*, and *Piano Music of Robert Schumann* played by Alicia de Larrocha. She also checked out several books, including a collection of supernatural tales from the nineteenth century. As she explained to the librarian, she planned to use these materials to prepare for her triple role in Hoffmann, steeping herself in everything fantastic and uncanny that she could get her hands on. Nothing in her manner seemed distraught or depressed, but within a few days she was dead. Miss Whipple was too discreet to mention the overdue books and records, and after a few weeks her patience was rewarded. Avery Morgan himself came to the library to return them. She thanked him sympathetically and waived the fines, even overlooking the absence of one of the records, the Schumann piano music, which was never returned. It wasn't until after he left that she discovered the letter stuck in one of the books.

Nothing too surprising about that. Letters, postcards, shopping lists—even obscene photographs—come flying out of returned books all the time. Miss Whipple had amassed quite a collection over the years and learned a great deal about her neighbors in the process. But to find a letter addressed to Maria Morgan so soon after her death, and postmarked shortly before it, was almost too poignant. Miss Whipple's first instinct was to call Avery Morgan and offer to hold the letter until he could pick it up. Certainly not to open it or read it. What kind of person would do that? But her second instinct—and it was the one that soon prevailed—was to stuff the letter into her purse and take it home so she could read it without being observed. At home she discovered that it was a love letter and it did not come from Maria Morgan's husband. When she thought about some of the things mentioned in the letter and who it was that must have written it, she had to catch her breath. She read the letter over a few times, just to make sure there was no misunderstanding, and then she buried it deep in a locked file cabinet and tried never to think about it again.

"I don't know if there's much of a story here," Dubin told Miss Whipple one morning as he followed her shelving cart between the stacks. "Maybe Maria Morgan really committed suicide. She'd been depressed—"

The librarian snorted derisively as she squeezed a copy of *Reversal of Fortune* onto the top shelf in the True Crime section.

"You disagree?"

"If she was depressed," Miss Whipple said, "I certainly never noticed it. She was in here checking out books the day before she died."

The librarian started to say more but instead she avoided looking at Dubin and concentrated on her reshelving. Her eagerness to cooperate with Dubin had been flagging; it cut against the grain of her natural discretion. She was not the kind of person who went around telling secrets to strangers, even in a good cause.

And of course there were some places she absolutely would not go, secrets she'd kept too long to tell them now.

Dubin followed her around the corner to the History section. He picked up a book off the cart and tried to locate where it went, but she snatched it out of his hand.

"I'll do that if you don't mind."

"No problem," he smiled, taking a step back. "According to the articles you gave me, she was being treated for depression."

There was a long pause as Miss Whipple made an opening for the book and slipped it in. "All I can say is I was very surprised to hear that," she finally said.

"So did she kill herself?"

"I never believed it."

Dubin watched her carefully. "In that case she must have been murdered."

The librarian seemed to shiver when he said that word. "Don't say that!"

"Well, I think it's the only alternative. She didn't die a natural death."

"If you don't mind, I've got work to do."

Dubin gave her his most winning smile, the one he reserved for old ladies and government bureaucrats. "I'm sorry. I'm just trying to run through the logic of whether I ought to be spending my time on this or not."

She smiled grudgingly and pushed her cart around a corner and halfway down the next aisle. "Okay, go on."

"The question is why would anyone have wanted to kill her," Dubin said. "Money had nothing to do with it. I checked out her will. Her money went exactly where you'd expect it to go—to her husband in trust for the kids, with a small bequest to a sister in California."

"Avery Morgan certainly didn't kill her for her money, if that's what you've been thinking."

"What did he kill her for, then?"

"I didn't say he did. I just meant, he's already got so much money of his own."

"You suspect him, though. Don't you?"

"I didn't say that."

"You do suspect him. Everybody around here does. But is it based on anything other than speculation? What was his motive?"

She lowered her voice almost to a whisper. "Maybe she had a lover."

"More speculation."

"No. Maybe I know she had a lover."

"You know that for a fact? It's not just some gossip you heard?"

"I think I know the difference between fact and gossip."

"How do you know? Did you catch them in the act?"

"No." She hesitated. "I—I saw a letter."

"To Maria Morgan?"

She nodded.

"Who was it from?"

Miss Whipple swung her shelving cart around so that it stood between herself and Dubin, and with that barricade between them she faced him defiantly. "I'm afraid you're going a little too fast for me, Mr. Dubin."

"I thought you wanted to help."

"I'm trying to help, but I have my limits. You're going to have to do your homework and see what you can find out for yourself."

"All right. I can think of two other people who probably know at least as much as you do."

She smiled skeptically. "Who's that?"

"The nurse. What's her name? Mrs. Paterson? She was with the family even in those days, wasn't she? And Dr. Palmer. He was the one who treated Maria Morgan for her so-called depression."

"I doubt if either of them would talk to you."

"Well, there's no harm in asking, is there? I'll let you know what happens."

When Dubin and Miss Whipple stepped out from behind the stacks they came face to face with Avery Morgan, who stood at the desk waiting to return an overdue book. Morgan seemed shocked to see Dubin and angry with the librarian for allowing him in the library.

"What have you been telling this man?"

The librarian blushed and nearly toppled over. "Mr. Morgan. What do you mean?"

"You know what I mean. He's been asking you about Maria, hasn't he? What have you told him?"

"Nothing, really. I haven't told him anything."

"He's a blackmailer."

"A blackmailer?"

"That's right "

She turned to Dubin, who again tried his most winning smile. She did not smile back this time. "But he told me he was a writer."

"The only thing he writes is extortion notes."

"But who is he blackmailing?"

"He's tried my wife and me, but since he doesn't have anything to blackmail us about he's shopping around in the neighborhood for whatever he can find." Morgan's lower lip was quivering. "No one in this town is safe with a man like that walking around."

Dubin drove past the train station and parked in the shady spot where he often sat watching for Nicole. He thought about her often, much more often than about Susan Avery. Sometimes, in her flimsy running clothes, she flitted out the door and flew away before he could even think about following her. There was no sign of her that day, which was just as well. His encounter with Avery Morgan had left him in a foul mood. He knew what he was and made no excuses for himself, but still Avery Morgan had wounded his pride. No one in this town is safe with a man like that walking around. It infuriated him to be spoken of that way, even if it was true.

* * *

Miss Whipple spent a sleepless night, angry and upset with herself as much as with Dubin. What had she done? After keeping her secret for seven years, what had possessed her to confide in a stranger? He called himself a writer—and he looked like a writer, with his thoughtful eyes and his delicate moustache and the wavy dark hair that he wore a little too long—and somehow she must have thought she could trust him. She thought he'd write a book that would eventually find a place in the True Crime section, and she'd be mentioned in the Acknowledgements—"The author extends his warmest gratitude to Miss Francine Whipple, without whose tireless assistance this book could never have been written." Was that what she'd been hoping? Was she that much of a fool? All she'd accomplished was to expose the town and everyone in it to the machinations of a blackmailer.

Miss Whipple tossed and turned for three more hours before she fell asleep. By then it was almost dawn and she knew exactly what she would have to do. Don't worry, she told herself. The letter is in a safe place.

I feel I should say more about Hunter and Antonia, because this is their story, not mine. And I could do that easily enough by sticking to the jargon of my trade, substituting clinical data for the kinds of observations we normally make about the people around us. But to say very much about them as human beings—to describe them in the same terms as I've described Olympia or Nicole or even Jeff Gottlieb—is frankly beyond my powers.

Hunter was a hard person to know. His social interactions consisted of incoherent ravings interspersed with long periods of silence. It's no accident that *Hamlet* was his favorite play. He spent his life brooding, reading books, talking to himself as he tried on his multiple personalities, shouting out random challenges and conundrums—and watching videos, endlessly watching videos, often the same one for hours at a time. I could record all this as clinical data, but I would have to be Shakespeare to go beyond the pathological in my rendering of it. And he had spent most of his life so heavily sedated that, unlike Hamlet, he could not express himself in actions any better than in words. You could have watched him for a hundred years without coming any closer to knowing his innermost thoughts. I wanted to bridge the gap by reducing his dosages, but on that I had been overruled. For Antonia the situation was even more hopeless. Gibberish would have been an improvement over the seven years' silence her illness had imposed on her. In her bright blue eyes you could glimpse a beautiful soul, like a tropical fish in an aquarium, trying to escape through the clouded glass.

Just three weeks had gone by since Hunter first sat down to play the piano, but so much had changed in those weeks that it seemed a different world. Hunter's illness had shown some improvement; Nicole had turned out to be more seriously troubled than anyone imagined; and I—not to be outdone by my patients—had become the victim of frequent nightmares and migraine attacks that left me feeling unable to cope with the demands of my job. I considered calling Dr. Neuberger, the therapist who, during my residency, had helped me overcome these and other symptoms before they spoiled my chances for a successful career. But what would I say to Dr. Neuberger? How could I spare the time to travel into the city to see him on any kind of regular basis? Frankly, there were things going on in my life that I would have been reluctant to discuss with him. I had been drawn into a relationship with Olympia that even I could recognize as a dangerous sexual obsession. I had lost my judgment and self-control and was beginning to lose my grip on reality. Only that could account for my fateful decision to yield to Olympia's blandishments and allow her father, Dr. Peter Bartolli, to conduct a hypnotic past life regression on Hunter Morgan.

Dr. Palmer would have been furious if he'd known what we were doing behind his back. Not only because it involved Peter Bartolli but because to him the whole subject of past life regression was completely beyond the pale. I'd had the same reaction when Olympia first brought it up, but under her prodding I did enough research to convince myself that the idea wasn't utterly mad. A scientist named Stephenson at the University of Virginia has published several volumes of carefully documented studies on the past life regression phenomenon, having traveled throughout Africa and India collecting first-person narratives for many years. For example, Stephenson relates the story of a small boy in India who specifically recalled being murdered in a past life, describing his killers, their weapons, and numerous details that no one in his village could have known. It turned out that a crime corresponding exactly to the boy's "recollection" had been committed in a distant village about six months before he was born. My research uncovered many stories of a similar nature. And I discovered that past life regression through hypnosis has been used as a therapeutic tool by a wide variety of practitioners, including many who don't believe in reincarnation or any other mystical claptrap. It's no more unbelievable than Freudianism, I told myself—and probably no less therapeutic. And so I pretended to have an open mind, though deep down I knew it was nonsense. The truth is that I was being guided not by sound medical judgment but by my obsession with Olympia. In her mind anything labeled "New Age" might as well have been proven beyond a reasonable doubt—she herself had experienced several previous lives, she told me, all of a glamorous and historically significant nature. And at the merest hint of skepticism on my part, she would turn away coldly and challenge me to argue the point with her father.

I had never actually met Peter Bartolli until the night appointed for the hypnosis session with Hunter. It was a rainy, moonless night, with the north wind whisking in the first shudder of an autumn chill. Bartolli appeared in my office shaking the rain from his black umbrella after having been spirited into the Institute's service entrance by Olympia. The umbrella was almost as large as he was and it seemed to enfold him like a pair of black wings. He kept it furled around him as he made his way down the darkened corridors to my office, presumably to avoid being identified by the staff. But no one who'd ever seen him before could have failed to recognize his wiry frame or the agitated, insistent movements of his long, slender hands. As he shook the rain off the umbrella and reached out to greet me, a wide smile stretched beneath his bottomless eyes. "Dr. Hoffmann," he said with an air of satisfaction. "Peter Bartolli. I'm so very pleased to meet you."

Bartolli wore black shoes, black wool slacks and a black turtleneck. But in spite of this lugubrious color scheme he projected a warmth that made me like him immediately. He spoke perfect English—almost too precise to be perfect—but there was something Old World, possibly Middle European about him. I tried to remember what Olympia had told me about his background. "I'm delighted to meet you, doctor," I said. "Olympia has told me so much about you."

"That's unfortunate," he said, making a face at his daughter. Then he laughed, "I hope she didn't tell you any of my secrets."

Olympia joined in his laughter, and I took the cue and laughed too. "Even though," he winked, "she has told me all of yours."

Olympia and her father enjoyed another round of laughter, though I felt like squirming out of the room. Fortunately Hunter, who had been sitting quietly in the wing chair across from my desk, with his back turned to the door, chose that moment to make his presence known. "Dr. Palmer!" he called out. "Where's Dr. Palmer!"

"Dr. Palmer is out of town," I answered. "He's at a meeting in London. He won't be back till next week."

Bartolli stepped forward and leaned around to face Hunter. "Do you know me?"

"Excellent well, sir. You are a fishmonger."

"Ha!" Bartolli smiled. "Still playing Hamlet!" He pulled up a small chair and sat down. "No, Hunter, I'm Dr. Bartolli. You remember me, don't you?"

"Have you a daughter?"

"Yes. You know Olympia, don't you?"

"Let her not walk in the sun."

Bartolli knew the script. "Still harping on my daughter!"

Hunter laughed. "Gone, far gone!"

Bartolli took his hand and squeezed it lightly. "Yes, you're gone, far gone, but you can come back if you do as I say. You feel better lately, don't you, Hunter?"

Hunter nodded.

"Well, tonight we're going to try something a little different, and I think you'll feel even better than you do. We're going to try to go back in time. Would you like to do that?"

Hunter nodded again.

Bartolli signaled to Olympia and me to take seats in the back of the room where Hunter wouldn't see us. Before I sat down I pushed a button to start the tape recorder beside my desk. "What I'd like you to do is just relax," Bartolli said, gently laying Hunter's hand on the arm of the wing chair. "Close your eyes and just listen to my voice and relax. You know what 'relax' means. It means not to worry about anything or care about anything or think about anything. So just relax. That's right. Just relax."

Bartolli's voice was so entrancing that even Olympia, sitting beside me in the back of the room, seemed to be drifting under his control. I squeezed her hand and she jolted awake just as her father glanced in our direction to let us know that Hunter had fallen into the desired hypnotic state. "Now let's try to think back to an earlier age," he said softly, "a time when everything was different. You're still you, although you're different too, and there you are and there's everyone else and it's an entirely different time and place. Just relax, and in your mind look around you and try to tell us what you see."

Hunter's voice sounded low, almost growling. "Dark," he said. "Dingy."

"It's a dark and dingy place. Where are you?"

"Noisy too. Lots of men." He rolled his head from side to side, growling in that strange voice that none of us had ever heard before. "Dancing in circles, drinking out of mugs."

"You're someplace dark and dingy and noisy where there are a lot of men dancing around drinking. And are they saying anything?"

"Shouting. Singing. Drinking and singing and shouting."

"Are they speaking English?"

"English, sure. They're speaking English."

Bartolli leaned forward and lowered his voice. "Can you tell us what you're doing?"

"I just walked in. I'm looking around."

"When is all this happening?"

"Oh," Hunter whispered, as if he didn't want the men to overhear. "It's a long time ago. A big barrel, men in funny clothes, drinking beer and jumping around singing and drinking beer."

"Now if you could just go back and give us the whole picture again."

"It's a place like a bar, sort of dark, no windows, noisy..."

And so it went. Bartolli had the uncanny ability to draw a coherence out of Hunter's "past life" that was completely absent from his present one. Hunter answered his questions in meaningful phrases, sometimes even complete sentences, with none of the breathless gibberish that usually poured out of him. It was as if he'd recaptured a life in which he was not schizophrenic—though the world he described was a very strange one indeed. It was all as Olympia had predicted, but I could hardly believe my ears. And as for Olympia: I had my hands full just trying to keep her out of Hunter's trance. She sat with her eyes closed, smiling, bobbing her head as she listened, and more than once I had to clamp down on her arm to keep her in her seat.

We recorded and transcribed the entire session, filling thirty-five pages with Hunter's disconnected answers to Bartolli's questions. Let me try to give a condensed version, without all the fits and starts:

"I'm in a dark, dingy tavern filled with noisy men dancing and shouting, drinking and singing. It's a long time ago, I don't know where it is. They're speaking English, but their clothes look funny and old fashioned. They're singing some kind of drinking song, waving their beer mugs around in the air as they sing. They shout at me when I arrive—it's like they all know me—and I sit down at a big round table and drink a glass of wine, keeping my eye on an evil-looking man who wears a cape and a hat like George Washington's. Everyone's laughing at a weird little midget who looks like a court jester. The men light a fire in the middle of the table—it's some kind of flaming punch—and we drink toasts and smoke pipes and talk about women. Everyone looks at me, and I offer to tell the story of the three women I have loved."

At this point Hunter started shouting incoherently, almost violently, and Bartolli had to calm him down and renew the painstaking process of drawing out his memories one by one. In fragmentary moments of lucidity over the next half hour, Hunter described the following scene:

"A beautiful young woman lies sleeping on a swinging couch, dressed in a kind of ballet dress. I walk in with an old man, who refers to the young woman as his daughter, though she doesn't wake up. Another old man runs into the room, with white hair and long eyebrows that stick out in front of his face. He shows me a pair of eyeglasses, and when I try them on the room comes to life. The girl wakes up and the two old men fight over her—apparently each of them thinks she's his daughter—and she starts dancing like a ballerina. I'm in love with her, and before long we're dancing together, she's spinning me around and we whirl wildly down a long staircase. Her father chases after us, shouting for us to stop."

Hunter grew increasingly agitated as he related these events, and by the time the "father"—I couldn't tell which one—started chasing them down the stairs, he was shouting and gasping for breath and all the color had drained from his face, as if his deepest fears were being realized. Bartolli had no choice but to pull him back from the regression and release him from the trance, and in a few minutes he had caught his breath and sat gazing around the room with his accustomed lack of affect.

I had never seen anything remotely like it. To be sure, the second half of the narrative sounded more like a fantasy or a nightmare than a historical recollection, but for Hunter even that was a momentous leap forward. He had gone "back in time" into a world that he could describe and other people could begin to understand.

It was time for Hunter to return to his room and go to bed. I rang for Mrs. Paterson and she appeared so quickly that I wondered if she'd been listening outside the door. She took Hunter's hand and spoke softly to him, almost as if she were soothing a horse. "Okay now Hunter. It's time to go back to your room. Can you stand up?" With Olympia's aid, she stood him up, and the two of them walked him out of the room.

Dr. Bartolli found his umbrella and stood by the door waiting for Olympia to return. "You've seen something here tonight," he said, "that I hope will change the way you think about your work with Hunter. We've already brought him a few steps closer to the real world. Don't you agree?"

"The real world?" I laughed. "What he described was some kind of bizarre fantasy world that's not a whole lot different from the one he usually lives in."

"No. But at least it was describable. At least he could paint a picture of himself dancing with the girl and trying to escape."

In Olympia's absence I felt I could speak freely to Bartolli, as one physician to another. "It seems to me," I said cautiously, "that you're just layering one form of delusion on top of another."

"This is no delusion."

"Surely you don't expect me to believe in reincarnation?"

Bartolli nodded respectfully, dismissing my skepticism with the authority of his imperious eyes. "Not in any literal sense," he allowed. "But psychologically each of us is reincarnated many times a day, forging new personalities that operate outside of our own experience. You see the extreme forms of this in bipolar disorder, multiple-personality disorder, the savant syndrome. Schizophrenia, or spirit possession as it is known in some cultures."

Before I could respond, Olympia appeared at the door and took her father's hand. "We've got to be going," she said.

He smiled at his daughter and then back at me. "Memories are built along the same lines as dreams," he said. "Little pieces of the past are floating around in the world we experience, waiting to coalesce into a memory in the same way that little pieces of memory coalesce into a dream."

Olympia tugged at his arm. "Come on, Dad. It's ten o'clock."

"In other words," he smiled, disappearing with his daughter out into the rainy night, "we are such stuff as dreams are made on. And right now it's time for my little life to be rounded with some sleep."

10

Dubin had been brooding about the Offenbach letter he'd found circled in the Stephen Witz catalog at the library. "There was someone who really wanted it," Witz had told him—and it was probably someone right here in Egdon who had kept Maria Morgan's obsession with *The Tales of Hoffmann* alive for seven years. That letter, if he could find it, might be the kind of tangible evidence he needed to link the past to the present. In his business suspicions, beliefs, even certainties, had no value: letters, diaries, photographs, were the only things you could put a price tag on, and they usually turned up in the same place. Who bought the Offenbach letter? Was it Avery Morgan? The dealer would never tell, and Susan probably didn't know. There was only one thing left to do. He would have to ask Avery Morgan himself.

He called the house—luckily the au pair answered—and asked to speak to Mr. Morgan.

"Who's calling, please?"

"This is Stephen Witz, in New York. I have personal business with Mr. Morgan."

Morgan took his time coming to the phone. "Hello?" He seemed surprised, even a little annoyed, to receive the call. That was a good sign, Dubin thought. It meant he didn't speak to the autograph dealer very often.

"Mr. Morgan," Dubin said, "this is Stephen Witz in New York. The autograph dealer?"

"Oh, sure. How are you?"

"Very well. And yourself?"

"Fine, thank you. What can I do for you?"

"Mr. Morgan, I'm calling about the letter you purchased last year. A related manuscript may be coming on the market, the manuscript mentioned in the letter. It's an important item, and I wondered if—"

"I'm a little confused," Morgan interrupted. "What letter are you talking about?"

"The Offenbach letter you purchased last year. Jacques Offenbach to Albert Wolff, August 28, 1880."

A long silence. Morgan must have been more than a little confused. "There must be some mistake," he finally said. "I haven't purchased any Offenbach materials from you. Or from anyone else. You know I only collect Americana."

"Perhaps I'm mistaken, but my records show that you purchased the letter."

"You are mistaken. Mr. Witz. And your records are inaccurate."

"I'm sorry, sir."

"You know my collecting interests. If you get anything I'd be interested in, please send me a note. But if it's not in my area, I'd rather not be bothered."

When the conversation ended, Dubin picked up the phone again to dial information. There were two other people he wanted to talk to. One was Casimir Ostrovsky, the opera director who selected Maria Morgan for her last role as the female lead in Offenbach's *Tales of Hoffmann*. The other was Frank Lynch, the retired cop who investigated her death.

Frank Lynch had retired down to the Jersey shore and now occupied himself with fishing. He and his wife shared a mobile home in Toms River backing on a lagoon where he docked his 20-foot Grady. Dubin sat waiting for him on the patio behind the house, sipping a glass of lemonade supplied by Mrs. Lynch, a talkative lady who quickly made it clear that she had no interest in fishing. When Dubin told her why he wanted to talk to her husband she also lost interest in talking and disappeared into the house, leaving Dubin to pass the time with a restless labrador retriever who eyed him expectantly but seemed totally at a loss for words.

It was an unusually warm day for October, and unusually humid for that time of year. The afternoon sun slanted through the heavy salt air, stifling the lagoon in an oppressive silence. A few seagulls hovered indifferently while others waited on the pylons that marked the entrance to the bay. Dubin stood up to peer through the mist and across the bay to the barrier island with its amusement rides and white vacation homes crowded along the shore. After half an hour Frank Lynch chugged into the lagoon standing in the rear of the Grady like a gondolier cruising the canals of Venice. He was in his mid-fifties, tall and a little ungainly, with a toothy smile that had a couple of blank spaces in it. His smile faded when Dubin told him why he was there.

"You a private cop?"

"No. I'm a writer. I'm writing a story about her for *New York* magazine."

Lynch ignored him while he finished mooring the boat and cleaned a coolerful of fish in an outdoor sink. The seagulls swooped around him but he didn't seem to notice. "Could you use a couple of bluefish?"

Dubin shrugged. "Sure."

"We've got enough in the freezer to make it to the next Ice Age. How about a beer?"

Lynch took his fish into the house and came back out with a six-pack of Coors Light. They sat in folding chairs facing the steamy lagoon, as if they were talking about fishing or baseball.

"So what do you think I can tell you about Maria Morgan that you don't already know?"

"I've heard a lot about her, but it's all the official version. I thought maybe you could give me a few more details."

"Details." Lynch tilted his head upwards and poured one of the beers down his throat. "You want to know what color her face was? Were her eyes bulging out? That sort of thing?"

Dubin took his time answering. "I might be interested in those types of details if you think they're significant."

"Significant?"

"Yeah. Significant."

Lynch crushed his empty beer can with one hand and popped open another one. "Why don't you talk to the police?"

"I did," Dubin said. "The new chief"—Dubin pretended to be searching through his notes—"what's his name?"

"Wozniak."

"Wozniak. He seemed to think your investigation left something to be desired, and he said you'd retired and moved away. I had the feeling he was trying to get rid of me."

Lynch sat quietly for along time, emptying and crushing one beer can after another until the whole six pack was gone. "Stay here," he finally said, and he went inside the house.

When he came back out he was carrying a cardboard box full of files and loose papers, which he set down next to the patio table. "I kept copies of all my notes." A mischievous grin flashed across his face. "You know, to wrap fish in and stuff."

Digging through the box, he found a manila folder labeled "Morgan" and handed it to Dubin. "You can look at the stuff in this file," he said, "but don't ask to take it with you."

When Dubin opened the file, the first thing he saw was Maria Morgan's autopsy report.

"And if you find something," Lynch went on, still grinning, "and you tell anybody you got it from me, I swear to God I'll cut your balls off and use them for bait."

Dubin spent the next hour reading—and in some cases, copying into his notebook—the documents in Lynch's file. There was the death certificate, the autopsy report, the police incident report, notes of dozens of interviews Lynch had conducted after Maria Morgan's death. He had talked to everyone—Avery Morgan, Mrs. Paterson, the twins Hunter and Antonia, the opera director Casimir Ostrovsky, and a "Susan McGuire," identified as a "babysitter" but presumably the current Mrs. Morgan, as well as a number of other people Dubin had never heard of. At the bottom of the pile Dubin found Lynch's notes on the room where the death had occurred, the upstairs studio in the barn Dubin had visited twice with Susan. Lynch had made a meticulous inventory of everything he saw in that room, including the title of every book and the length of all the scuff marks and dents on the floor and furniture, and Dubin spent twenty minutes copying it word for word into his notebook.

While Dubin worked, Lynch hosed off his boat and tinkered with the engine, whistling some old tune that Dubin didn't quite recognize. Each note of the tune seemed to hang in the heavy air like a seagull before drifting away.

"Can I ask you some questions?" Dubin asked when he had finished.

"You can ask but I probably won't answer," Lynch said.

Dubin ignored his warning. "This autopsy report—"

"You can forget about that," Lynch interrupted.

"What do you mean?"

"It's a piece of crap."

It was a little less still now. Dubin could hear waves nibbling at the edge of the lagoon.

"Here," Lynch said. With his big hands, he picked up the bluefish he had cleaned for Dubin and wrapped it in the autopsy report, sealing the package with white freezer tape. "I told you that's what I saved this stuff for."

Dubin thanked him and said good-bye. The smothering air, the stinking fish, the jeering gulls—all this made him want to get as far away from there as possible. Lynch wasn't going to tell him anything he didn't already know.

After a few minutes he stopped his car and dumped the bluefish in the weeds by the side of the road. He salvaged what he could of the autopsy report, but most of it was illegible. The seagulls, which must have followed him from Lynch's house, swooped down and encircled him with their shameless gaze. Like blackmailers, he thought. Predatory but always afraid.

* * *

I really didn't know what to make of Peter Bartolli. Was he a wise, all-knowing Prospero, as he pretended—that little quote from *The Tempest* about "such stuff as dreams are made on" was totally predictable—or just a fatuous windbag, a Polonius, as Hunter implied in his quotations from *Hamlet*?

Those questions, I admit, came from Nicole, not from me. She's the one who recognized the quotations and proposed some analogies between certain Shakespeare plays and recent happenings at the Institute. I had been unable to resist telling her about Hunter's past life regression at her next session. After a bit of maneuvering on her part, I even let her read the transcript. Admittedly this was unprofessional, even unethical, but I felt I needed her input—the only other person I could have confided in was Gottlieb, and that would have been suicidal. Nicole seemed fascinated by my depiction of Hunter falling under Bartolli's hypnotic spell and she read the transcript with total absorption in about five minutes. But her main interest in the event seemed to be what it showed about my relationship with Olympia.

"Are you sure you want to be going down this path?" she asked, boring her eyes into mine.

"What do you mean?"

"This whole thing was Olympia's idea, wasn't it?"

"No, not at all. Her father's been wanting to do a regression on Hunter ever since he worked here."

"Uh, huh," she nodded. "But it was Olympia who got you involved."

"Sure, she's the one who asked me. I'd never met Bartolli until the other night."

"Don't you see? That's why he sent her here in the first place."

"Sent her?"

"Of course he sent her. To get power over you—and it worked. Are you going to let him come back and finish the job?"

"I'm thinking about it. You realize"—I lowered my voice, realizing at once how absurd that was since we were sitting in my office with the door shut—"that this is not for public consumption. Dr. Palmer doesn't know anything about it and he would be furious if he found out." I glanced at my watch, even though I could see the wall clock behind my desk. "I'm afraid our time is up."

She stood up awkwardly, perhaps embarrassed by the abrupt way I had dismissed her. I realized at once that I had overreacted.

"Nicole," I said gently, "I'd like you to come back sooner than a week this time. Today's Wednesday. Could you come in again on Saturday?"

"I think so."

I reached for my calendar. "How about Saturday afternoon? Would two o'clock be all right?"

As I wrote up my notes of that session with Nicole, I realized that she was tottering on the edge. Some of the things she'd said when we were discussing the past life regression—not to mention her fixation on Olympia—told me that trouble was on the way. My intuition was borne out on Saturday afternoon when she returned for the visit we had scheduled for 2:00 o'clock. Since Nicole's actions leading up to that visit are so important—and since she described them to me in detail on several occasions—I will try to relate them just as they occurred, saving my own comments for later.

She left her apartment a little after 1:00 o'clock and stopped at a specialty market to pick up a few things she needed. When she returned to her car it was after 1:30, and the weekly broadcast of the Metropolitan Opera was on the radio. According to Nicole, the featured work was *The Tales of Hoffmann* by Jacques Offenbach with an all-star cast. Nicole could hear the audience buzzing and the orchestra tuning up as the announcer delivered a synopsis of the first two acts. "The curtain rises on Luther's tavern in Nuremberg," the announcer said, "where a chorus of lively spirits celebrate the arrival of the poet Hoffmann and his servant Nicklausse...."

As Nicole listened she felt her head swimming and her chest tightening. She pulled the car over to the side of the road, her mouth parched, her face flushed, and tried to concentrate on what the announcer was saying: "Act Two begins in the home of the inventor Spalanzani, who has constructed a mechanical doll so lifelike that he introduces it to Hoffmann as his daughter Olympia...."

When the announcer finished his introduction, Nicole threw the car into gear and raced the fifteen minutes to the Institute, hurtling into my office at exactly 2:00 o'clock with a look of panic in her eyes. I could tell at a glance that her condition had worsened. She described her drive to the Institute in minute detail, as if she were afraid that I might miss some critical point. Then, noticing the stereo receiver on the bookshelf beside my desk, she turned on the radio and tuned it to the station she'd been listening to in the car. "Listen!" she said. "Wait till you hear this!"

All I could hear was some insipid classical music, violins punctuated by high-strung singing in a foreign language and bursts of wild applause. As I've mentioned, I have no use for opera, especially *The Tales of Hoffmann*, which is what this turned out to be. "What's this all about?" I demanded.

"When I was driving over here," Nicole said, "the announcer was giving a synopsis that was almost exactly the same as what Hunter related in his past life regression."

"And?"

"Don't you see? Hoffmann wrote these fantastical stories and became so famous that Offenbach put him into an opera, surrounded by the characters he'd created. They seem like fantasy figures but Hoffmann was a real person who probably knew real people who were the models for the characters in the opera."

"All right. That makes sense so far."

"And who was Hoffmann? He was the same person who inspired Schumann to write his *Kreisleriana*, which Hunter can play without having ever touched a piano before."

"OK. Go on."

"And now Hunter does a past life regression, and the past life he remembers turns out to be Hoffmann's, as related in the opera."

"Or," I said, "his so-called past life is nothing but the plot of the opera, which he heard on one of these Metropolitan Opera broadcasts, or saw on television."

"That's possible," she admitted. I was surprised that she acceded so readily to what I intended as a devastating blow to her argument. And I was even more surprised when she leaned forward with a condescending smile; not for the first time, she looked as if she were the therapist and I the patient. "But there's more," she said in a low voice, "and this is where things start to get weird: The life that Hoffmann is living in the opera, and in Hunter's past life regression—isn't it a lot like your life?"

"My life?"

"Yes. Yours."

"Mine? What are you talking about?"

"It's as if you were the protagonist of Hunter's past life regression."

It took me a moment to grasp the significance of what she'd said. Her illness had evidently deepened into a full-blown delusional psychosis that was somehow connected with the dissertation she was writing. And in her delusional state she had come to believe that I, her psychiatrist, was actually living the fantasized past life of Hunter Morgan, another of my patients. What could that even mean? Did it make me part of Hunter's delusion—or Nicole's? My hands suddenly felt clammy, my face hot and drenched with sweat. "Why do you think that?" I asked, as casually as I could.

"Don't you see? A man named Hoffmann falls in love with a beautiful dancer named Olympia, and although people have warned him that she's an automaton, he ignores them, seeing her through the lens of his infatuation. At last she captures him in her frenzy, whirling him round and round until"—here Nicole broke off, seemingly unwilling or unable to continue the story. "What does this sound like, if not your obsession with Olympia? Don't you see?"

I chose my words carefully, swabbing the sweat from my cheeks and forehead with a handkerchief. "You mean the story Hunter is telling—and the story of the opera—are really about me?"

"Or you're about them."

I smiled reassuringly, as I always did in such situations, in order to show that I meant no rejection or disapproval. But I was beginning to feel desperate for the session to end. "Well," I asked, "how does the story end?"

"I can't tell you that," she said, avoiding my eyes. "You'll have to find that out for yourself."

So many times during that crucial period I wanted to snap my fingers and say: "Listen up! Time for a reality check! People can't remember past lives or experiences that happened to somebody else. Ideas aren't transmitted through crystals or viruses, and real people's lives aren't recapitulations of operas or literary texts." That's what any sensible person would have done. But when you're a psychiatrist you can't behave like a sensible person. You have to go with the flow, keep the patient talking, encourage her to take you on an all-inclusive tour of the world she's constructed for herself. Once you're in that world you can guide her toward the light—at least in theory. In the real world such a suspension of disbelief can be dangerous, especially when the therapist has issues of his own. Had I been able to talk to Dr. Neuberger, everything might have turned out differently.

The problem, I thought at the time, was that the person leading the flight from reality was Olympia, who wasn't my patient. Nicole tried to warn me about the path we were headed down. I thought my skepticism, my professional training, my adamant disdain for supernatural explanations of any kind would protect me. And in a sense they did: I never for one minute believed in any of Olympia's New Age nonsense. There was a perfectly sensible explanation for everything that happened. Hunter had obviously seen or read about the same opera that Nicole heard on the radio. The resemblances to my life were mere coincidences, fancifully embroidered by Nicole like the influence of the ubiquitous Hoffmann. And there were even a number of more sinister possibilities: Nicole claimed that Peter Bartolli had sent Olympia to seduce me into this dangerous exercise, and it had crossed my mind that all the events of the past few weeks might have been an elaborate charade orchestrated by Bartolli for some purpose known only to himself. Thus my own thoughts, under the pressure of trying to grasp the unknown, veered off into fantasy and speculation. The nightmares, the headaches, and now the sudden attacks of sweating I had been experiencing, came to me like visitations from another world. Reality would eventually rear its ugly head, but by then it would be too late.

11

It was just after noon when Dubin arrived at Casimir Ostrovsky's apartment building on Central Park West. The doorman, who looked like a Third World strongman in military attire, seemed to recognize in Dubin a fellow impostor. A contemptuous smile stole across his pitted face when Dubin asked for Ostrovsky.

"Fifteen," he said and turned away.

Ostrovsky greeted Dubin politely but skeptically. He wore an ascot and a navy blazer and spoke with the faintest trace of a Russian accent. He looked about sixty years old and his clear blue eyes were passionate and proud. Dubin followed him into a spacious living room overlooking the park. "I can give you five minutes," Ostrovsky said. "I hate *New York* magazine, by the way."

"So do I. It's a rag."

"I'm surprised they would want to print an article about Maria Morgan and my ill-fated production of *Hoffmann*."

"It was my idea."

Ostrovsky poured two glasses of white wine and they sat down facing each other on leather armchairs. "From the minute I met Maria I knew I wanted her to sing *Hoffmann*," he said. "She had this fantastical streak, maybe a little bit of a split personality, that enabled her to throw herself into the three soprano roles as if they were the same role, which obviously they are."

"Obviously."

"She steeped herself in the role until she became possessed by it. And I always wondered which character she was when she killed herself. Was she the automaton, the virgin or the whore?"

The telephone rang and Ostrovsky glided away toward the kitchen as he murmured into the receiver. He closed the kitchen door behind him and Dubin could hear his voice rise to a whine, but apart from a few sharp words he said nothing Dubin could understand. The living room was informed by a neat masculine hand, its back wall occupied by built-in bookshelves filled with bound musical scores, its side walls hung with framed drawings and photographs on operatic themes. In the light from the picture windows overlooking Central Park stood a white Yamaha grand piano with its lid discreetly raised a few inches.

"Would you like some more wine?"

Dubin said no but Ostrovsky poured himself another glass and sat back down on the leather chair. "Where were we?" he asked, his eyes a little more lively than when he'd left the room.

"Your production of *Hoffmann.*"

"Right." He took a sip of his wine. "It never happened, of course. When Maria died the whole project fell apart—the rest of us were too distraught to continue that season—and we were never able to get it up and running again. Which of course is exactly what might have been expected."

"What do you mean?"

"There's been a curse on that opera from the moment of its conception. It destroyed Maria and I knew there would be other victims if I persisted with my plans."

Dubin watched him carefully. "Possibly yourself."

"Quite possibly myself."

The telephone rang again. This time Ostrovsky stayed in the room as he paced around murmuring into the phone. Something about a meeting or an appointment that involved several other people. On the phone he sounded authoritative, almost dictatorial.

Dubin stared out the window as he waited for Ostrovsky to sit back down. "By the way," Dubin said, "have you heard of the letter that Offenbach wrote on his deathbed claiming that he was composing a secret version of the opera to foil his wife?"

The question caught Ostrovsky off guard. "How," he stammered, "how—how did you know about that?"

"All I know is what the Witz catalog said about it. Do you know more?"

He coughed, took a sip of wine, cleared his throat. "I've read the letter."

"Are you the one who bought it?"

"No," he laughed, a little too quickly. "I wish I could say I was. The buyer—who will remain anonymous—asked me to authenticate it."

Dubin took his time before asking the next question. "Is the letter authentic?"

"Unquestionably."

"Then—"

"But I think poor Offenbach was a little off his rocker by the time he wrote it and didn't know what he was saying. I don't think his wife was trying to kill him. She desperately wanted him to live long enough to complete the opera so she could profit from it."

"What about the secret manuscript?

"There wasn't any secret manuscript."

"How do you know?"

"The letter went to Wolff, who was also supposed to get the manuscript. If the manuscript existed, it would have come to light at the same time as the letter."

"Unless the wife intercepted it before it ever got to Wolff."

Ostrovsky shrugged. "Anything's possible." He looked at his watch. "Now if you don't mind, I have another appointment."

Dubin stood up and thanked Ostrovsky for the interview. Then, as they stepped toward the door, he asked, "What if I told you I know where the manuscript is?"

"I'd probably say you were lying," Ostrovsky said as he opened the door, "because obviously you've been lying about everything else."

"You'd be making a mistake," Dubin said.

"Who are you? You're obviously not really a writer. You've just been pumping me for information and I don't like it."

"I used to be a writer. Now I'm living in the real world and I'm trying to make a living. I know where that manuscript is but frankly all I care about is money."

Dubin thought he saw a flicker of something like fear in the Russian blue eyes. "You don't have anything on me," Ostrovsky said.

"Not so far. But you've given me some leads. Thanks." Dubin turned and slipped through the door.

Ostrovsky caught his sleeve. "What do you want?"

"Talk to your friend who bought the letter. If he wants to talk to me about the manuscript, you can help get us together." Dubin pulled away and headed toward the elevator.

"Get out of here!" Ostrovsky hissed.

"I'll be in touch."

Sometimes Nicole felt as if she were destined to become a character in somebody else's nightmare—or worse yet, a footnote in somebody else's dissertation. Her own nightmares often centered around her thesis advisor, Professor Henry "Boog" Crawford. He was a leering drunk and a notorious womanizer who infuriated Nicole by peppering her with questions and then interrupting before she could answer. In his younger days he'd been an unsuccessful novelist—with his short white beard and his desk covered with snapshots of fishing in the Florida Keys, it was obvious who he was trying to emulate—and Nicole had no idea what he was doing in Literary Theory, a subject he professed to despise. At the end of the previous year, Nicole's advisor had fled the department for a job at Berkeley, leaving Crawford, whom everyone avoided, as the only professor willing to take on new students. He treated her with an avuncular familiarity and insisted on holding their meetings at the Morro Castle, a shabby watering hole a couple blocks from campus that conjured up the faded glory of Havana under the *ancien régime*.

"'Authors as Characters, Characters as Authors,'" Crawford read aloud from the title page of her thesis proposal, gulping a mouthful of expensive tequila from a shot glass. "'The Semiotics of Authorship in Literary Romance.' I like the title."

"Thank you. I—"

"It sounds like it means something." He slapped the proposal down on the table and laughed. "Even if it doesn't!" Then he threw back the rest of his tequila and leaned forward confidentially. "You know, you're halfway there if you have a good title."

"I know that." Nicole took a sip of her beer. "I gave it quite a bit of thought, and—"

"But what the hell is it about?"

She felt her face burning and it wasn't from the alcohol. "Well, you see—"

"Isn't this idea—the idea of authors becoming characters in their own fictions—isn't it a little old by now? I mean, for Christ's sake, they all are, aren't they?"

"They're all what?"

"Characters." He slapped the table again, only now he wasn't laughing. The waiter came running to bring him another tequila. "In what they write. Aren't they all characters whether they say so or not? Sometimes they're the only character."

"Of course. But—"

"You know, in all that post-modernist crap."

"But you see"—she held up her forefinger to silence him before he could interrupt again—"this is a little different. It's about authors becoming characters in what somebody else writes, and then meeting up with the characters they created themselves in their own works."

Crawford eyed her skeptically. "Come again?"

"In the Dumas story I was telling you about, the young Hoffmann arrives in Paris during the Reign of Terror—he's only eighteen years old—and meets up with some of the characters he'd write about years later, who were presumably based on people he hadn't even met yet."

"How could he do that?"

"Well, because Dumas was writing the story, you see, about fifty years later."

Crawford handed the proposal back to her—unread—and flashed his most ingratiating smile. "It doesn't make a whole lot of sense to me, but what the hell? When it comes to dissertation topics, Christ!—none of them make any sense, do they?"

"I think—"

"By the way: What the hell is semiotics?"

Nicole had a great deal of work to do before she could even visualize the outlines of her dissertation. It had all started with Hoffmann, the writer, as fictionalized by Dumas, and a little research explained the link between Dumas and Offenbach, the composer. Dumas's tale had been serialized at the height of the Hoffmann craze in Paris, and the next year a play was produced along similar lines, with Hoffmann among characters of his own creation. That was the play Offenbach spent twenty years turning into *The Tales of Hoffmann*. Nicole desperately needed to see a complete performance of the opera. As always, Miss Whipple had just the thing: a video—three day rental, $2.00 fine for each day overdue—of the 1951 film version directed by Michael Powell and Emeric Pressburger, with Moira Shearer as the first of Hoffmann's three ill-fated loves. Nicole checked out the video and took it home, and that night as she sat in her easy chair munching popcorn she was enthralled by its beauty, frightened by its surrealistic imagery—and shocked by its resonance with certain themes she'd been discussing with her therapist.

Nicole had a secret that she had kept since she was fourteen years old. That fall she was sent away to boarding school about forty miles from her home in Ballanchree on the northwest coast of Ireland. Her father owned a prosperous farm, with pastures that rolled out to the sea cliffs and a sawmill and feed store in town that put everyone in his debt. There was no one in the county who wasn't afraid of him and his temper, least of all Nicole's mother, who had trained her daughters in the twin arts of evasion and obedience.

When Nicole heard the news and was suddenly called back from school, all she could see was her little brother, brown-haired Sean, age 10, at the bottom of a cliff, looking straight up at her. Two black eyes. A swollen mouth. Bruised and broken, hungry water swirling beneath him. Dead. They brought him up wrapped in the rug from the front hall and hid him in a box. No one was allowed to see him. Rushing home from school, crying on the bus. Ballyshannon, Kilcar, Carrick, endless muddy trek through the rain, crying. No one can see him, the coffin is sealed. Father drunk as usual, sullen, staying away. Mother brisk, businesslike, as if she was afraid to cry. Houseful of women, neighbors, cousins, aunts. The unctuous Father Meagh, trying to sound consoling. Nausea, anger, pain. Crying face down on the pillow in the cold room.

The funeral was on Friday morning and the whole town turned out in their black raincoats and hats. The closed wooden coffin rested on a low scaffold in front of the altar. After the Gospel reading Father Meagh stood behind the coffin and gestured over it mechanically. "In times of sorrow," he began, "many people ask: How could God allow this to happen? And the answer is always the same: God is not responsible for this. Like everything else that is evil, this is the Devil's work." He gazed over the congregation as if expecting to see Satan crouching in the back pew. "God gave us the bountiful earth, with its meadows and streams, its mountains and valleys—and yes, its rocks and treacherous cliffs—and the freedom to decide how we would use these gifts for our own human purposes. But only through the intervention of the Devil did evil come into the world..."

Nicole closed her ears and her mind to the rest of Father Meagh's homily. It was in English, of course—the Devil's tongue, as her grandmother would have said—and maybe that was the reason it made so little sense. It seemed to be all in code, an indictment of the Devil in his own carefully chosen words. Nicole sat between her mother and her father, who measured his approval of the sermon with a series of somber nods, and as the priest went on she felt her mind closing to her parents and to Ballanchree and everything it had ever meant to her. She stopped crying and when it came time for communion she stayed in the pew. She could sense her mother's confusion and her father's anger but there was nothing they could do. That afternoon, when the last of the nauseating meals had been eaten and the cousins and the aunts were starting to drift away, she slipped out of the house without saying goodbye and walked into town through the rain to catch the bus back to her school.

At school she accepted the condolences of her teachers but told them nothing of what had happened at Ballanchree. They took her silence for grieving and assumed that she was adjusting well to the tragedy. But at her next confession she surprised even Father Ahearn, who for many years had made a pastime of coaxing descriptions of their sins from adolescent girls.

"Forgive me, father, for I have sinned," she began.

"And how have you sinned, child? Did you touch yourself?"

"I don't know the name for it, father."

"Then do your best to describe it."

"Does the Devil really exist?" she asked.

"Yes, child. The Devil exists, just as surely as you and I. That is the teaching of the Church."

"Then is it a sin not to believe in the Devil?"

"It is a heresy, yes, and therefore a sin. In the Middle Ages, men were burned for denying the existence of the Devil."

"Then that is the sin I wish to confess."

Father Ahearn imposed a small penance and arranged for Nicole to come to his office in the rectory the next day. She dreaded the stone silence of the rectory and its dim halls and she was determined not to repent. But she knew Father Ahearn would be hard to resist. He was a cheerful, pasty-faced Dominican who could talk anyone out of being a sinner. "There has to be a Devil, don't you see?" Father Ahearn told her, smiling amiably. "Because if there's no Devil, then where would evil come from?"

"I don't know," she admitted.

"Sure there's plenty of evil in the world, though, isn't there? And it must come from somewhere. Because nothing comes from nothing, does it?"

She shook her head.

"Now I know what you're thinking," he went on. "I know what happened to your little brother, and my heart goes out to you and your family. That was a great tragedy, and it was evil, to be sure, for something like that to happen to an innocent young boy, falling off a cliff like that. And that evil must have a source, and its source must be the Devil."

"I don't think so."

Father Ahearn's smile darkened. "You don't believe in the Devil?"

"No."

"But if there is no Devil, then there must also be no God, because then God would have to be the source of both good and evil. And as such, God could not be God."

She turned away to avoid the priest's sanctimonious gaze. His office, she realized, was decorated entirely with paintings of St. Anthony being tortured by demons.

"Therefore, to doubt the Devil is to doubt God," he concluded. "It is a very great sin. A mortal sin, my child. A mortal sin which you must renounce and repent."

Through several interrogations Nicole held her ground, refusing either to repent or to explain herself. There were other girls at the school who openly admitted that they did not believe in God; this was treated as youthful folly that could be remedied by proper instruction. But not believing in the Devil was a far more serious matter, so unusual, so obviously willful and perverse, that it could not be overlooked. In the mind of Father Ahearn and the other school authorities, a person would practically have to be in league with the Devil to deny his existence. And so Nicole was asked to withdraw from the school, and in the middle of the term, without returning home, she went to live with an aunt in London.

The headmistress called her parents and they agreed to this arrangement without even asking to speak to Nicole.

Nicole's secret, which she never revealed to anyone, was that she knew who killed her brother and it was not the Devil. It was her father.

12

Nicole's theory that *The Tales of Hoffmann* provided the key to both my own life and Hunter's fantasies made little sense to me. Of course I didn't know—I still don't know—if the synopsis she related after listening to the radio broadcast bore any relation to what really happens in the opera. It did resemble the fantasies Hunter described during his past life regression, the transcript of which I had foolishly allowed Nicole to read. And as I told her, Hunter could have seen the opera on TV or video, just as he had seen *Hamlet* which also stood out in his mental landscape. But I still couldn't see how either the opera story or Hunter's fantasy world had any connection with me. True, my name was Hoffmann and I'd become obsessed with Olympia almost from the moment I laid eyes on her. She was a dancer and I suppose you could say she had two "fathers" who contended over her, and she had an odd, otherworldly quality that made her seem a little detached from reality. But that was about as far as the resemblance reached. Nicole's perception of a mystical connection between myself and Hunter's fantasies or Offenbach's opera must have stemmed from an intense jealousy which her illness had magnified into a delusion. She loved me, or thought she did, and she saw Olympia as a major threat to her happiness. That much I could have expected—should have expected—based on psychoanalytic theory alone. What I wasn't prepared for was Olympia's insistence that she too played a role in Hunter's past-life experiences.

It was about a week after the regression, a couple of nights after Nicole had heard the opera broadcast and tried to warn me about Olympia. I had slipped into Olympia's room when all the patients went to bed and was surprised to find her fully dressed and wide awake, reading a paperback novel under a small bedside lamp.

She smiled and stood up, pulling me into a long, deep kiss. I needed her more urgently than usual, but I wanted to avoid any discussion of the past life regression issue until after we had made love because I'd decided to discontinue the treatment and I knew she would try to change my mind. I peeled off her dress and stood caressing her in the dim light.

"We've got to finish Hunter's past life regression," she said matter-of-factly.

I tried to stop her mouth with a kiss. "Let's talk about that later."

She kissed me eagerly, then pulled away. "It's important to me. We need to talk about it now."

A feeling of sudden breathlessness, even suffocation, came over me. "Why?" I gasped.

"I think I was the woman in Hunter's past life."

"What do you mean?"

"The dancer."

"You mean he was fantasizing about you?"

"No, I mean I was actually there."

I sat her down next to me on the bed and took a long, desperate breath. My heart, which had been fluttering with amorous excitement, was now pounding with an almost violent frustration. "Olympia," I said, "let's not get too carried away with this past life stuff. You went under hypnosis—I know that because I had to shake you out of it—and you heard what Hunter was saying and—"

"No," she objected. "I didn't go under hypnosis. But I knew what he was going to say before he said it."

"Dammit!" I jumped to my feet and circled the room. "I thought it was supposed to be Hunter's past life we were regressing to—not yours!"

"Why couldn't it be both?"

"How could it be both?"

She reached out her hand and pulled me back to the bed. I sat down and she kissed my neck and unbuttoned my shirt and pulled it off and rolled me onto my back. "When I was sitting there listening to Hunter I had the feeling, just like Hunter, that I'd seen it all in another life. I was the woman he was in love with, the beautiful young woman sleeping on the swinging couch. I was the one who danced with him and spun him around and whirled him down the staircase."

"That's where it ended," I said helplessly.

"That's when my father had to bring him back," she corrected me. "But that's not really the end of the story. There's more. I know that because I was there."

I can't begin to describe how defeated and humiliated I felt at that moment. In my professional judgment I'd decided to put an end to this nonsense before Dr. Palmer found out about it and expelled me from the Institute.   But my good intentions—as Nicole predicted—had been undone by my obsession with Olympia. I had fallen literally into her clutches and now I lay beneath her strong and irresistible body as she rolled her kisses over me.

"What happens next?" I ventured.

"My father chases after us, shouting for us to stop.   And then—"

"What happens?"

She shook her head. "I get dizzy even thinking about it."

Her face hovered over mine. It struck me that she really did look more like a doll than a living woman, but I didn't care.

"We've got to go back," she smiled. "We've got to go back and finish what we started."

And so I agreed, against my better judgment, to allow Hunter Morgan's past life regression to continue. Olympia beat me into submission using the oldest weapon in a woman's arsenal. But that night our torrid relationship reached the melting point: I played along with her mad plan while plotting in my mind to get rid of her.

You know you're in trouble when just getting through the day requires a willing suspension of disbelief, as if instead of living your life you were reading some far-fetched novel. That was the way I'd begun to feel in the time I spent with Olympia. But which was the novel and which was my life? Were things really as weird as they seemed or was I losing my mind? From the moment I met her, my life had entered the realm of the improbable; now it seemed to be veering off in the direction of the impossible. I was haunted by nightmares, migraines, sweats, and now this desperate sense of suffocation that left me willing to accept anything, to actually believe anything, if only it would end. I had imagined that I could protect myself from the destructive energy swirling around me simply by rejecting Olympia's crackpot supernaturalism. There's a natural explanation for everything that happens in this world—so I believed, and so I reminded myself when I agreed to let Peter Bartolli continue his hypnotic therapy. What I lost sight of was that nature itself can exert a terrifying and astonishing force. And soon we would all be reminded that there's nothing more natural than death—even a most unnatural one.

It was less than twenty-four hours before Dubin heard back from Casimir Ostrovsky. He sounded calm, businesslike, quietly hostile. "I've spoken to the person who bought the letter," he said. "He's interested in hearing more about the manuscript."

"That's nice. Is he interested in buying it?"

"He wants to talk to you."

"Does he want to buy it or not?"

A long, silent pause. Ostrovsky might have been talking to someone with his hand over the receiver. "I don't want to be involved in this," he finally said. "He'll call you." The connection went dead.

An hour later, when the phone rang again, the voice on the other end was not Ostrovsky's, though it did show a trace of a foreign accent.

"Do you have the item our Russian friend mentioned?" the voice asked.

"I can get it when I need it," Dubin said. "If you're interested."

"I'm interested, but I need to know who I'm dealing with. Who are you?"

"My name's Dubin. No first name, no address."

"Dubin," the man repeated. "Where did you get it?"

"You're not listening," Dubin said. "I said I don't have it but I can get it."

"Are you a dealer?"

"No. Listen, you want to talk about it, I'll meet you somewhere and we can talk. And I'm going to need a down payment."

Silence.

"We can make it a public place if that makes you feel better."

They arranged to meet at four o'clock in the food court at the Blythedale Mall, about thirty miles from Egdon. "They have a McDonald's there," Dubin said. "Carry an umbrella so I'll know who you are."

"An umbrella? There isn't a cloud in the sky."

"That's the point. I'll see you at four."

Dubin arrived at the food court at 3:30 and bought a Big Mac and some fries and a large coffee and settled down to wait with the *New York Post* spread out in front of him as he drank his coffee and nibbled his fries. He paid no attention to anyone and was careful not to gaze around as if he were expecting someone. A little before 4:00 he noticed a small, gray-haired man who looked slightly familiar walking around conspicuously clutching an umbrella. The man, who wore a navy sport coat over a yellow knit shirt, peered straight at Dubin and even waved his umbrella but Dubin ignored him and went back to his reading with a suppressed thrill of excitement. He knew where he'd seen the man before: it was the night he'd stopped in the woods behind the Palmer Institute and peeked through the fence at the ethereal dance on the lawn. His visitor in the food court was the otherworldly voyeur with the cavernous eyes who'd been watching the strange performance when he arrived.

For over an hour the man waited with increasing impatience, marching around the food court brandishing his umbrella like a sword. When he finally decided to give up, Dubin followed him outside and watched him climb into a blue Saab sedan. He trailed the Saab for almost an hour over roads that led farther into the country, past the traffic jams and strip malls onto smaller roads and finally over the narrow blacktops that wound through the wooded hills near Egdon like a hidden network of underground caverns. There were no people in that country, only rural route mailboxes and trees. The houses near the road looked dark and unoccupied.

The blue Saab turned suddenly into a long gravel driveway that disappeared into the woods. Dubin sped past and pulled into the next side road, about a quarter mile farther. He parked along the side road and found a path back through the woods toward the driveway where the Saab had disappeared. It was late October and the sky was already darkening. Dubin peered ahead, stepping through a thicket of brush and vines and fallen timber, and soon found himself at the edge of the driveway looking at the hulk of a Victorian mansion silhouetted against the fading sky. The blue Saab was parked by a side door, where there was a light on inside. As Dubin watched from behind the bushes, the man he'd been following came back to the door and opened it. A slender black cat slinked outside and at first Dubin thought the cat was running towards him. But after a moment it rolled in the dirt, then darted off in pursuit of some imaginary prey, while the man stood watching from the doorway.

Dubin slipped back down the path and into the woods. He had learned enough for one day.

The next two days were chilly and dismal with intermittent rain. Dubin was following two leads and all he could do was keep following them, even if it meant spending most of the day standing in the woods watching wet leaves fall to the ground. The man who'd bought the Offenbach letter stayed in his shadowy mansion, venturing out in the blue Saab only for one short trip to a convenience store on the edge of town with Dubin prowling along behind him. He must have had some connection to the Palmer Institute or the Morgan family, and by watching him day and night Dubin could find out what it was. He kept his vigil through the day but could only make it through part of one moonless night before the rain-soaked woods seemed to be closing in on him. He ached like a caged animal when he stayed in the car and shivered with cold when he stood in the mud listening to the wind rattling the last few leaves off the trees. About three in the morning he gave up and drove back to his apartment and poured himself a double shot of tequila and soaked himself in a hot shower before dropping into bed.

The next morning—actually closer to noon—he drove back through the village and this time he parked along the road leading to the Institute, within sight of the entrance gate. There he watched through the rain and his steamed-up windshield for Mrs. Paterson, the Morgan twins' nurse. A few minutes of internet research had shown that Mrs. Paterson owned a black Toyota Corolla. When he saw the Toyota leaving the compound at about four in the afternoon he followed it cautiously into town, staying right behind Mrs. Paterson as she parked and walked toward the old brick post office with her umbrella up. He hurried up beside her, his face spattered by the rain, and put on his most disarming smile.

"Mrs. Paterson?" he said. "My name's Dubin. I'm writing an article on Maria Morgan for *New York* magazine. I've been talking to people who knew her, trying to get a sense of what she was like as a person."

Mrs. Paterson kept walking. "I don't want to talk to you."

"Don't run away. I just want to chat with you for a couple of minutes."

"I don't feel like chatting. I'm in a hurry, can't you see?"

"So am I. I'll walk along with you if you don't mind. Like I said, I've been talking to people in town, just trying to get a sense of what kind of person Maria Morgan was."

She turned her head and peered at him from under her umbrella. There were no answers in her dark, ageless face. "She was a wonderful person, and that's about all I'm going to say."

"That's what I've heard all over town. A warm and wonderful person, with a smile for everybody. People around here really loved her, maybe some a little more than others."

She ignored him and kept walking.

"Her husband—he's sort of a cold fish, isn't he?"

"I wouldn't know about that."

"Well, you worked for him, didn't you?"

"Yes, and he's always treated me fairly."

They were a few feet from the post office and Dubin knew he would lose her if she stepped inside. He leaned closer and lowered his voice. "Mrs. Paterson, I know she had a lover. And I know who it was," he lied, "as I'm sure you do."

She stopped and for an instant her eyes widened inquisitively. They didn't ask who the lover was—she already knew that—but how Dubin had found out.

"There were letters," he explained.

"How'd you get them?"

"You don't want to know. I'm a writer. I make it my business to find things out."

She pulled him aside, lifting her umbrella over his head as if to make a place where they could talk privately. There was anger in her tired eyes but it was mixed with fear and sadness and a plea for help. "What do you want from me?"

"I'm trying to understand what happened," he explained in a low voice. "Her career was just taking off, with her first role at the Met. So if she was depressed it must have had something to do with what else was going on in her life. In other words, with him."

"I took care of the kids, that's all. I wasn't involved in her life. If she was having an affair I don't know anything about it."

"But you lived with the family. You must have seen things, known what was going on."

"I keep to myself and don't stick my nose where it doesn't belong."

"I'm the opposite," he smiled. "I always stick my nose where it doesn't belong. And right now I'm sticking it all over this town trying to find out why Maria Morgan killed herself—if she did kill herself."

Mrs. Paterson pulled away, leaving Dubin standing in the rain. "What are you talking about?"

"Come on. Nobody really believes she committed suicide."

"You better get out of here before I call the police."

"The police? They're in on it too, aren't they?"

She headed for the door and Dubin said something he regretted as soon as he said it. "Doesn't your conscience bother you, Mrs. Paterson?"

At least once a day Nicole had to stop what she was doing for a few seconds to marvel at the unaccountable strangeness of life.

She worried about this habit because she knew it was probably a symptom of something, but there was nothing she could do about it. The sensation could come at any time. She might be standing in line at the ATM or pumping gas at the Exxon station or cruising into the city on the commuter bus—she might even be right in the middle of a conversation with someone she knew—and suddenly there it was: she had to stop and catch her breath because all at once it struck her how incredibly strange life is—how strange people are, how strange they look and sound, how strange all their activities appear if you step back and watch them for a moment. Just look at these odd-shaped animals, she would say to herself, standing here wrapped in fibers made from petroleum or plants or the skins of other animals, barking out arbitrary sounds to which they attach so much meaning and importance. Yet sometimes it didn't seem strange so much as magical, as if she had turned a new page in the book of the world where everything was connected to everything else in some occult fashion and if only she could find the hidden footnotes that explained the connections she would know everything there was to know. That Saturday afternoon as she sat listening to *The Tales of Hoffmann* on the car radio she was struck by its resemblance to Dumas's *The Woman With the Velvet Necklace*, to which she had been led by Hunter Morgan's playing of Schumann's Kreisleriana. The same characters had migrated for almost two hundred years through the brains of Hoffmann, Schumann, Dumas and Offenbach and all their readers and listeners, and now there they were, speaking to her through radio waves from the stage of the Metropolitan Opera in New York. Could anything have been more strange? Could anything (and this is where things get really strange) have been more predictable?

She had to stop at the library to return the *Tales of Hoffmann* video that Miss Whipple had recommended the day after the radio broadcast. It was a spectacular, surrealistic movie and she'd kept it out for a week, even though it was due after three days, watching it again and again until she knew every scene by heart. Now she felt guilty about returning it so late.

"I'm returning this," she said sheepishly. "It's overdue." She had her wallet out, ready to pay the fine.

"Don't worry, dear." Miss Whipple interrupted her conversation with another library patron to smile at Nicole and reject her attempt to pay the fine. "How did you like it?"

"It's very beautiful."

"Yes. It's a beautiful, beautiful work."

The librarian was talking to someone Nicole had never seen before, a small, wiry man of about fifty whose deep-set eyes seemed to sparkle when he looked at her, as if he already knew who she was. "There's a more interesting version than this one," the man said, smiling. "Just as beautiful in its own way."

"Really?" asked Miss Whipple. "Which one is that?"

"The Kent Nagano production that was done in Lyon in 1993.
I believe it's available on video."

"Well, we don't have it."

The man ignored Miss Whipple and concentrated his gaze on
Nicole.   "It's set in an old-fashioned lunatic asylum," he said.
"Hoffmann is a madman who keeps falling in love with the female
inmates until finally he thinks one of them is a prostitute who has
stolen his reflection and he stabs her in a jealous rage."

"What have they done to my favorite opera?" cried Miss
Whipple.

"They've restored the insanity and brutality its composer
intended," the man answered, still smiling. He bowed slightly. "By
the way, I'm Peter Bartolli."

"Oh! Dr. Bartolli!" Nicole extended her hand.

He nodded again. "You've heard of me, perhaps?"

"I... I know some people at the Institute."

"Have you been out there?"

"Oh, yes.   Visiting some friends.   Hunter and Antonia
Morgan."

"Ah." He raised his eyebrows. "Hunter and Antonia don't get
many visitors."

"I know. That's why I go often."

He must have known the real reason for her weekly visits,
Nicole realized later. He was a psychiatrist, Dr. Palmer's brother—
of course she'd heard of him. Had he heard of her? Was that why
he suddenly introduced himself—to cut off the conversation
before it got anywhere, the way psychiatrists always do? They can't
let the patients get anywhere near the truth or they'd be out of a
job.

But these thoughts came later. At that moment Nicole was
confused and embarrassed and all she knew was that there was no
point in continuing the conversation.

"I didn't mean to interrupt," she said. She glanced toward the
librarian, but Miss Whipple stood with her back turned arranging

some books on a cart. "I've got to be going. Very nice to have met you."

She moved toward the door. "I was just leaving myself," Peter Bartolli said. He waved good-bye to Miss Whipple and followed Nicole out to the parking lot. They exchanged a few pleasantries— Nicole really did like him; he seemed a warm, humorous man, the kind she'd like to know better if the circumstances were different— and then they each climbed into their cars and went their separate ways.

Dubin had spent the afternoon following the man who attempted to buy the Offenbach manuscript. Followed him from the Victorian mansion in the woods along the narrow roads that wound their way into town. Followed the blue Saab to half a dozen destinations—a bank, a gas station, a couple of strip malls, a dry cleaner—before it finally slipped into the library parking lot. There, remembering his last visit, when Avery Morgan had denounced him to the librarian as a blackmailer, Dubin stayed in his car listening to NPR. When Nicole drove up a few minutes later he pulled down the sun visor and looked the other way, his heart racing. She didn't seem to notice him as she emerged from her car and flitted inside.

He turned off the radio and moved his car so he had a better view of the library entrance. Ten minutes later Nicole emerged with Dubin's quarry shuffling after her, his arms laden with books. He and the redheaded angel stood chatting like the best of friends. Then they exchanged a few parting words, climbed into their cars and drove away in opposite directions.

Dubin cruised out of the parking lot behind them, but this time he didn't follow the blue Saab. He followed Nicole.

13

There came a knock, and without peering through her peephole Nicole opened the door. She wondered if she ought to be alarmed. It was the man with the thin moustache and the dark wavy hair who'd spent the last two months turning up wherever she happened to be.

"You're here again," she said. "Edgar Allan Poe."

"Dubin," he corrected her.

"Of course. Dubin. The mysterious detective. Won't you come in?"

Again she led him into the dingy apartment and offered him a seat at the table, pushing a pile of books to one side. "Is there something I can help you with?"

"I'm hoping there is," he smiled. "I'm handling the sale of a valuable manuscript for some clients."

"I doubt if I can help you with that. What's the manuscript?"

"It's the final score of *The Tales of Hoffmann*."

Nicole felt a little chill when he said that. How did he know about the work she'd been doing? Had she told him about it the last time?

"My clients want to sell it," he went on, "but they're very particular about who they deal with."

"So they hired a detective?"

"Last year someone bought an autograph letter that Offenbach wrote on his deathbed, claiming that he was working on a secret final version of the opera. He was afraid his wife would destroy the manuscript or even kill him in order to suppress it. That letter belonged to my clients and it was sold through a dealer to an unidentified collector. Now someone—probably the same collector—wants to buy the secret manuscript."

"Nothing unusual about that, is there? I mean, naturally the person who bought the letter would be interested in the manuscript."

"Remember we talked about Maria Morgan?"

"Sure."

"When she died she was rehearsing *The Tales of Hoffmann*. I'm convinced there's a connection between that and her death."

"A connection?" Nicole felt her pulse racing. "What do you mean?"

"It was more than a role to her. It was an obsession—an obsession that seems to be shared by our unidentified collector."

She pushed the pile of books a little farther from Dubin's line of sight. "What does all this have to do with me?"

"There's a man who's interested in the manuscript and I saw you talking to him this afternoon outside the library. Sort of a small man—"

"Oh, you mean Dr. Bartolli. That was Dr. Bartolli I was talking to."

Dubin seemed taken aback to learn the man's name. "I need to know a lot more about this Dr. Bartolli. Who is he? How do you know him?"

"He used to be Associate Director of the Institute. He's Dr. Palmer's half brother. I never saw him there, though. I just met him this afternoon."

Dubin studied Nicole's face as if deciding whether to believe her or not.

"You're really trying to find out if someone killed Hunter's mother, aren't you?" she asked.

"My clients hate publicity," he answered, ignoring the question. "They don't want to be connected with any crimes, even after the fact. Especially a celebrity murder. So they asked me to clarify that point before the transaction is completed."

"You can't blame him for what happened," Nicole said.

"Can't blame who?"

"Hunter." She gazed around the room distractedly. "You can't blame Hunter for what happened to his mother."

Night had fallen by the time Dubin left Nicole's apartment. Naturally if someone had murdered Maria Morgan she would want to help in any way she could, as long as she was sure it wasn't Hunter. And she was sure, she was utterly certain that Hunter could not be blamed. He was a victim, he and Antonia were victims—Dubin had agreed with her on that. But it troubled her to think that *The Tales of Hoffmann* was somehow linked with what had happened seven years before. All the work she'd done on her dissertation, all the connections she'd uncovered between Hoffmann and Dumas and Offenbach and the other nineteenth-century Romantics, even her chosen thesis topic itself, had taken on a sinister flavor and it frightened her.

When she went to bed and closed her eyes she saw her brother's broken face staring up at her from the rocks below and she knew that whatever happened she had to protect Hunter. She couldn't protect her brother anymore but she could protect Hunter.

"Hunter, you remember when we were here last week, don't you? You were telling me a story about something that happened a long time ago. Do you remember?"

It was another rainy night and Hunter Morgan's second past life regression was about to begin. The lights in my office were low; they flickered occasionally as the driving rain rattled the power lines that connected the Institute with the outside world. Peter Bartolli straddled a stool in front of my desk purring softly to Hunter, who sat in the wing chair facing him, with his back to Olympia and me. Despite my misgivings, everyone assumed that the process would be more or less the same the second time around. Dr. Palmer had flown to Chicago on personal business, and Gottlieb had the night off. None of us realized that we stood on the edge of an abyss.

Olympia could hardly wait to finish what she had set in motion. She sat beside me in the back of the darkened room, squeezing my hand in her excitement.

"Do you remember the story you were telling me?" Bartolli asked Hunter.

Hunter turned away, covering his eyes with his hand.

"We're going to try to go back to that same time and place," Bartolli said, ignoring this reaction. "We want to find out what happened next. Is that OK with you?"

Hunter groaned indistinctly and Bartolli took it as a yes. "So to start out, like last time, just relax. Close your eyes and listen to my voice and don't think about anything. That's right. Just relax."

Olympia went limp in her chair, dropped my hand and fell into a hypnotic trance. This time I didn't even try to stop her. If she was determined to join Hunter in his fantasy world, there was nothing I could do about it.

"I want to take you back to where we were last time," Bartolli told Hunter. "You remember, don't you? A beautiful young woman in a ballet dress lies sleeping on a couch. You walk in with her father. An old man. Another old man runs into the room, with long eyebrows that stick out in front of his face."

"The two old men," he muttered. "Fighting. Fighting over the woman."

"The two men are fighting over the woman? What does she do?"

"Dancing. Dancing."

"She starts dancing?"

He nodded.

"Do you love her?"

He made a deep growl. "Love her. Love her. Lover."

"Are you one of the men?"

He shook his head violently. "No! I'm not an old man!"

"You love her, but you're not one of the old men?"

And that was how it went, slowly, painstakingly, Bartolli drawing each thought out of Hunter's mind until he finally started to babble. It was still a little incoherent but it made a kind of dramatic sense. He was dancing with the woman, spinning around and whirling down a long staircase with her father chasing after them, shouting for them to stop. The other man was chasing them, too, and the two men fought with each other, tugging and pulling at the woman and Hunter to try and make them stop.

As this story poured out of Hunter's mouth, Olympia stumbled to her feet and started to dance. Slowly at first, but then with increasing confidence and speed until she was whirling feverishly in the small space between Hunter and Bartolli and myself, her arms poised above her head like a ballerina's. When one of the old men in Hunter's narration would pull on the woman's arm, trying to stop her from dancing, Olympia's arm would shoot out to the side and she would start to lose her balance. Then the other man, according to Hunter, would lurch at her from the other side and Olympia would twirl away, escaping from both her pursuers to a different spot on the carpet where she resumed her *pas de deux* with the invisible Hunter.

Suddenly something terrible seemed to be happening. Hunter's voice dropped into a low-pitched growl and as he gasped for breath he described one of the men pushing the other aside and leaping violently onto the woman, knocking her down to the floor and strangling her as she shattered into half a dozen pieces. Her head fell off, though her eyes still blinked as if she were alive. Her limbs twitched their way across the floor as if she were still dancing. Hunter watched from a distance, powerless to protect her, his screams stifled by his fright.

As Hunter reached this crisis in his narration, Olympia had thrown herself down on the floor and begun to thrash wildly, apparently reliving the horrors he was describing. Of course her head and limbs remained attached to her body, but they twitched and flipped in ways that seemed to defy human anatomy. I was reminded of the scene in *The Exorcist* when the girl's head spins around—Hunter's guttural narration even sounded like the girl's voice as she succumbed to demonic possession in the movie. Then he let out a high-pitched scream—something about a belt, something about hanging her with a belt—and Olympia arched her back and twitched as if she were in her death throes.

"Stop this!" came a shout from the doorway. "Stop this at once!"

Miles Palmer burst into the room, his face an oven of fury. He glared at his brother, then at me, then at poor Olympia who was still writhing and whimpering on the floor, with a wrath that was almost divine in its intensity. My worst nightmare had come true. I felt queasy, desperately out of breath.

Bartolli stood up in alarm. "Do you realize what you're doing? They're under hypnosis. You can't just—"

"Get out of here!" Palmer commanded.

"Hunter—"

"I'll take care of Hunter. You get your daughter out of here!"

Olympia had stopped writhing but she gave no sign of life or understanding. It was as if she had really broken into a dozen pieces that were scattered on the floor. Bartolli tried to revive her and raise her to standing position, but she was far too heavy for him to handle.

"Dr. Hoffmann!" Dr. Palmer pointed at me. "Help him get her out of here!"

I stumbled to my feet, and while Bartolli and I struggled to lift Olympia into a standing position and walk her out the door, Dr. Palmer stepped over to Hunter, who had sat quietly through this volcanic eruption as if nothing had happened. He crouched down beside Hunter, one knee on the floor, and wrapped an arm around his shoulder, murmuring to him in the kind of soft, reassuring voice you would use to comfort a child.

"Hunter," he said gently. "Are you all right?"

14

The night before his world would change forever, Dubin stared at the TV screen surrounded by a mob of football fans whose beery excitement buoyed him in his own desperate anonymity. It wasn't his usual bar but he was sipping his usual drink and thinking his usual thoughts, and the more he thought the more he wanted to drink. What had he been doing for the past couple of months? Chasing a story that had no beginning, no middle and no end, a story that made no sense even to the people it was supposed to be about. He told himself he was only in it for the money—but that wasn't true and he knew it. He was in it for the story, just as he'd been back in his days as a journalist. And even then he couldn't resist the temptation to delve into the story a little deeper than necessary, even to start making it up if he couldn't get all the pieces to fit together. The missing Offenbach manuscript—that was something he'd made up, wasn't it? And now people were talking about it, acting on it, weaving it into the plot, as if it really existed. He had to be careful.

As always it was the women he had to be most careful about. The librarian had turned against him and that was a bad sign—she was like a Greek chorus, knowing all, predicting all, ultimately judging all. And his new friend Nicole—what was he to make of her? She was beautiful and young and brilliant and probably as mad as a hatter, with enough crackbrained ideas to send his story into post-modernist hell and ruin his chances of success as a blackmailer. Yet he found her hauntingly attractive and he knew he wouldn't be able to stay away from her. Susan Morgan? She was as alluring and dangerous as thin ice glistening on a pond. He knew he couldn't trust her and she knew she couldn't trust him and in that mutual distrust they'd found a common bond. Obviously she wanted to sleep with him and just as obviously he was determined to resist. He still hadn't cashed her $5,000 check and he probably never would. She'd left him several messages, and the next morning when Avery Morgan was out of town he'd visit her again and go upstairs to take another look at Maria Morgan's studio and then he'd leave without giving her what she wanted. But none of this mattered to Dubin as he knocked down his third Grey Goose martini and thought about going home to bed. It wasn't Susan Morgan, or Nicole either, who troubled his dreams. Of all the women he'd met in the past two months, the one he had to try to forget wasn't Nicole or Susan, it was poor old Mrs. Paterson, whose frightened face he could still see peering out from under her umbrella as he dogged her steps up to the post office peppering her with questions. It made him think of his mother, who had suffered for months before she died. There was sadness and pain enough for ten lifetimes in that face, and he'd become one of her tormentors.

Susan Morgan stood at the top of the stairs watching Dubin impatiently as he inspected Maria Morgan's studio as if for the first time. "Haven't I seen this movie before?"

"Not exactly."

"No. Last time it was enlivened by witty dialogue." She turned away to gaze out the window at the bare crazed trees around the duck pond. "Are you looking for something?"

"Not exactly."

"I'm going downstairs."

Dubin spent another ten minutes checking the contents of the room against the list he'd copied from Frank Lynch's files. He checked every knick-knack, every book title, every poster. There were only three things missing—a publicity photo of Maria Morgan, a kaleidoscope, and a phonograph record and its jacket. Just one out of dozens of records and CDs on the list, and that struck him as interesting. He lifted the sheet that covered the old record player; the turntable was empty. Plugging the record player into a wall socket, he saw that it still worked in spite of its battered condition.

Then looking across the room he noticed something he'd missed before: a little loft in the shadows at the far end, reachable by climbing a grid of boards arranged like steps on the wall. He pulled himself up the ladder and peered in through the dim light. The loft was about eight feet wide and filled almost entirely with a double mattress moldering beneath a wool blanket and a couple of dirty pillows. The whole space was littered with soda cans, snack food bags, a scattering of tape cassettes and a Walkman whose battery had burst and leaked over one of the pillows. If you didn't mind crawling into that low berth you could lie there and watch everything that went on in the studio while you ate potato chips and drank Coke and listened to your own music—the tapes were all heavy metal and rap—instead of operas or whatever your mother was playing on the turntable, and if you were quiet maybe she wouldn't even know you were there. That's what it was, Dubin realized as soon as he peered into that dusky space—a teenage hideout, known or unknown to Maria Morgan, apparently unknown to Frank Lynch, since there was nothing about it in his report. Was it Hunter or Antonia? Dubin wondered. Or maybe both? Had they been eyewitnesses to their mother's death?

Back downstairs, he brushed the dust off his clothes and decided not to mention it to Susan. She smiled at him with a mixture of irony and vulnerability that told him the next move was up to him. "Can I get you something to drink?"

"I've got to be going."

"Is that a 'no'?"

He turned around to wash his hands in the sink, and when he turned back around her smile had frosted over. She stood with her arms crossed, anxious to get on with her life as Mrs. Avery Morgan. There were charity balls to be planned, well-known names to be bandied about, contractors and caterers and tennis instructors to be abused or appeased as the occasion demanded.

The telephone rang and after she answered it she leaned over the sink as if she was going to vomit. "What? What do you mean? Oh my God! Avery's not here. No, he's traveling. I can't reach him until his plane lands."

She hung up and stood facing Dubin.

"What's the matter?" he asked.

"Mrs. Paterson hanged herself."

"What?"

"She's dead. Mrs. Paterson's dead."

Susan was crying now, choking on her tears. "She's dead. And—oh my God! Hunter's gone."

"What do you mean?"

"Hunter's gone."

"Where did he go?"

"He disappeared. They can't find him."

II. Julietta

15

The morning death came to the Institute, like so many other unforgettable moments in my life, had an air of unreality about it. Time and the retelling have made it my own. But on that dour November morning it all seemed to be happening to someone else.

The day began routinely enough. Breakfast was served to ambulatory patients in the dining room beginning at 8:00 o'clock. At that hour Mrs. Paterson would arrive with Hunter and Antonia and they'd help themselves to cereal and orange juice—cream of wheat and coffee for Mrs. Paterson—from the buffet. But that morning they were late, which was so unusual that at first no one noticed it. A little before 8:30 a nurse named Eileen made a joke about Mrs. Paterson oversleeping and went upstairs to look for her. We didn't hear a scream but what we heard was even worse: Eileen gagging on her tears as she staggered back into the dining room to say that Mrs. Paterson was dead. I ran up to her room with some of the others, half-expecting a false alarm, and found the poor woman strung up to the light fixture like an old coat, still swinging from Eileen's panicked touch. Her eyes were wide open and when we took her down she was limp and heavy and cold. I ran through the usual emergency procedures and noticed something surprising, even before I had any reason to think about it: her eyes were open but not popping out, her face wasn't bloated or purple—in other words, she bore none of the signs of strangulation. But there was no doubt she was dead.

I sent Julietta, the receptionist, who'd run upstairs with me from the dining room, back down to call the police and hospital security. Then I went looking for the twins. Antonia was sitting up in her bed, smiling patiently as she waited for Mrs. Paterson to rouse her for breakfast. Hunter was nowhere to be found—not in his room, not in the dining room or in the patient lounge where he spent so much of his time. I met Gottlieb and we searched every room and ran back upstairs, where three security guards had gathered to wait for the police. We told them that one of the patients was missing and they called out on their radio. Then we went back to Hunter's room and found that he'd taken his shoes and his jacket and a few odds and ends.

"Don't touch anything," Gottlieb said.

"Why not?"

"How do you know Hunter didn't kill her?"

I felt a little sick when I heard Gottlieb say that. "This isn't a joke."

I headed back to Mrs. Paterson's room and found Dr. Palmer, ashen-faced, his voice quivering as he conferred with the police. There were two or three cops with their radios chattering, taping off the area as they helped the EMTs remove the body. "I can't understand why she would have done this," Dr. Palmer told the officer in charge. "We didn't find a note."

"Sometimes they don't leave a note."

"Especially when somebody else kills them," Gottlieb said.

Dr. Palmer looked sick. "What are you talking about?"

"Did you examine the body?"

"No, I just got here. Is there something I don't know?"

The officer took a step forward and lowered his voice. "I don't want to prejudge the situation," he said to Dr. Palmer, "but there's evidence of a struggle. The back of the victim's head is bloody and her face doesn't display the usual signs of strangulation."

"In other words," Gottlieb said, "she was already dead when she hung herself."

It was a shock to learn that Mrs. Paterson may have been murdered—and an even greater shock to realize that Hunter Morgan, suddenly on the loose after seven years, was the leading suspect. Dr. Palmer was unable at first to accept the implications of what the officer had told him. "No," he sputtered, visibly shaken, "this is not possible! Hoffmann? Did you hear this?"

"Let's go down to your office," I suggested.

"That's not a bad idea," Gottlieb agreed.

We followed Dr. Palmer downstairs to his office and closed the door behind us. I'm embarrassed to admit that we were all thinking more about Hunter—and about ourselves and our careers—than his victim.

"Do the police know that Hunter's gone?" Dr. Palmer asked.

"We told security," I said. "I don't know if they told the police."

He reached for his phone and dialed security. "Have you found Hunter Morgan yet?" he demanded. "All right. But you don't need to involve the police. He can't be far."

We each took a seat and watched each other unsteadily. I felt almost sick to my stomach with the growing realization that I might have contributed to this disaster. Gottlieb's eyes darted between Dr. Palmer's and mine, as if he was waiting for the right moment to strike.

Someone knocked on the door. It was the police officer. "I understand one of your patients is missing," he said. "Do you think he's dangerous?"

"Hunter?" Dr. Palmer exclaimed. "No, absolutely not. He's just a boy."

"Have you got a picture of him?"

"Listen, you don't need to worry about Hunter. We'll find him. He's probably still in the building."

The officer looked to me for support but didn't find any. "Dr. Palmer," he said. "This woman didn't kill herself. She was murdered."

"What does that have to do with Hunter?"

The officer turned and headed for the door. "We're putting out a bulletin on him."

When the officer left, Dr. Palmer buried his face in his hands and we all sat trying to grasp the implications of what was happening. Finally Dr. Palmer looked up and said, "I've got to call Avery Morgan."

He picked up the phone and dialed a familiar number. Apparently Avery was not at home and he spoke with his wife. "Avery's traveling," he said when he hung up. "His wife can't reach him until his plane lands. In a way that's good, because by then we'll have Hunter back."

"I hope you're right," Gottlieb said.

"He can't be far." Dr. Palmer closed his eyes. "God, I hope she can reach Avery. I don't want him to see this on the news."

For Nicole the day began like any other, with two cups of coffee and a half hour of BBC news, which kept her remarkably well informed about Africa and the Middle East but serenely ignorant of anything that might touch her own life. She lived in superstitious dread of distraction. At that stage of work on her dissertation, anything—a stray phone call, a random meeting with a friend, a news story on the internet—could entice her away from her topic, or worse, set her research in a new direction, adding months, possibly years to the project. Her encounter with Peter Bartolli at the library and the subsequent visit from Dubin had set her back a week or longer. She'd spent two days on the internet reading recent scholarship on *The Tales of Hoffmann* and another day locating a video of the 1993 Lyon Opera production in which the characters are inmates in a lunatic asylum and Hoffmann degenerates into a psychopathic killer. This, according to Dubin, wasn't even the worst of it: there was a monstrous final Hoffmann who was so brutal and degraded that Offenbach, on his deathbed, had to smuggle his tale out of the house to keep it from being burned by his wife. Before long, Offenbach would probably be a character in someone else's fiction, composing further iterations of his masterpiece with a new and different Hoffmann in every one. And so Hoffmann and Offenbach would recycle endlessly on the wheel of birth and rebirth that we call literature.

That's good, Nicole thought. The wheel of birth and rebirth that we call literature. She wrote it in her notebook.

After lunch, which consisted of tuna fish and biscuits and a cup of tea—she was trying to lighten up on the coffee—Nicole decided to stroll down to the library for a chat with Miss Whipple. It was a bright, crisp day and the walk put her in good spirits. But the moment she stepped into the library her world changed, as if she'd slipped into darkness. Her throat tightened, her breath faltered and she tasted the dizzying terror she would live with in the days to come. All this from one glimpse of the librarian: Ms. Whipple's usually cheerful face, peering up grimly from behind her desk, was the face of death. "Have you heard the news?"

Nicole tried to remember. Was there something in the Middle East. "What news?"

"About Mrs. Paterson."

"Mrs. Paterson?"

"She was found hanged in her room at the Institute. They're saying it was suicide, but—"

"Suicide?"

"—I have my doubts."

In fact Miss Whipple had more than doubts. She was convinced beyond a shadow of a doubt that the poor lady had been murdered. "There's no way it was suicide," she went on. "A sixty-year old single woman who spent all her spare time reading the Bible—what could have led her to commit suicide?"

"What could have led someone to murder her?"

The librarian's face darkened again into a mask of death. "There are things. There are things that could have happened."

"There are?"

She nodded. "Nicole, I want to ask a favor." She reached into her desk drawer and pulled out a small manila envelope and handed it to Nicole. "I want you to take this and keep it for me."

"What's in it?"

"Never mind what it is. I don't want you to open it. But if anything happens I want you to have it."

"If anything happens? What do you mean?"

"I don't know. After this, anything's possible."

I was amazed how quickly the police did their work and moved on. After a couple of hours, apart from the yellow tape across the door to Mrs. Paterson's room, you would hardly have known anything was amiss at the Institute. Hunter was gone, of course, but the other patients—including his sister—required the usual attention. The staff needed more than the usual attention, since it was one of their number who had died. At that point they still thought it was suicide, that Hunter had fled in horror after discovering the body, and naturally I said nothing to imply the contrary. But Julietta, the receptionist, who'd been with me when I found the body, seemed to have suspicions of her own. She came from a rougher background than most of the people who worked there—it was rumored that she moonlighted as an exotic dancer or worse—and she proved to be surprisingly well informed about the forensic aspects of hanging.

"Mrs. Paterson didn't look bloated or anything," Julietta said. "Her face wasn't, like, puffed out or purple or anything."

"That's true," I admitted, keeping my voice low. I glanced around to make sure no one was watching us. Under the circumstances I felt awkward, even a little guilty, chatting with Julietta in front of the reception desk during my afternoon break. I told myself there was nothing to feel guilty about—we all needed something to take our minds off the horrors of that horrible day. And at that moment in my life what I needed was sympathetic female companionship. My relationship with Olympia was over. She had fallen apart at the end of Hunter's second past-life regression, or I should say in the middle of it, when Dr. Palmer burst in and interrupted the hypnosis, leaving Hunter somewhere back in the nineteenth century and Olympia writhing around on

THE RULES OF DREAMING   143

the floor in a trance. I'd had a premonition of that catastrophe in one of my recurrent nightmares, in which I dreamed I was a patient of Dr. Palmer, who was explaining that Olympia was a symptom of my illness, not a cure. For all her fragile beauty and her compulsive interest in sex, she wasn't the woman of flesh and blood I needed and deserved.

Julietta, by contrast, was the real thing—a sensuous creature who knew how to attract and love a man, even a loser like Gottlieb. A large mirror filled the wall behind her desk and another mirror hung on the wall across from it, creating the illusion that she ruled an infinite space in which her charms were endlessly replicated. She slept with Gottlieb—everyone knew that—and it was a revolting thing to contemplate. But even on that depressing day I found a certain excitement in the notion of beating Gottlieb at his own game, making him as jealous of me as I was of him.

"I hope you weren't too upset when we found the body," I said.

"Not really," she said. "I had a girlfriend who hung herself in the locker room after Larry Barbato gave her a handful of downers. She looked horrible. All puffed out, you know what I mean?"

"Yes, I've seen people like that."

"And purple as a plum. Not that Mrs. Paterson would be, you know, the same color."

"No, not exactly."

"So that means she didn't choke, doesn't it?"

Had Gottlieb been talking to her? I wondered. "I guess that's something the police will have to figure out."

"And now there's a madman on the loose."

"Oh, I wouldn't worry about that."

The phone rang. "Palmer Institute," she said in her receptionist voice. "How can I help you? Please hold while I ring his line."

My break time was up. I started to walk away.

Julietta put her hand over the receiver and jiggled her eyelashes at me. "You've made me feel a lot better, Ned."

I could see my face in the mirror behind her, and it surprised me. My shy smile, reverberating through the infinity of mirrors over her head, was twisted into a concupiscent leer. It was as if I had freed myself of Olympia but not of the obsession she had led me into. I cast my eyes down and hurried back upstairs.

At three o'clock that afternoon, Dr. Palmer summoned me back to his office. His attitude seemed to have hardened as the shock of the morning wore off.

"I just spoke with Avery Morgan," he said. "He's beside himself."

"I can understand that he would be upset."

"Upset isn't the word. He's furious. He blames the Institute and he blames me. He's threatening to get a lawyer if we don't find Hunter by tomorrow morning."

"I'm sorry."

Dr. Palmer glared with a ferocity that surprised me. "You're sorry? You ought to be, because this is all your doing. First you wanted to lower his dosages, and then—I don't even want to think about that absurd satanic ritual or whatever it was you were performing with my half-wit brother."

"It was hypnosis."

"Hypnosis, for God's sake! On a schizophrenic!"

There was nothing in Dr. Palmer's accusations that I hadn't reproached myself for a hundred times. That didn't make it any easier to listen to what he was saying. "I realize now that it was a serious error of judgment on my part. I've told you that."

"I swear to God, if you say anything to Avery Morgan or anyone else about that business with my brother—"

"I won't."

"Or about anything else, for that matter." The sweat was pouring off his forehead like tears from a howling child. I could see that his career, everything he'd worked for over a quarter century, was on the line. "Do you understand?" he continued. "If you talk to any reporters or lawyers or anybody else about anything it's going to be the last thing you do as a licensed physician. Do you understand? Even the police—I don't want you talking to the police. There are patient privacy issues, family privacy issues, reputation issues, all sorts of issues that you wouldn't be sensitive to. I'll do the talking. Do you understand?"

"If you feel that way, then I should resign."

"You're not going to resign. That would only attract attention and be seen as an admission that we did something wrong. You're going to stay here until I tell you to resign. Do you understand? I won't have a scandal."

Nicole was shaken and sad when she left the library that afternoon. Mrs. Paterson was a kindly lady who'd befriended her when she stayed at the Institute. It was hard to imagine her hanging herself, and even harder to imagine anyone else doing it for her. Miss Whipple was undoubtedly wrong about that—she refused to explain her suspicions or why she was giving Nicole the mysterious envelope. The big question was how Hunter and Antonia would get along without the nurse who'd cared for them since the day they were born. Nicole thought about driving out to the Institute but she remembered the work she'd planned for the afternoon and decided to wait until the next morning. It was already late, and the war against distraction had to be fought one inch at a time.

Back in her apartment, she sat in front of the computer but the words would not come. Instead of literary theory all she could think about was Mrs. Paterson dead and Hunter and Antonia sobbing around her. She tried to distract herself from her distractions by thinking about the unmade bed and the dirty dishes in the sink and the trash scattered around the apartment, and before long she couldn't think of anything else. She made the bed and washed the dishes and then she gathered the trash into a plastic bag and carried it down to the dumpster, where she had one of her dreaded meetings with the landlady, Mrs. Gruber.

Mrs. Gruber was condescending, nosy and cheap, convinced that Nicole was using her apartment for immoral purposes but willing to look the other way if it gave her an excuse to raise the rent. That afternoon she wore a pink housecoat over her shapeless torso and a pair of velveteen slippers on her feet. At the sight of Nicole she raised her eyebrows as if expecting to find something scandalous in Nicole's garbage bag.

"Did you hear about your friends at the Institute?" Mrs. Gruber never missed an opportunity to remind Nicole of her stay at the Institute.

"My friends?"

"The nurse was killed—"

"Yes, poor Mrs. Paterson."

"And that boy—the Morgan kid—he's the one who did it."

Nicole caught her breath. "What? What Morgan kid?"

"Hunter Morgan? Isn't that his name? He killed her and flew the coop."

Dubin had lost count of the Grey Goose martinis and the beers he'd chased them down with. He sat in a corner booth in a cheap Italian restaurant called Dino's along Route 17 where he was sure nobody would recognize him. Mozzarella sticks were as close as he could come to eating. Families came and went—young couples, teenagers, some quiet, some noisy, all acting as if nothing had happened. Waiters took their orders and brought their pizzas swooping down on enormous trays. A football game unfolded silently on the TV over the bar. Dubin paid no attention to any of this or even to his own thoughts. He sipped his martinis seriously, as if he were taking medicine, but the alcohol only aggravated his remorse. He'd thought of blackmail, the way he practiced it, as a victimless crime, or no crime at all, since he only tormented the guilty and extracted money from the rich. The pursuit of journalism by other means, he called it. A highly profitable game. Now Mrs. Paterson was dead, the victim of his victimless crime.

He didn't know who killed her or exactly why, but he was sure it was a deadly move in the game he'd set in motion. There was no question of ever forgiving himself. That would never happen. The only thing he could do was drink and when he stopped drinking find whoever killed her. That was the only way the game could end.

16

He knew enough to stay out of sight until it was dark. The first day he hid in a barn behind a pile of lumber and when the owners came in to feed the horses he held himself perfectly still and they never knew he was there. When the sun went down he found some rotting apples on the ground and shoved them into his mouth until he felt like vomiting. Then he ran away and spent the night prowling the woods and the ditches along the dark roads on the edge of town. In the morning he found a dilapidated shed that was full of rusted farm equipment and slept on the wooden floor until dark. On the third morning he ventured closer to town and watched from behind a tree as an elderly woman climbed into her Subaru Legacy wagon and backed down the gravel driveway to the street. He found a way into the house through the cellar door, ate some food he knew she would never miss—some crackers and a raw hot dog and a can of soda—and watched TV until he heard her coming home. He turned off the TV and crept back downstairs to the cellar, where he curled up on the floor behind the furnace and listened to the old woman creaking around upstairs, light as a feather. Then he started to think about Nicole. He wondered what she would say when he found her. Would she be afraid? When it got dark he would slip back outside, sneak through the town to try and find Nicole. He wondered if she would be expecting him.

Sleeping was hard on that cement floor, and punctuated by nightmares. When he woke up he had the sensation that he'd been dreaming someone else's life. It must be the drugs, he realized. The drugs are finally wearing off.

Upstairs he could hear the old woman moving around, probably cooking her dinner. She seemed harmless enough. He doubted if she could even make it down the cellar stairs without breaking her neck. But the dinner—was there some way he could get his hands on the dinner? Then he remembered the rotten apples and felt sick to his stomach.

17

Frank Lynch was slowly bringing the Grady up to the slip when his wife came out of the house with the cordless phone and handed it to him. It was windy and almost too cold to be out on the water. In another couple of weeks he planned to pull the boat out and put it in the shed, where he could work on it during the winter. Anything to get out of the house. His wife didn't usually bother him when he was outside.

On the phone he heard the voice of Mayor Lester Kapp, his former boss, who told him about the apparent suicide that turned out to be a murder. "I'm shocked and saddened by this tragic event," the mayor said, repeating a line from his statement to the press. "We're going to need you up here, Frank."

"What the hell are you talking about?"

"Frank, I know you're retired but the guys we've got now—not that there's anything wrong with them, they're doing a fine job— they're just a little green, that's all."

"A little green?" Lynch laughed. Calling the current police force a little green was like calling the mayor a little fat. "They've got at least five years experience between them. That ought to be enough to find a crazy kid who's running around out in the cold."

"Frank," pleaded the mayor, "we need you here. Can I count on you?"

At eight o'clock the next morning Frank Lynch, newly deputized, sat in the front seat of the town's only police cruiser—an aging Ford Crown Victoria—trying to explain his strategy for finding Hunter Morgan. Captain Tom Wozniak, 28 years old and a former security guard at the Wal-Mart in Port Jervis, tuned the radio and fiddled impatiently with his keys. "Do you know something I don't know?" Wozniak demanded. "Because if you do, tell it to me now so I can do my job."

"The mayor thought I might have something to contribute," Lynch said evenly, "because I was here the last time. You know, when the boy's mother died."

"His mother? They have her down as a suicide. Did I miss something?"

"Tom, you weren't here then, so you actually missed the whole thing." Lynch showed Wozniak his jagged smile. "Relax. I'm here to help."

It took another half hour of diplomacy before Lynch could make Wozniak grasp who was in charge of the investigation. Once that was out of the way, they were able to concentrate on Lynch's search plan. Initially it would cover a radius of five miles from the center of town, through terrain that was hilly and wooded and still sparsely populated. Wozniak and his two assistants had already covered the obvious places, the secluded spots along the creek and the railroad tracks where they'd taken girls or gone to drink as teenagers. Of course Hunter wouldn't have known about any of those places, but Wozniak thought they were worth a try. Some of the local fire departments and rescue squads were sending men to aid in the search, and the Morgan family—you could hardly tell them no, with their kind of money—had brought in a bunch of do-gooder organizations that only got in the way. What they failed to appreciate, Wozniak told Lynch, was that the kid was dangerous. He killed a defenseless old woman and God only knows what he would do if he was cornered. "Yeah," Lynch agreed, "maybe he'll string up the rescue team with the nylon cords on their pajamas."

Lynch opened the door and hoisted himself out of the cruiser, remembering the years of back pain he'd endured driving around in that car. "Listen," he said, leaning down to talk to Wozniak through the window, "let's get this organized as soon as we can. We can use the civilians if we give them radios and tell them to keep their distance if they spot the target. Does that make sense?"

"Sure."

"And Wozniak, when you get a chance, there's something else I'd like you to do."

"What's that?"

"There's this stranger been hanging around town for the past month or two. Maybe you've seen him. Late thirties, moustache, high forehead, dark hair longish in the back."

"Drives a Beamer?"

"That's the one."

"Yeah," Wozniak smiled, "I've seen that guy hanging around."

"He goes by the name of Dubin. No one seems to know him or what he's doing here."

"I've seen him."

"I'd like you to check him out. Find out who he is and where he came from and what he's been doing here."

"You want me to pick him up?"

"No." Lynch was quick to wave that idea aside. "Not yet. Let's start by calling *New York* magazine to find out why it's taking him so long to write his article."

At seven o'clock Miss Whipple locked the library door and walked the six blocks to her home, a tidy bungalow at the edge of town surrounded by gnarled trees and an impenetrable thicket of shrubbery. At the end of a long day she was grateful for her sensible shoes and her excellent eyesight, especially now that daylight savings time had ended. There were still enough leaves on the trees—the oaks in particular clung to their leaves well into November—that on a cloudy night like this the sidewalk seemed to be lost in shadows. Her little house, all but invisible in the gathering darkness, called out to her with the sound of a porch screen banging in the wind. She needed to ask the neighbor boy to take down those screens and replace them with the storm windows, to trim the shrubs and rake up all these leaves that were rustling under her feet. She was fond of this neighborhood with its overgrown, desolate atmosphere—it reminded her of something out of the Gothic Romance section. But even with sensible shoes it was hard to climb the steps without slipping on those leaves.

Once in the house Miss Whipple turned on all the lights and stoked the TV up to a volume that drowned out the wind whistling outside. She had no pets—they were a nuisance—and surprisingly few books, other than those she brought home from the library. On a typical night she would heat up a frozen dinner in the microwave, watch a couple of her favorite shows on TV, and read herself to sleep with a book checked out from the True Crime section. But on that particular night—it was the night after Mrs. Paterson's death—she had no appetite for frozen fish sticks and even less of one for True Crime. She sat in the upholstered wing chair she'd inherited from her mother many years before, gripping her remote control as if she could use it to click reality on and off like one of her TV shows. Her conscience interrogated her more insistently than any police officer. Was she responsible for what had happened to Mrs. Paterson? Could she have done something to prevent it? And now what about Nicole? What had possessed her to give that letter to Nicole?

She clicked the mute button but the scenarios running through her head filled in the silence. Then she turned the sound back on and sat in the wing chair as if waiting for something to happen. Would there be a knock on the door? she wondered. A plea for help? Or something more violent and irresistible? With the TV so loud, and that screen banging, would she be able to hear it?

Anything could happen, she'd told Nicole. Anything.

"I'm to blame for this! I'm the one who's to blame!"

Nicole sat in front of me sobbing and digging her fingernails into her red hair as if she wanted to tear it out. She looked terrible—pasty and pale and sagging like a corpse—from not having slept the past two nights. I wasn't in the best of shape myself. It seemed like an eternity, but it had only been three days since Hunter disappeared. Mrs. Paterson's autopsy had told a gruesome but unsurprising tale: head battered from behind with a blunt object, enough to knock her out and possibly to kill her; then she had been choked and hung from a light fixture with the nylon belt of her bathrobe. In this last detail there was a resemblance that was sickening in its specificity: Mrs. Paterson had ended her life mimicking Hunter's mother's suicide of seven years before. Why? we all asked ourselves. Why had a young man who had never exhibited any violent propensities suddenly been driven to this terrible recapitulation? And who was responsible? On that score, there was more than enough blame to go around and it was going around like the flu. Avery Morgan blamed Dr. Palmer, Dr. Palmer blamed me, and Nicole—who had the least of anyone to do with it—blamed herself.

She sat in my office berating herself because she hadn't been able to prevent me from allowing Peter Bartolli to conduct the second past-life regression, which in her mind had led to the tragedy. I'd told her about that terrible night when Dr. Palmer surprised us in the middle of Hunter's hypnotic trance and suddenly pulled him back from wherever he had traveled, furiously expelling Bartolli and Olympia from the Institute and removing Hunter from my care. "Don't you see?" Nicole demanded. "It's just what I told you would happen. Your obsession with Olympia was completely predictable and so was its outcome. That's how the first act ends."

"The first act?" She seemed to think we were still talking about *The Tales of Hoffmann.*

"Olympia is shattered by the two men claiming to be her father, while her lover stands by helplessly and realizes that she was never anything but a soulless automaton. That's exactly what happened, isn't it?"

I swallowed uncomfortably and took a deep breath. "We're talking about real life, not an opera. And we're not here to talk about Olympia."

"We're talking about you. Olympia's irrelevant at this point."

Nicole was making it difficult for me to help her, by focusing on my life instead of her own. She needed to be supported and humored even in her most bizarre notions, including her fantasies about me, but I had let her go too far in that direction and now she had become impossible to deal with. And the shock of the murder had pushed her illness into dangerous territory.

"Now it's Julietta you've become obsessed with, isn't it?" she said.

"Julietta? The receptionist? That's ridiculous."

"You need to understand how dangerous this can be for both of you."

"Nicole, that's enough! We can't sit here discussing my obsession with the receptionist—which by the way I don't have. Let's try to concentrate on your illness and what we can do about it."

She was crying again. "We have to find Hunter. We have to find him before they catch him and hurt him."

I was relieved when Nicole finally left my office that afternoon. Frankly I had enough on my mind without having to humor someone who couldn't tell the difference between real life and an opera. Things had been getting strange lately, but not quite as strange as an opera, where the characters might as well be living in a madhouse. Perhaps that was what Nicole was trying to tell me—after all, I was living in a madhouse. Don't the patients always start to think of their physician as one of the inmates? In fact I was trying to get my life back to some semblance of normality, which was not an easy task. Glad as I was to be rid of Olympia, I dreaded spending the long nights without her. Sometimes I would awaken not knowing who or where I was, and I'd make it all the way to the bathroom—where I'd finally see my face in the mirror—with the conviction that I was someone else. An identity disorder, Dr. Neuberger had called it, and until then I thought I'd left it behind me. The police officer in charge of the search for Hunter had been calling and leaving messages on an hourly basis; he wanted to ask

me about Hunter's course of treatment, medications, habits, and so
forth. I would have been perfectly willing to accommodate him
but I was under strict orders from Dr. Palmer not to talk to
anyone. It was almost as if I were the murderer and Dr. Palmer
was afraid I was going to incriminate myself.

Nicole's house loomed over the narrow street like a black hole
swallowing the few stars that penetrated the clouded night sky.
From where he sat in his car across the street, Dubin could just
make out the jagged roofline of gables and chimneys and the
untrimmed cypress trees that sheltered the old house from the
wind and concealed its decay. The lights had gone out long ago
but Dubin stayed behind, watching, listening, wondering whether
Nicole was asleep in her garret or watching him from one of the
mullioned windows. Every now and then he would ease out of the
car to prowl through the shadows closer to the house, listening for
movement near the darkened side entrance. Once he tried the
door and found it unlocked, slipping inside and up the stairs to the
third floor. It was quiet there, deserted—no sign of Hunter
Morgan or any other madman or intruder. Just himself and the
mortal silence of people dreaming behind closed doors. A cat ran
down the stairs and out the door. Dubin clicked the latch behind
him as he went out.

Back into the shadows. Encircling cypresses, evergreens that
looked full and black even in the darkness, invisible tentacles with
thorns reaching out to snag him as he passed. He moved carefully
but not furtively. Out of the corner of his eye he saw something
move. He turned quickly, ready to pounce or run, he didn't know
which. A man lurched in front of him.

"Hold it!" the man said.

A flashlight shined into Dubin's eyes, then quickly turned
upward, revealing the front of the man's torso and the
undersurfaces of his face. Dubin saw a tall, slightly lopsided figure
with thinning gray hair and a politician's smile. It was Frank

Lynch, the retired cop he'd last seen cleaning bluefish at the Jersey shore.

"Remember me?" Lynch asked.

"Sure. You're Frank Lynch. My name's Dubin."

"I remember you," Lynch said. He held out his hand. "How you doing? Let's step over into the light."

They walked about fifty feet to a spot where the neighborhood's only street light drooped over the sidewalk. "Still working on that article?" Lynch asked in a friendly, insinuating tone.

"I sure am."

"It must be a long one."

"Too long," Dubin agreed. "And it's getting longer all the time."

"Why's that?"

"The murder here in town. I've got the feeling it's somehow connected with Maria Morgan."

Lynch pretended to feign surprise. "Whatever gave you that idea?"

"You're a detective. You must have noticed the similarities."

Lynch laughed noiselessly, displaying his missing teeth. Dubin had forgotten about the missing teeth.

"Or maybe since you retired," Dubin went on, "you don't think about such things, just boats and fishing and the like. By the way, aren't you a long way from home?"

"I've been called out of retirement, believe it or not. Special assignment just for this one case."

"So you're a cop again?"

"You could say that. But I'll be back down the shore soon. We expect to pick up Hunter Morgan within a couple of days."

"You think he did it?"

"Let's just say that right now he's the one we're most interested in talking to."

"You think he killed his mother too?"

"You're a writer. You must have noticed the similarities."

It was Dubin's turn to laugh. Lynch was the kind of cop he feared the most—warm, witty and apparently on the level. Someday he'd like to hear the story of how each one of those missing teeth had fallen out of his smile.

"Who are you working for?" Lynch asked, a little less amiably.

"I'm free lance. As I told you. A free lance writer."

"You have a license?"

"Does a writer need a license?"

"They ought to, in my opinion. But you're not a writer."

"What do you think I am?"

"I don't think you're a writer. I think you're a private cop. Or maybe something worse."

"Something worse?"

"Something like a blackmailer."

Dubin laughed again. "Why a blackmailer?"

"The similarities are obvious. Even I can figure that out."

Nicole had given up trying to sleep at night. At eleven o'clock she turned out the lights and lay on her bed fully clothed, shivering with cold because that was better than trembling with anxiety. Someone was stalking her; she knew that. But she didn't call the police because if it was Hunter she wanted a chance to talk to him before they caught him and locked him up someplace where she'd never see him again. Had Hunter really killed Mrs. Paterson? She didn't believe it but there was only one way to find out. Search parties had spread across the countryside in every direction but she knew he couldn't be far. And she knew she didn't need to search for him. He would find her.

A couple of nights earlier she'd spotted a dark figure prowling in the bushes around the house. The man—she assumed it was a man—let himself in the downstairs door and crept up the stairs as she stood motionless at her door listening and holding her breath, both hands clamped on the doorknob as if she expected him to wrench the door open and burst inside. She heard him come slowly up the stairs, one step at a time, stopping when the stairs creaked, taking another step when nothing stirred in response. There came a sudden hiss as a cat leaped away from the landing and bolted down the stairs. The man stood outside Nicole's door a minute or two, not touching the door knob, listening, possibly sensing her presence on the other side of the door, before he turned around and retreated down the stairs. Nicole nudged the door open and peered down the dark staircase, half expecting to be grabbed by the throat and dragged back into her apartment, but all she could see was a dead mouse left by the cat. She stood listening until she heard the outside door click shut. The rest of that night she sat by the window, watching for any movement among the black cypress trees that crowded the house. Nothing moved, not even a cat, but in the morning when she peeked back into the hall the dead mouse had disappeared.

During daylight hours—and each day brought fewer and fewer of them—she tried to do her work, writing compulsively but not productively. The coffee she drank to stay awake only fed her anxiety. After a few hours of this she would often drift into that twilight state on the edge of dreaming where she did her best thinking, only to be brought abruptly back to reality by a barking dog or the clatter of a passing truck. Every unexpected sound triggered a fresh jolt of fear and a fresh attempt to argue herself out of it. All fear is fear of the unknown, she would type on her screen. If you know what's going to happen, there's nothing to be afraid of. And then she would add, as if it were an afterthought: Try to keep from going crazy.

She had stashed the unopened envelope from Miss Whipple in a place where no one would ever find it. She didn't know why she felt she had to do that, or why she'd even been afraid to read it. If anything happens, Miss Whipple had said—in the meantime she wasn't supposed to open it or read it. But isn't something always happening? What could Miss Whipple have meant by anything? Did she mean what people who say that usually mean: if I die a sudden and unexplained death, then you should open this letter?

But if it's that important, why not open it now? What if it implicates Hunter in Mrs. Paterson's death? Or on the other hand, what if it implicates someone else—wouldn't that absolve Hunter? She could open the envelope and take a peek, then hide it again until it was really needed. If it implicated Hunter, which was impossible, she would have to figure out what to do. No, she decided. Leave it alone. Wait until after you've talked to Hunter.

But that night, when it was so dark and so quiet that her mind seemed as bright and noisy as an arcade, when sleeping was out of the question and the stalker, whoever he was, seemed to be keeping his distance from her door, she stood up from her bed and groped her way through the darkness into the kitchen, where she climbed on the counter and reached behind a cabinet to the spot where she'd stashed the librarian's envelope. Unwilling either to turn on the lights or to wait until morning, she opened the envelope with a bread knife and found another, smaller envelope inside, which was already opened. Inside the smaller envelope she found a folded, handwritten letter, which she read by the eerie light of her computer screen.

> Dearest,
> Plane held over in Boston due to bad weather so I'll take this time to drop a note. Hope you're over your cold and the rehearsals are going well. I'm keeping my head above water but I can't imagine the current situation continuing much longer. A. is a fool to think he can keep you away from me—if he succeeds I may do something drastic. There are worse things than unhappiness. I think about you constantly, even when I'm supposed to be concentrating on my work. A textbook obsession, I'm afraid. Like Hoffmann in the Venice act, or my little friend Nero, racing around and wagging his tail when he sees me coming and moping when I'm gone. You must decide soon, my love. XX

Nicole read the letter three times. Obviously a love letter of sorts, but why had Miss Whipple confided it to her? Why was it suddenly important for Nicole to know that the spinster librarian had a secret, romantic past? In her youth, of course—but no, the letter didn't seem old enough for that. Nicole squinted at the postmark and as she held the envelope up in the dim light she realized that it wasn't addressed to Miss Whipple at all. It was addressed to Maria Morgan and it was postmarked a week before she died.

18

Dubin drove up the driveway rehearsing a lie he'd never have to tell because Avery Morgan was nowhere in sight. Susan crouched in front of the barn combing her golden retriever as if she'd been expecting him. She seemed glad to see him but he could tell from the look in her eyes that something had changed.

"I've tried to call you about a dozen times," he said as he climbed out of his car.

She smiled and led the dog into its pen next to the barn.

"It was always somebody else who answered the phone."

"Not surprisingly," she said, "I've been busy."

"Out searching for Hunter?"

"About twenty-three hours a day. I'm working with the police around here while Avery's upstate helping the state troopers."

"Then you're here by yourself?"

"My mom has the kids."

"Are you afraid?"

She shook her head. "I don't think there's anything to be afraid of. Hunter isn't a killer."

"Somebody is," Dubin said.

"Is it you?"

"No."

"Good. Then I have nothing to worry about for the next thirty minutes."

She poured Dubin a cup of coffee and sat down across from him in the little kitchen in the barn.

"I thought you would've left town by now," she said.

"I wanted to make sure you were all right." He stirred a spoonful of sugar into his coffee and took a sip. "And I want to help."

"Help?"

"Help find the killer. I feel responsible for what's happened. If I hadn't been snooping around—"

"It's not your fault," she interrupted, a little sharply. "Whatever happened had nothing to do with you."

"I wish I could believe that."

"You're just a detective without a client, remember?" She was teasing him. "You're just in it for the money."

Dubin smiled, but he felt belittled. He was annoyed that his moral seriousness wasn't being taken seriously. "How do you know it has nothing to do with me? Don't you think this death is related to the one seven years ago?"

"I don't see how it could be."

They sat quietly for a while, and then Dubin said: "Can we go upstairs?"

"Haven't you been up there enough?"

Upstairs, Susan perched uncomfortably on a wooden stool while Dubin crouched beneath the overhead light, brushing away the dust on the floor until he found the dents and scuff marks that Frank Lynch had noted in his report. When he stood up he examined the record turntable, noting the dented corner where it had evidently landed on the floor. He studied the light fixture over his head and imagined Maria Morgan kicking the turntable off its stand as she swung and thrashed in her last moments. "Three items are missing that were here when Frank Lynch took his inventory," he said. "A photograph of Maria Morgan, a kaleidoscope, and a record."

"You mean a CD?"

"Not a CD—an old fashioned vinyl record."

"I remember the picture. It was a glossy black and white publicity photo. She used to keep it tacked up on the wall over there."

"Do you remember the kaleidoscope?"

"No, I never saw that."

Dubin glanced back up at the light fixture. "How was the turntable found?"

"What do you mean?"

"Was it set up like it is now or knocked onto the floor?"

"I don't remember. There were some things on the floor that she'd kicked over when—you know. The turntable might have been one of them."

"Then somebody must have set it back up."

"I think Avery picked up the stuff that was on the floor."

Dubin stepped over to the window and looked out over the brittle winter landscape. "What about the record?" he asked. "Do you remember the record that was on the turntable?"

"No. Was there a record on the turntable?"

"Frank Lynch listed a particular record on the turntable and its jacket on the shelf."

She rolled her eyes toward the bookshelf. "Maybe they're still over there."

"No, I checked the last time." He turned back around to face her. "What I'd like to find out is, where did the record go? And the picture and the kaleidoscope? Did Avery take them?"

Susan was getting bored with his questions, even annoyed. "He might have," she said. "This is his house, you know. He could clear out the whole place if he wanted to. But he's always said he didn't want to touch the studio. He wants to leave it the way it was when Maria died."

"Then who else could have taken those things out of here?"

"Anybody could have. We didn't used to keep it locked."

"What I'm wondering is why anybody would have taken the trouble to remove just those three items."

"I don't see what difference it makes."

"What about Hunter or Antonia? Could they have done it?"

"Done what?"

"Taken those three things."

Susan slipped off the stool and stood facing Dubin defiantly. "That's ridiculous. I would have found them in the house when— when they left to live at the Institute."

Dubin accepted her answer and changed the subject. "How long did they stay here after their mother died?"

"Not very long," she said, still sounding argumentative. "And Avery didn't let them come up here, I remember that. He told me to keep them out of here."

"When were they institutionalized? How long after Maria's death?"

"Not very long afterwards. They both went off the deep end and Avery had no choice but to put them in the Institute."

"How long?"

"Like about a week later."

"And they never came back?"

"No. They've never come back."

"Why not? Couldn't you—"

"Because I didn't want them to."

She turned her back and headed down the narrow stairs. "Turn off the lights when you're done."

"I've seen what I needed to see." He turned off the lights and followed Susan down the stairs, wondering what she had to hide. Was she just being protective or was there more to it than that? She was tall and athletic and completely amoral as far as he could tell. She could have done anything Hunter or Avery could have done.

By the time he caught up with her she was outside the barn sweeping some rotting leaves off the driveway. "I'm sorry if I ask too many questions," he said.

She turned it into a joke. "I know you're supposed to be a detective," she laughed, "but I'm the closest thing you've got to a client. Can't you give me a break and pick somebody else's brain for a change?"

Dubin would have joined in the joke but he needed to ask one more question. "Has Frank Lynch been here?"

"Sure he's been here. He's been called back to work on the case."

"Why?"

She hesitated. "I don't know. Because he worked on the last one and he knows Hunter, I guess."

"Did he know Maria?"

"Everybody around here knew Maria." She turned away with a mischievous smile. "Some a little better than others."

Nicole was right about one thing: I was growing more and more obsessed with Julietta. And the more obsessed I became, the more Gottlieb preyed on my mind. There was something frightening about Gottlieb, something unkempt and unpredictable that made him as menacing as a drooling ape. The idea of his touching Julietta almost made me sick to my stomach.

And something strange had been happening whenever I looked in a mirror. In the morning, I'd had trouble shaving because the glass was always steamed up from the shower. I could never seem to wipe away the steam well enough to see myself, and whenever I passed in front of a mirror, the man I saw staring back at me seemed ill-defined and only vaguely familiar. One afternoon as I stood chatting with Julietta, I couldn't recognize myself in the endless regression of mirrors that opened behind her desk. Was this the price of my obsession? I wondered. Had Julietta captured me so completely that I'd lost the part of me I show the world?

One morning I heard something extremely disturbing: Gottlieb was scheduled to be on vacation at the same time as Julietta. The nurses were making jokes about it—they all seemed to assume that Gottlieb and Julietta would be vacationing together. The very idea sent me into a panic. Where were they going? I remembered that

Julietta had told me she was going to Venice. Was Gottlieb going there too?

When no one was looking I did a little snooping around Gottlieb's desk. It looked like a pig sty, not surprisingly, heaped with unopened mail and magazines and confidential patient records that should have been kept under lock and key. In the top drawer I found a thin manila folder labeled "Italy" and in that folder a color brochure describing a "Romantic Getaway Vacation For Two" in Venice. My hand shook as I hid the folder back in the drawer.

Since she couldn't sleep, Nicole tried to do her work at night. By the light of her computer screen, she would arrange her books and research notes on the desk and sit typing from midnight to dawn. She left the downstairs door unlatched in the hope that Hunter would find her, but her only visitors were Dumas, Hoffmann, Offenbach and other refugees from the Romantic Era whose phantasms loomed around her in the eerie shadows cast by the computer screen. Sometimes, when she was falling into that half-dreaming state that comes just before sleep, she imagined that she heard her uninvited guests whispering furiously, arguing with each other about their lives and works and what she would write about them. Suddenly, with her heart pounding, she would catch her breath and sit up, frightened by her lapse into hallucination, and in the darkness she'd find that the phantasms had disappeared, their insinuating words hushed by a car swooshing past, the landlady's cat mewing on the stairs. But on one such occasion the visitor did not vanish when she blinked her eyes. Instead he hovered in the doorway, with his thin moustache and his high forehead and his ravening eyes boring into her like a messenger from another world.

"Oh, my God!" she blurted, shaking herself awake. "It's you again! Edgar Allan Poe!"

"I'm sorry. I didn't mean to scare you."

The man was holding himself perfectly still, as if expecting her to leap out at him. "And it's Dubin," he added.

"I beg your pardon?"

"My name's Dubin."

She studied him quizzically. "Of course," she said. "Dubin. The manuscript detective. Do you have a first name?"

"You can just call me Dubin."

She stood up and stepped toward him. "I'm so sorry I keep mistaking you for Edgar Allan Poe. I've been thinking about him a lot lately."

"I understand."

"Are you still trying to find out if there's a connection between your manuscript and what happened to Maria Morgan?"

He hesitated. "Yes, but the plot has thickened since we spoke."

"The plot?" That was an alarming turn of phrase. "What do you mean?"

"The murder at the Institute," he said. "Mrs. Paterson."

Nicole took another step closer to the doorway, half expecting Dubin to disappear when she turned on the overhead light. Instead he blinked, smiled and asked if he could come inside. She moved a pile of books and papers to make room for him on the couch and sat down across from him in the incredibly uncomfortable wooden armchair she'd bought at a yard sale. "I don't understand," she said. "How is Mrs. Paterson connected to your manuscript?"

"Through her death, obviously. And Hunter Morgan."

She waited for an explanation but none was forthcoming. "Hunter had nothing to do with her death," she said.

"How do you know that?"

"I know Hunter."

"That's what I'm worried about."

"What do you mean?"

Dubin leaned forward and pulled her into his intense gaze. "I don't want to alarm you," he said, "but I do want you to listen to me. I think you're in danger. You know Hunter and he knows you.

That's enough right now that you should be taking reasonable precautions, like not leaving your door wide open."

"Precautions against what?"

"Against Hunter showing up when you're here alone."

"Don't you understand?" She flew out of her chair, gesturing wildly. "I want him to show up here so I'll have a chance to talk to him before they take him away. I want to find him before he gets hurt. That's why I've been leaving the door unlocked."

"You're using yourself as bait?"

"You could say that," she said defiantly.

Two hours later Dubin and Nicole were the best of friends. She served him Irish whiskey while the night was still dark and English breakfast tea after the November light crept around the edges of the curtains. Something about her half-wild but fiercely sympathetic spirit made him want to talk. He told her everything that had happened since he first stumbled into that miserable town—his meetings with Avery Morgan, Miss Whipple, Mrs. Paterson, Peter Bartolli, even Susan. She asked all the right questions and when he answered she listened with a concentration that gave him the hope that with her help he might be able to find his way out of the maze he'd been wandering in for the past three months.

"Wait a minute," she said, a little sheepishly. "I want to show you something."

With a leap, she climbed on top of the kitchen counter and groped behind a cabinet, locating a manila envelope which she brought down and handed to him. "Open it."

Dubin removed the smaller envelope addressed to Maria Morgan and studied the postmark before he pulled out the anonymous letter, which he read two or three times before looking back up at Nicole.

"Where did you get this?"

"I can't tell you that."

Dubin frowned and read part of the letter aloud: "'A. is a fool to think he can keep you away from me—if he succeeds I may do something drastic. There are worse things than unhappiness. I think about you constantly, even when I'm supposed to be concentrating on my work. A textbook obsession, I'm afraid. Like Hoffmann in the Venice act, or my little friend Nero racing around and wagging his tail when he sees me coming and moping when I'm gone.'" He read it again silently and smiled. "So the opera singer was having an affair."

"Evidently."

"And 'A.'—obviously that's Avery Morgan—found out about it and was trying to stop it. And the lover was threatening to do something drastic if he succeeded."

"Do you know exactly when she died?"

Dubin stuck the letter back in its envelope. "About a week after this letter was postmarked." He lurched to his feet and paced around the little room like a tiger in a cage. "Avery Morgan is an autograph collector but this is one priceless item that he let slip through his grasp. Where did you get it?"

"It was entrusted to me. I can't tell you any more."

"Do you realize how important this is? It's the smoking gun that gives Morgan a motive for murdering his wife."

Nicole looked a little queasy. "Maybe I shouldn't have shown it to you." She took the letter from Dubin's hand and tried to put it back in its hiding place, but she was too shaky to climb back up on the counter. Instead she stuck it inside a cookbook and buried the cookbook in a pile of papers next to the stove.

"There's no way Avery Morgan will ever know you have that letter," Dubin reassured her.

"And the other man? The lover?"

"Whoever he was, he had a dog named Nero. That shouldn't be too hard to nail down."

19

One afternoon after a heavy rain, when clouds of mist were still drifting over the landscape, I put on my raincoat and walked along the gravel path that sketched the perimeter of the Institute's grounds. Inside the iron fence, the lawns and gardens had been raked and put to bed for the winter, but the other side was a thicket of thorns and hemlocks that encircled the Institute like a forest closing in on an abandoned castle. As I walked through the mist I thought back over the bizarre series of events that had unfolded in the three months since Hunter's first performance of Schumann's Kreisleriana. My affair with Olympia, which had burned so brightly and so briefly that in retrospect it almost seemed like a dream. A brutal murder, leaving Hunter at large and my brilliant career hanging in the balance. My own troubling symptoms—lately I'd been hearing voices, dimly, as if a radio had been left on in a nearby room, warbling in some foreign language that was impossible to understand. And all the while the figure of Nicole hovering over me like some half-crazed Cassandra, warning me that my life was being taken over by an opera plot. Now it was the growing obsession with Julietta that threatened to send me off in new and dangerous directions. What could I do to keep things from getting worse? How was I ever going to find my way out of this labyrinth?

On the other side of the iron fence, in the densest part of the thicket, a man in a hooded parka stood staring back at me. My heart leaped—it was Dr. Neuberger! My innermost wish had been fulfilled. At last I could breathe free, at last I could unburden myself of the crushing weight that had been building over me these past three months.

I stepped closer, wondering who would be the first to speak. He pushed his hood back and instead of Dr. Neuberger I recognized the dark, angular face of Peter Bartolli. He smiled and called my name.

"You're not supposed to be here!" I yelled.

Bartolli shrugged. "I've often spoken with Hunter here." He looked over my shoulder, as if hoping to catch a glimpse of Hunter coming up the path.

"Where's Olympia?"

"Gone. You won't be seeing her again."

"Hunter's gone too, as I'm sure you know."

He nodded. "Is my brother blaming me for that?"

"Mostly he's blaming me."

He smiled sympathetically. It was the same smile he'd aimed at Hunter when he was hypnotizing him. I tried to look away but found myself being drawn into the depths of his chthonic eyes. I wondered if I could trust him the way I trusted Dr. Neuberger.

"You should search for Hunter yourself," he said. "He won't run away from you."

The idea made me uncomfortable. "I can't," I objected. "I've got other responsibilities, other patients..."

"But finding Hunter must be your highest priority."

"I can't leave here."

"You want to stay with Julietta," he said. It wasn't a question.

"Who's been talking to you about Julietta?" I roared, amazed at how deftly he'd been able to play on my emotions. "Is it Gottlieb? Have you been talking to Gottlieb?"

"I know about Julietta," he nodded, without answering my question. "But Gottlieb—I wouldn't waste my breath talking to that man. You're right to be afraid of him."

"I'm not afraid of him."

"Then you ought to be. He's the main obstacle keeping you from Julietta."

I was starting to feel desperate, as if one of my panic attacks was coming on. "What can I do?"

"Keep your eye on him. And be careful: he can be violent at times."

"Violent?"

He lowered his voice to a whisper. "Do you have a weapon? A small knife, perhaps, that you can carry in your pocket?"

A knife? Was I hearing him correctly? "Yes"—I remembered the paring knife I'd lifted from the kitchen—"I have a small knife. But I... I wouldn't know what to do with it."

"You've already lost Olympia. Are you going to let Julietta sail off into the sunset with a man like Gottlieb?"

He turned and disappeared into the thicket and I found myself gripping the iron bars of the fence as I caught my breath and tried to frame my answer to his question. I felt like one of the inmates, peering through the bars into the woods and wondering whether I'd been hallucinating. Had Peter Bartolli been standing there a moment before—or was it really Dr. Neuberger?

"No," I finally said, calling after him. "I'm not going to let that happen. Did you hear me? I'm not going to let that happen!"

Miss Whipple stayed late at the library, afraid to venture out in the darkness, afraid most of all to spend another night alone in her bungalow. The previous night she'd heard something—or someone—rattling around in the basement, having entered (she supposed) through the bulkhead in the back. It could have been a raccoon or even a fox—such varmints had been known to pilfer from her basement pantry at this time of year—or it could have been an intruder of a more dangerous sort, even a creature of her own fevered imagination or her guilty conscience: entering in the nighttime, lying in wait by day, ready to torment her when she returned home to sleep. She gave scant credence to the theory that Hunter Morgan was still in the neighborhood. Even a madman would know enough to head north into the mountains, and with all the search parties about he surely would have been caught by now. No, it wasn't escaped lunatics she was worried about, but the other kind, the kind who don't have to escape because no one knows they're mad. No one but her, that is. No one but her

Miss Whipple locked the library door and turned off the outside light. Then she sat down at her desk and loosened the laces of her sensible shoes, which, to tell the truth, had begun to feel like a pair of steel vices by the end of the day. Luckily she found a container of yogurt and an apple in the little refrigerator beneath her desk, and after consuming these she hoisted her reading glasses to the bridge of her nose and sat back to relax with a copy of *In Cold Blood* by Truman Capote, one of her favorite books. After a chapter or two she dozed off and fell into a dreamless sleep, awakening in confusion and panic two hours later. Eleven o'clock! An hour earlier she could have called one of the women from church to drive her home, but now she'd slept too long. There was no one she could call at this hour. She gathered her belongings—her purse, her knitting and the Capote book, even though she was unlikely to read any more of it that night—and quietly eased herself out into the darkness, locking the library door behind her. Then with an air of resolution she shuffled through six blocks of shadows and fallen leaves until she came within sight of her bungalow. There were no lights on in the surrounding houses: all the neighbors must have gone to bed or been murdered like the Clutter family so long ago. Her house looked the same as it had looked the night before—dark, sequestered, the porch screen still banging in the wind—but she stopped in her tracks when she saw it. Without the rustling of the leaves beneath her feet, the house stood all the more forbidding in its silence.

It was too late for second thoughts. All she had to do was brush her teeth and put on her nightgown and go to bed, which she'd done ten thousand times before. Why should this night be any different?

* * *

"What'd you get on Dubin?"

Frank Lynch sat in the police cruiser with Captain Tom Wozniak digging into a couple of Spicy Italians they had just extracted from the proprietor of Val's Sub Shop. It was five in the afternoon, near the end of a gloomy, tedious day. The cruiser hovered like a space ship in Val's parking lot, its defroster roaring uselessly as the two men steamed up the windshield with their exhalations of prosciutto and onions and hot Italian peppers.

"It's like you thought," Wozniak said, taking a sip of his Coke. "He's not really a writer."

"*New York* magazine never heard of him?"

"They've heard of him, all right."

"What are you talking about?"

Tom Wozniak proved to be a more resourceful detective than Lynch had expected. On the phone with *New York* magazine, he'd pressed his inquiries from one desk to another until he hit pay dirt—an old timer named Brad Cornelius who not only knew Dubin in his previous life but seemed to have an axe to grind against him.

"Dubin used to be an investigative reporter for the *Times*. A regular boy wonder. Won all the awards. Then he got caught up in one of those scandals."

"Plagiarism?"

"No, the opposite. He was just making the stuff up. Falsifying his notes and travel records and writing fake articles for the paper. He denied it, claimed he was only guilty of sloppy recordkeeping, but the paper fired him anyway. And after that none of the other papers would touch him. He made some noise for a while, threatened to sue, even got into a brawl with a couple of editors from the *Times*. And then he just disappeared off the face of the earth."

"What do you mean, disappeared?"

"Nobody knew what happened to him. He'd been drinking heavily, his wife left him. They figured he had a breakdown or went into rehab somewhere."

"How long ago was that?"

"Seven, eight years."

Lynch lowered the remains of the Spicy Italian to his lap and wiped his hands with a napkin. "I thought he looked familiar."

"What do you mean?"

"Never mind." He crumpled his garbage into a paper bag and wiped his hands again. "So your friend Brad never heard of him again?"

"I told you, this Brad guy—I don't know if I believe everything he says. He seems to have it out for Dubin but he wouldn't say why. He says he's heard rumors that Dubin showed up back in the area and was going around doing research."

"Research?"

"The same kind of research he used to do for the newspaper. Remember that state senator down in Staten Island whose secretary went missing a couple of years ago? Well, according to Brad, a lot of people saw Dubin snooping around down there, looking things up in the court records, asking a lot of questions for a month or two. Then he just disappeared like he did the last time."

"Sounds like he's got his disappearing act down to a T."

"Yeah."

Lynch crushed his Coke cup, shoved it into the garbage bag, and handed the bag to Wozniak. "You never know," he said, slipping the cruiser into gear. "Maybe he's getting ready to disappear from around here too."

Nicole awoke with a feeling of certainty that Hunter had been found. This knowledge must have come from a dream, though she couldn't remember it. But she did remember hearing Miss Whipple's voice, as clearly as if it were an announcement on the radio. Miss Whipple had told her not to worry, that Hunter had been found. Nicole called Dr. Hoffmann at the Institute and left a message but he never called back. Finally she called the general switchboard, which opened at 8:00 o'clock. The woman who answered—it was the sexy receptionist Julietta—wouldn't tell her anything.

"Have they found Hunter?"

"I'm sorry, I can't discuss that with you."

"Is he still missing?"

"I said I can't discuss it with you."

At 9:00 o'clock she found herself on the library steps, waiting for Miss Whipple to open the doors as she always did at that hour. She waited what seemed like an eternity but Miss Whipple never arrived. A little before 10:00, a police car pulled into the parking lot. A fat policeman climbed out and walked up squinting suspiciously at Nicole.

"You want something here?"

"I'm waiting for the library to open."

"The library's closed today."

"How do you know that? Miss Whipple always—"

"Miss Whipple won't be coming in today."

"Why not?"

He hesitated. "Miss Whipple's dead."

Nicole felt the world swirling around her. She felt her lips moving but no words were coming out.

The policeman peered at her curiously. "Can I see some I.D., please."

Nicole found her car and somehow navigated her way to the Institute, though she felt almost as incoherent as she'd felt the first time she went there. Only this time, she thought, it's the world that's gone mad. First Mrs. Paterson and now Miss Whipple—how could that be? The policeman wouldn't provide any details. Instead he wrote down her name and address and said she might be needed later for questioning. He referred to her as a witness.

"A witness to what? What happened?"

"I can't give you that information."

The Institute looked surprisingly normal, but that was an illusion. Everything that seemed real and normal right now was an illusion. The ivy climbing the front of the building was an illusion. The well-trimmed bushes around the walkway and the steps. Julietta, at the receptionist's desk, chewing gum and polishing her nails.

"Can I help you?"

"I need to see Dr. Hoffmann."

"Do you have an appointment?"

"No, of course not. I'm here because of Hunter. Have they found him?"

"I can't discuss that with you." Julietta smirked because she'd said the same thing on the phone. She looked down at her appointment book. "You have an appointment scheduled for Thursday. Can't you wait until then to see Dr. Hoffmann?"

"I want to see him now."

"He's really busy."

"I'll just go to the cafeteria and wait for Antonia."

Julietta narrowed her shadowy eyes. "You can't do that."

"Look, I come here all the time. I'm a patient."

"If you're an out-patient you need an appointment." Julietta was smirking again. "Or would you rather be an in-patient?"

Nicole caught a glimpse of her own crazed, desperate face in the mirror over Julietta's head. Her eyes bobbed like wild green flames. Her lips were set for a scream. Her red hair seemed to be trying to escape in every direction. She did not look normal and that was reassuring. Unlike everything around her, she looked real.

"No. I'll come back for my appointment on Thursday."

Dubin heard the news about Miss Whipple from Susan, who left a desperate message on his answering machine. When he called her back he learned the details that had shocked the Morgans and everyone in town. The librarian had died in exactly the same fashion as Mrs. Paterson: her head had been battered from behind with a blunt object and then she had been hung from a light fixture with an extension cord disconnected from a lamp.   Again the similarity to Maria Morgan's suicide was too obvious to mention or ignore.   Even Susan sounded unnerved, though she denied the possibility that Hunter could be the killer.

"Be careful," Dubin said, too stunned to say anything meaningful.

"Thanks," Susan said. "We're not going to stop searching for Hunter."

"Even if it isn't Hunter, there's already a pattern and you could be part of it."

"What do you mean?"

"I don't know. Just be careful."

Early the next morning Dubin drove past Miss Whipple's house. It was a bungalow on a wooded lot about six blocks from the library. Through the dense shrubbery he could see yellow police tape stretching across the doors and windows, blocking access to the screened porch. He wanted to stop and peek in a window, or even slip inside, to see where the librarian had been found. Everyone was saying Hunter Morgan killed her but Dubin didn't believe it. In Dubin's guilt-ridden mind, that theory had a fatal flaw: it let him—Dubin—off too easily. He knew he was guilty. He knew his own actions had led to the deaths of both Mrs. Paterson and Miss Whipple. How could what he felt so remorseful about be explained by a random force like Hunter Morgan's madness? There had to be more to it than that; it had to be connected with the train of events he'd set in motion.

But he couldn't just stop and peek in the librarian's window. If the police were watching him, which they probably were, they might accuse him of the murder—and there would be some justice in that. But then he would never be able to find the killer.

Mrs. Paterson, Miss Whipple. Who would be next? Who else had Dubin compromised?   The obvious candidates were Susan and Nicole. Both women, both vulnerable, both knowing more than they should know. It would be difficult to protect Susan. She seemed to be in constant motion, working with her husband day and night to find Hunter. But Nicole lived by herself at the top of that rambling old house. She'd been a patient at the Institute and grown close to Hunter and Antonia. The killer might try to find her.

At night, Dubin thought. That's when these things seem to happen. At night.

It was two o'clock in the morning and Nicole sat at her desk trying to keep from going crazy. She had spent most of the last two days crying about Miss Whipple and desperately trying to reach Dr. Hoffmann at the Institute, who didn't return her calls. It never occurred to her that she was in any danger.

She tried to focus on her work, though at the moment she was thinking about Dubin. There was something inevitable about Dubin, something archetypal if not quite déjà vu, that made him turn up in her thoughts more often than she would have expected. Like Edgar Allan Poe himself, she mused, who haunts our literature like the raven in his own poem, appearing periodically to reclaim his obsessions from those who have appropriated them.

She scrolled anxiously through her notes and started nodding off to sleep. Suddenly there came a tapping and she looked up to find Dubin watching her from the doorway.

"Everything OK?"

She knew he would come back. "Come on in," she said, trying to sound cheerful. "I was just about to make some tea."

They sat at the little table sipping tea and talking about how quiet it was at three o'clock in the morning. "I didn't mean to leave the door open," she said sheepishly. "It was because the landlady's cat kept scratching to go in and out."

"Somebody ought to tell that cat where she lives. Do you feed her?"

"I serve her tea sometimes." As soon as she said that she realized how odd it must have sounded. "With milk," she added.

Dubin smiled. "You've got to be more careful now."

"Now that what?"

"Now that—I assume you've heard what happened to the librarian."

"Sure," Nicole said. "I'm a wreck from crying about it."

"I'm sorry."

"She was a wonderful lady."

Dubin nodded. "You've got to be more careful. There's a pattern to these deaths and it could lead to you."

"To me?"

"Maria Morgan, Mrs. Paterson, and now Miss Whipple—"

"It could only lead to me if the killer is Hunter."

"We won't know what the pattern is until it's complete."

"Until the last act?" she smiled, a little cryptically. "When all the bodies have been counted?"

Nicole stood up and carried the teapot back to the stove to refill it with hot water. The cat had appeared beneath her feet and she stooped down to pour some milk into its bowl. "Have you thought any more about that letter?" she asked Dubin as she slipped back into her seat.

"I've thought about the letter a lot," Dubin admitted, relieved that she had brought it up. With Miss Whipple's death, the letter had taken on a new and possibly crucial significance. "Do you think I could see it again?"

"Sure." She found the letter where she'd hidden it on the counter and handed it to him. Then she sipped her tea while he read it for what seemed an eternity.

"Do you think Maria Morgan was murdered?" she finally asked.

"That's the hypothesis I've been going on."

"And do you think the same person killed Mrs. Paterson and Miss Whipple?"

"It's very likely."

"Then Hunter shouldn't be a suspect in any of the killings."

Dubin looked up from his reading for the first time. "Why not?"

"For one thing he was only fourteen years old when his mother died. And when you read that letter you realize there was this whole thing going on between Avery Morgan and the secret lover, and if anyone killed her it was probably one of them. Which means it was also probably one of them who killed Mrs. Paterson and Miss Whipple."

"Why?"

"They must have known something. I think it was Avery Morgan."

"Why do you say that?"

"Because it would explain Hunter's madness."

Dubin set down his teacup and spread the letter carefully on the table. "You're going to have to explain that one for me."

"Hunter thinks he's Hamlet. He's constantly watching videos of *Hamlet* movies and he's got all of Hamlet's lines memorized. Everyone thinks he goes around ranting and raving like a madman, but when I was there I realized that what he was doing most of the time was quoting from *Hamlet*."

"And that's not crazy?"

"It may be crazy but it's not insane. It's a disguise, don't you see? The madness is just a disguise, as it was for Hamlet."

"You think Hunter has just been faking it for the past seven years?"

Nicole shook her head. "I think Hunter, by playing Hamlet, is trying to tell us something. He's trying to tell us that his own madness is self-protective, like Hamlet's. If he saw his father kill his mother he must have known he would be next unless he rendered himself harmless. So that's exactly what he did."

20

Susan sat in the windowless kitchen at the back of the stone barn, sipping coffee as she thought about the irony of Dubin worrying about her safety. The kids were staying at her mother's with the au pair and with them had fled any semblance of normality. Halloween, with its festive images of death, had come and gone. It was too early for holiday cheer or long evenings by the fire—only November rain and moldy leaves clogging the drain spouts, boggy mists oozing up from the pond to smother the boxwoods and the wilting ferns. Mud everywhere, crusted with frost in the mornings, flowing like a stream by mid-afternoon. A cold wind whispering down from the north with a rumor of snow, more likely sleet and freezing rain. They might have snow in the mountains where Avery had gone to search for Hunter with his army of volunteers, but here you could be sure it would be nothing but rain and mud. If she was lucky the mud would engulf the boxwoods and swallow their sickly odor that she'd hated from the first day she set foot in this place.

No, she wasn't afraid although Dubin seemed to think she should be. Three women were dead, and if there was order in the universe, that pattern was likely to continue until the killer was brought to justice. But she doubted that there was any order in the universe that couldn't be overcome if you had enough money and knew the right people. When she'd come here ten years before, what was she? Just a baby sitter for two screwed-up kids she never much liked, hired to give them what their screwed-up mother couldn't provide because she was so obsessed with her career. After the mother's death it wasn't difficult to step into her shoes. Avery needed a wife and Susan was there for him, ready to comfort him in his loss. The terms of their bargain were clear but never openly stated. For him, a home, children, and no more sex than was absolutely necessary. For her all of the above, plus money—so long as she never asked how much he had—and the freedom to sleep discreetly with other men. The main thing was the money. Avery was old money which meant he never had to work for it. "I own things"—that's how he always answered when some nosy neighbor asked what he did for a living. And that was what Susan liked about him—he wasn't ashamed to be rich, even if the class he represented had been consigned to godforsaken corners of the world like this one where their only prerogative was to be left alone.

When darkness fell, she locked up the barn and dragged her mud-soaked golden retriever behind the house to hose him off. She locked the dog in the back hall to dry along with her muddy sneakers and washed up in one of the downstairs bathrooms. Then she cleaned up the dirty dishes in the kitchen, heated up some pasta and sat down at the kitchen table to read the local paper, which was breathless with the news of the two murders and Hunter's disappearance. The town was thriving on fear. Along with the search parties, it was reaching its tentacles out into the countryside, even to this rotting redoubt of old money and hereditary insanity. Yes, women seemed to be the target, and she knew that if trouble came knocking, her idiot of a dog would run off into the woods and disappear. But was she the one who ought to be afraid? Frank Lynch had told her all about Nicole—how Nicole had grown close to Hunter during her stay at the Institute, how she spent every night with Dubin in her apartment. That was a scenario Susan could not bear to think about for very long. Dubin was a cold fish but Susan was paying him to be her cold fish. How much would she have to pay him to spend the night with her? She liked the idea of paying a man for doing nothing— of owning him, in a sense. Sooner or later he would give her what she wanted—she knew that. That was her consolation for spending her life surrounded by these rotting leaves and that punky boxwood smell that had oppressed her for so many years. I own things.

There was nothing to be afraid of.

Dubin balanced uncertainly on his bar stool, chasing the last grey goose over a blurry landscape in his mind's eye.

"Last call!"

His vision dissolved and he found himself staring straight ahead, infinitely replicated in the mirror behind the bar. "Give me another one of these."

"Are you sure?"

"I'm sure."

In the turmoil of his anguished mind, Dubin had decided that his best course was to stick with the original plan. Using the fictitious manuscript as bait—though in a sense it had backfired— had brought him closer to the core of things than he could have ever imagined. He'd assumed Avery Morgan had bought the Offenbach letter and would also want the manuscript, but the bird he'd unexpectedly lured into his trap was Peter Bartolli, the banished co-founder of the Palmer Institute. There were fifteen messages on his answering machine from Bartolli asking about the manuscript. He had left them all unanswered. The longer he waited, the more desperate Bartolli would become. For Dubin it was a struggle of almost metaphysical proportions. He hated and feared psychiatrists the way a medieval peasant feared the Devil. You can't hide from them, you can't deceive them, you can't bargain with them except at the risk of your soul. If you think you're on a lucky streak, it's only because you've surrendered to the fate they have devised for you. Worse than blackmailers: collectors of souls.

Dubin drained the last of his Grey Goose and plodded steadily outside. The stakes were getting higher by the hour.

He stepped up to the wide front porch, wondering if Bartolli would answer the door. A black cat darted out from behind a bush and reared up at him, hissing silently as if trying to scare him away. Bartolli appeared and opened the door a crack to let the cat slink inside.

"My name is Dubin. You wanted to talk to me about the Offenbach manuscript."

Bartolli widened the opening and glared at him incredulously. "You're the man who was supposed to meet me in the food court."

"That's right."

"You were sitting there the whole time." He looked ready to fly across the threshold and knock Dubin to the ground. "Reading a newspaper. You let me wander around with my umbrella for an hour and didn't say a word."

"It was a test," Dubin said without blinking.

"What do you mean?"

"It was a test and you passed it. I followed you home and now that I've had a chance to find out who you are, we can continue our discussion."

"All this to buy a manuscript?"

"It's a very unusual manuscript. My client doesn't want it to fall into the wrong hands."

Bartolli stared at him unforgivingly. "All right, then," he finally said, swinging the door open. "Please come in."

Dubin followed him through a gloomy entrance hall decorated with primitive masks into an equally gloomy library lined with glassed-in bookcases. Bartolli unlocked a wooden cabinet and pulled out a buckram folder.

"Have a seat. Please. I want to show you something. This is one of my recent acquisitions. I think you'll recognize it."

He handed Dubin a clear plastic pouch labeled "Jacques Offenbach to Albert Wolff, 28 August 1880." Inside the pouch was a yellowed, ink-blotched letter in French covered with the impatient scrawl of a man in the last weeks of his life. Dubin nodded as if he knew all about it.

"I assume your client's manuscript is the one mentioned in this letter?"

"It's the one," Dubin assured him.

"Does your client realize what it is?"

"Absolutely. But she has little interest in such things, other than for family reasons."

"Then your client's a descendent of Wolff's? Or is she a member of the Offenbach family?"

"I'm not here to talk about my client. I'm here to talk about you. My client wants to know why you're so interested in this manuscript."

Bartolli fixed his all-consuming stare on Dubin for what must have been a full thirty seconds. "Then by all means," he said, suddenly smiling, "let me tell you something about myself." He put the pouch back in the folder and replaced the folder in the cabinet. "Shall we sit down in my office? It's stuffy in here."

He led Dubin down the hallway into a paneled study that looked like the captain's quarters in an old-fashioned ocean liner. This was the office, Dubin realized as he settled into a leather armchair, where the psychiatrist saw his patients. The lighting was soft, the artwork unobtrusive; there was even a couch along one of the walls. But the usual roles were reversed—it was Bartolli, ensconced behind his walnut desk, who had to give an account of himself. "I am the son of an Italian nobleman and an American heiress," he began. "I was born in Rome and educated in Italy and Switzerland—"

"But aren't you Miles Palmer's brother?"

"His half-brother," Bartolli corrected, his eyebrows arching scornfully. "Miles's father was a British distiller who made a fortune in real estate and dropped dead a year after he married my mother." He flicked an invisible piece of lint off his sleeve and ran a hand through his tuft of gray hair. "I can't account for her behavior. Miles spent most of his childhood in English boarding schools and in fact we have very little in common."

"You're both psychiatrists."

"True. And for a few years we were able to do some excellent work together at the Institute."

"Why did that end?"

"We have fundamentally different beliefs about the human psyche."

With a quick gesture, he waved aside any further questioning on that topic. "Now," he said, "as to the Offenbach manuscript: I bought the letter hoping that it would shed some light on *The Tales of Hoffmann*, but by itself it doesn't prove anything. I need the manuscript."

"But why?" Dubin asked. "I still don't understand where your interest is coming from."

Bartolli stared past Dubin at the bookshelves that lined the back wall of the study. "For the past several years, my work has taken me back to the early psychoanalysts and their studies of literature and folklore. Freud, of course, wrote a famous essay about Hoffmann." He shot an inquisitorial glance at Dubin. "You knew that, didn't you?"

"No, I didn't."

He eyed Dubin skeptically, as if convinced that he was lying. "It's well worth reading." He focused his gaze on Dubin and went on. "Offenbach's version of Hoffmann's tales has been bowdlerized since its inception with the purpose of concealing its true meaning. But in this letter—and in your manuscript, I assume—Offenbach tells us what he really wanted to do: to create a modern, existential work about a man driven to insanity and murder by sexual jealousy and obsession."

Bartolli had grown more and more breathless and excited as he spoke, his hands circling in broad spirals as if he were trying to conjure his words out of the air. Now he stood up, his face glowing, and walked around the desk to take hold of Dubin's arm. "If you want to know why I must have that manuscript, come with me! I want to show you something."

Reluctantly, Dubin followed him back toward the entrance hall and then down a narrow staircase to a dimly-lighted basement that smelled of sawdust and mildew. One end of the basement had been set up as a miniature theater, decorated with opera posters and kabuki masks. Rows of seats faced a low stage, most of which was occupied by some sort of structure draped with canvas.

"As you can tell, I am a man of many interests, many perspectives on life." Bartolli stepped onto the stage and pulled off the canvas, revealing a puppet theatre with a dozen marionettes grotesquely hanging in the proscenium, their heads drooping, their eyes bulging, as if they had been the victims of a mass execution. "I have many interests, but this," he said softly, "this is my passion."

21

The search for Hunter Morgan slogged into its second week in an atmosphere of grim determination, as morale among the staff sank to an all-time low. Julietta never left my thoughts as I agonized over her trip to Venice with Gottlieb. With each passing day I grew more angry and depressed. I wrote myself a prescription for Zoloft and took double the recommended dose, with no discernible effect. One morning—it was about nine days after Hunter disappeared—Dr. Palmer called me into his office. I was sure I was about to be fired. But he smiled paternally as I came in and offered me a seat in the leather chair in front of his desk.

"I can tell that you're very troubled by what's happened," he said.

"Yes," I admitted. Obviously he was thinking of Hunter, not Julietta. "I'll never forgive myself."

"It's not your fault."

It surprised me to hear him say that, but I thought I knew what he meant. The image of Peter Bartolli peering through the fence was still fresh in my mind. "You shouldn't blame your brother, either," I said.

"No," he agreed. "It's not his fault. These things happen sometimes. There's nothing anyone can do."

I appreciated his sympathy but it didn't alleviate my professional and spiritual crisis. Having been trained in modern psychiatry, I had no way of dealing with an event that went beyond any conceivable scientific explanation. It wasn't just that we didn't know yet what particular chemical imbalance could cause this type of thing to happen; it was whether we should even attempt to understand it in those terms. I had begun to feel that what Hunter had done could only be described as evil.

Dr. Palmer smiled grimly when I told him that. "Look on the wall behind you," he said.

I turned around and saw a framed print which I had often noticed but never examined in any detail. It depicted a fantastic scene that reminded me of Hieronymus Bosch, with a hideous dragonlike creature that must have represented the Devil hovering over a number of lesser demons and some cowering humans.

"What is it?"

"The Temptation of St. Anthony, by Jacques Callot. Seventeenth century etching."

"It's grotesque."

Dr. Palmer nodded in agreement. "Do you know the story of St. Anthony? He gave away all his wealth and lived as a hermit in the desert, where he was tormented by every kind of temptation imaginable, in the form of beautiful women, wild beasts and demons that tore at his flesh—and even the Devil himself, who appeared in this monstrous shape and proclaimed himself the ruler of the world."

"Why did he do it?"

"To find God he first had to find the Devil."

I laughed grimly. "Whatever that is."

"Today we know that the Devil is a human artifact, a superstition we created for ourselves. The same thing is true of evil itself. We know they don't really exist except in our minds."

Part of me couldn't accept that this was true. "Then why resist them?"

"That's the question a psychiatrist has to wrestle with every day of his life."

Dr. Palmer stood up and I assumed our meeting was over. But then he stepped toward me and put his arms around my shoulders and pulled me toward him for a brief embrace. I was deeply moved.

"I've had this print on my wall ever since I started practicing twenty-five years ago," he said. "As a reminder of how powerful these superstitions can be."

St. Anthony stared back at us from the print, terrified in the desperate isolation of his conscience.

"And I look at it every day—to remind myself that even though the Devil doesn't exist, that doesn't mean you can't be tempted by him. Tormented by him. And even destroyed by him."

Thinking back on the afternoon he'd spent with Peter Bartolli, Dubin wondered if his memory was playing tricks on him. It was almost as if he'd been dreaming, especially after he followed Bartolli down into his dank subterranean theater. There was the stage—and beside it a grand piano, of all things—and on the stage an elaborate puppet theater with a stage of its own, arrayed with a dozen hanging figures that looked like corpses on a gibbet. When Bartolli pulled the canvas cover off the puppet theater, announcing it as his passion in life, Dubin dropped into the nearest seat, sensing that he was intended as the audience. Bartolli had dimmed the lights, leaving only a single spotlight fixed on himself. Darkness poured in from the farthest corners of the room, which seemed impossibly far away, as if the basement were much larger than the house itself.

Bartolli's face throbbed under the lurid glow of the spotlight. "I personally designed all the marionettes," he boasted, "which were then hand carved by Austrian craftsmen." He climbed behind the puppet theatre and removed all the puppets from view; then he opened a little hatch above the proscenium so he could talk to Dubin as he introduced them. "The production I'm working on—in case you haven't guessed—is *The Tales of Hoffmann*."

The first marionette he brought out was a languid female with stringy blond hair and a ghoulish expression on her face. "This of course is Olympia. The ballerina Hoffmann falls in love with at first sight. She appears to be a woman but in fact she is a doll. Of course in the opera the actor who plays her is a woman. So in this case she's a puppet pretending to be a woman pretending to be a doll pretending to be a woman. She's specially designed so that at the flick of a wrist she falls apart and crumbles into a heap of cloth and sticks. I won't show you that just yet."

He left Olympia hanging while he selected another marionette. "This one's a real woman," he said, dangling another female form, darker and more sensuous than the first. "She can seduce a man into madness. Do you know her?"

The puppet's jet black eyes gleamed back at Dubin with lifelike penetration. "No," he whispered, without knowing why he was whispering.

"Her name is Giulietta."

Bartolli clattered around behind the stage for a few minutes as he raised some new equipment into position. "Now," he said, as if talking to himself. "Hoffmann. Who shall Hoffmann be today?" He peered at Dubin through the little hatch. "You see, the marvel of my invention is that I can move the heads around and change the characters' identities at will. I can make Hoffmann look like any number of men, depending on my mood. And that's fitting, don't you think? After all, Hoffmann could be anyone."

"How do you mean?"

"Even if—as your manuscript undoubtedly portrays him—he's an obsessionally jealous serial killer, he could be any man, couldn't he? Or to put it another way, any man could be Hoffmann. He could even be you."

"I'm looking forward to seeing who he is."

"Oh, it doesn't really matter whose face he has. In fact, I think we'll keep it covered." He lowered the Hoffmann figure over the stage, and Dubin felt a chill when he realized that the marionette's head had been covered with a neatly sewn hood, and that his hands—possibly because the strings were a little tangled—appeared to be tied behind his back. He looked like a man being led to the gallows. "It could be anyone," Bartolli said, peering down at Dubin through the hatch. "I mean, we all have a little of the Hoffmann in us, don't we?"

Dubin glanced over his shoulder toward the stairs, which had been swallowed in darkness.

"Maybe it's just because I'm a psychiatrist," Bartolli went on, "but I like to think of my little puppet theater as a microcosm of the human mind."

"The human mind? I don't understand what you mean."

"Then let me explain," Bartolli said pleasantly. "Contrary to popular belief, the mind does not function like a machine. The parts of a machine are all subordinate to one overall purpose." He marched the marionettes across the stage in a lockstep formation. "But the mind has a multitude of parts which each want to function autonomously, forming their own purposes and personalities, the goal of which is to dominate all the others"—he jiggled the strings and the three marionettes skittered helplessly across the stage—"like a ruthless tyrant."

"Personalities?"

"Plural, yes." Bartolli shook the strings and each of the marionettes danced a different dance, knocking into each other erratically. "Remember, we're here as the result of evolution, which has bequeathed us with a collection of fragmentary selves, each of which is perfectly willing to sacrifice all the others for the sake of its own survival."

As he thought back over this conversation, Dubin could almost feel the magnetism of Bartolli's gaze and the magisterial certainty of his voice. But what he remembered most was his reaction to Bartolli's ideas—they made him feel queasy, restless, eager to escape, as if the puppet theater was indeed a microcosm of his own mind and they were the strings that were entangling him under the puppet master's control. He wondered: Who is that hooded figure on the stage? What does he mean by saying it could be anyone?

"Nothing is ever lost in evolution," Bartolli went on. "Each part of the brain is a survivor. We have the brain of a lizard, a rodent, an ape, and all the stops along the way. Each has its own complete vision of the world, and can operate independently as a complete self if the need arises. And each has the Darwinian will to survive, even if it can do so only by suppressing or extinguishing all the others."

Bartolli disappeared from the hatch and the Hoffmann figure trudged painfully across the stage and turned his hooded face toward Dubin, raising his hands as if in a silent plea for recognition. "In our darker moments we perceive these separate selves for what they are, but for public consumption we try to integrate them together into one big personality that we present to the world as if it were a coherent whole."

The Olympia puppet danced out to pirouette beside Hoffmann, leaving him spinning in his attempt to follow her movements. "When people can't do it well enough, we call them schizophrenics. They're incapable of normal social functioning because each one of their fragmentary selves must have its own way, contending with the others like lunatics in an asylum."

Bartolli's face popped into the hatch, smiling his ironic smile. "Or, if you prefer, like prima donnas in an opera company." He ducked down again as the salacious Giulietta slithered on stage beside Olympia. "Our minds shelter a whole repertory company of small, self-important characters, each competing to be the center of attention. There's usually a king, or a duke, and a beautiful princess. Or perhaps a courtesan or an artiste." Olympia took an awkward bow as Giulietta tried to shove her aside. "Every one of them wants to be the center of attention at all times."

Bartolli lowered the curtain, leaving the puppets to their jealous machinations, and stepped down onto the main stage, his face sober. Dubin lurched to his feet, but Bartolli had ensnared him in his ideas; there was no possibility of escape.

"They are the gods," Bartolli concluded, "the angels, the demons, the furies, the inner voices we are all familiar with. And although you may imagine yourself pulling the strings, or sitting in the audience, I will tell you something: There isn't any audience and there isn't any puppeteer. There isn't any 'you' other than them. They are who you are."

22

The search parties were easy to avoid. He watched them through the leafless trees in the harsh light of the early winter landscape, plodding across the countryside in their orange vests like dull-witted insects. With the drugs finally out of his system, he felt as if he were discovering the world for the first time. Every day there were new shapes, new colors, all as bright and sharp at the edges as the knife he'd stolen from the old woman's kitchen. He knew they would never catch him. He spent the day sleeping in a culvert and at night he'd roam the woods searching for food. Avoiding the paved roads, he'd make his way to the edge of town, where a surprising number of people slept with their doors unlocked. He didn't know what he would do if anyone caught him sneaking into their house. He always kept the knife in his pocket, and sometimes he'd take it out and watch it glisten in the moonlight but that was all. He remembered hiding in the barn and eating the rotten apples and it made him sick to think about it. What had happened before that? His mind teemed with memories but they seemed to belong to someone else.

Nicole, he thought, watching the knife glisten in the moonlight. Eventually she would find him, or he would find her.

23

At our next session I told Nicole about my conversation with Dr. Palmer on the subject of evil. Her reaction was surprisingly angry, and it led to a major breakthrough in her therapy. "A superstition?" she scoffed. "Is that the scientific view? Then there's no reason why I shouldn't get a gun and blow your brains out."

"Why don't you?"

She glared back at me with a look in her green eyes that was almost enough to make me believe in supernatural evil. "I was expelled from school for not believing in the Devil," she said in a softer voice. "Did I ever tell you about that?"

And she proceeded to tell me the most extraordinary story about her girlhood in the west of Ireland, a subject she'd carefully avoided in all our previous sessions. I learned for the first time about the younger brother who died after falling onto some rocks and the sanctimonious priest who blamed her for not accepting the Devil as the agent of his death. For that sin she was expelled from school and sent to London to live with an aunt. She was fourteen.

"I don't understand why they sent you to London," I said. "So far away. Why didn't you just go home?"

"They didn't want me at home. They knew that I knew."

"Knew what?"

"Knew that my father did it."

"Did what?"

"Killed my brother."

I kept a poker face. "Your father killed your brother?"

"He beat him for every infraction. He beat me too, but not as badly because I was a girl and I was away at school. But Sean was only ten and when Father was drunk he used to slap him and push him around and I know as well as I know my own name that he pushed him or pummeled him off that cliff and down onto those jagged rocks. That's why they wouldn't let anyone see the body, there were marks on him and bruises that were already there when he died—doctors can tell that, can't they?—and it would have proven that Sean was being beaten and that he was pushed or chased or maybe he just jumped off out of desperation."

"How do you know all this?"

"I know it because I was sitting next to my father at the funeral and I could smell it on him, and on my mother as well."

"The alcohol?"

"No. The guilt."

"What does guilt smell like?"

"It smells like guilt. And I know what guilt smells like because I've plenty of my own. Don't you see? I should have helped him. I should have protected him. I knew it was going to happen and I did nothing to stop it."

She lowered her face and started to cry, the first time she had shed any tears in our many therapy sessions. The crying continued for several minutes, and I made no attempt to stop it or comment on it. When she seemed almost done I handed her a tissue and she blew her nose.

"Why haven't you told me about this sooner, Nicole?"

She raised her eyes blankly, aloof from her own emotions. "It has no relevance to my present life."

"It seems that it does, or you wouldn't be so upset."

She blew her nose again and smiled. "Perhaps you're right."

"Do you believe in the Devil now?"

"I don't think of it as the Devil. That's not my word for it. But I do believe in... something evil."

"What is it?"

"It's not something out of Dante or Milton or even Stephen King. It's not 'out there' somewhere. It's inside us—Dr. Palmer's right about that. But it's not a superstition. It's real."

"What is it?"

She shook her head, as if to deny that she could answer my question. "If you think evil exists only in your mind, it can take you over in a way that couldn't have happened to St. Anthony, who kept it outside of himself. Because when it gets inside you it doesn't let go. It can take over your consciousness and direct your actions and it can pass from one mind to another."

"How can it do that?"

"Through images, ideas, symbols. It can move from one mind to another and be passed forward through the generations along with language and literature and art. It can take over a person's life."

I had listened to Nicole with growing fascination. Her mode of expression was unique, reflecting her unusual background and verbal abilities, but the content of what she said was easily recognizable as a variation on one of the standard fantasies of deeply troubled patients: evil forces at large in the world, communicating magically from one mind to another, directing their words and actions. "This evil force," I asked her, "has it taken over your life?"

"No," she said, staring back at me with eyes that looked as tormented as St. Anthony's. "But I'm afraid—"

"You're afraid of what?"

"I'm afraid it's taking over yours."

Dubin was now spending every night with Nicole. At about two o'clock in the morning, lying hopelessly awake in his bed, he would finally admit to himself that he couldn't face another sleepless night. He would down a shot of reposado and drive the forty-five minutes to Nicole's apartment, where he would find her, as often as not, slumped over her keyboard with little to show for a night's work. Sometimes they would drink tea, sometimes white wine or whisky, talking and laughing and helping each other through the night, and then just before dawn—like Scheherazade, she said— she would discreetly fall silent and crawl into bed and he would lock the door behind him and drive back in a daze to his apartment. With her wild red hair and her restless green eyes, she was an intellectual street urchin, unlike any woman he'd ever known. He knew she could help him finish what he'd started.

They still talked constantly about the letter the librarian had given her. Dubin read it and reread it every time he came to the apartment. "There's something in here I don't understand," he said one night. "'A textbook obsession' was how Maria's lover described how he felt. I can understand that. But what do you think he meant by 'like Hoffmann in the Venice act?'"

"You don't know?" They were drinking Jameson's that night and Nicole had fueled herself to a cheeky defiance. "You ought to read your manuscript."

"What manuscript?"

"The manuscript of *The Tales of Hoffmann* you're trying to sell to Peter Bartolli. Remember? That's what you told me the first time you came here. Or was that just a ruse?"

"Absolutely not." Dubin gulped down the rest of his Jameson's and rapped his empty glass down on the table. "But the manuscript isn't mine—as a matter of fact I've never seen it."

"Well, if you ever get a chance to read it—assuming it really exists—you'll know what our distraught lover was talking about. But I'm surprised you even have to ask. Wasn't *The Tales of Hoffmann* the opera Maria Morgan was rehearsing when she died?"

"Yes, it was—and I ought to know more about it but I don't. What happens in the Venice act?"

Nicole smiled at Dubin's helplessness. "Hoffmann goes to Venice and becomes obsessed with a courtesan named Giulietta."

"A 'courtesan,'" he repeated. "I've always wondered what a courtesan is."

"It's a high-class whore."

"That's what I thought. All right, what happens next?"

"In the traditional version, Giulietta tricks Hoffmann into killing his rival Schlemiel and then sails away in a gondola to the music of the famous Barcarolle."

"What happens to Hoffmann?"

"He's left crying his heart out on the canal bank. But now we know that the traditional version was nothing but a bowdlerized afterthought. The Venice act was supposed to be the grand finale, with Hoffmann killing Giulietta and her gigolo boyfriend in an orgy of death and degradation."

Dubin reached for the Jameson's and poured himself another shot. "So much for comic opera."

"*The Tales of Hoffmann* was decidedly not intended as a comic opera," Nicole said, pulling the bottle away so he couldn't drink any more. "But you must know that. In that manuscript you're selling, it turns out even worse, doesn't it?"

In the hour just before dawn, when the night is supposed to be at its darkest, Nicole felt weighed down with alcohol and melancholy and fatigue and could think of nothing but collapsing into her bed. But Dubin had to wait, as he always did, until the first light of day before he would leave her there alone. He perched on the edge of the couch lost in thought, tapping his fingers on the boxful of books that served as her coffee table. "There's something else I meant to tell you about," he said suddenly.

"What is it?"

"You know I've been over Maria Morgan's studio with a fine-toothed comb, and I've compared what I found there with the inventory Frank Lynch made right after she died. There are three things in that inventory that are no longer there today—a promotional photo of Maria Morgan, a kaleidoscope, and an old fashioned phonograph record."

"You've told me that before."

"The question is, what happened to them?"

"All right." Nicole could not begin to answer any more questions. "What's the answer?"

"Anyone could have taken them from the studio. Susan says it didn't used to be locked. But she also says Avery Morgan wanted the place to remain just as Maria left it. So why would just those three things disappear?"

"The lover took them?"

"Exactly! Avery Morgan wouldn't have taken them, but the lover would have—because they must have some sentimental value to him. And if he went to the trouble of taking them for that reason, he probably still has them stashed away someplace."

Nicole stood up and stumbled toward her bedroom, hoping that the first light of dawn would light her way. "So all we have to do," she said, "is find someone with a picture of Maria Morgan, a kaleidoscope, and a phonograph record, who also has a dog named Nero."

"Exactly."

She turned to face Dubin, hopefully to say good night. "What record was it?"

"*Piano Music of Robert Schumann*, played by Alicia de Larrocha."

The sky suddenly lightened and Dubin stood up to leave. Nicole felt a little queasy.

"What's the matter?"

"Nothing," she said. "Nothing."

24

One morning Julietta greeted me wearing a gaudy new necklace. "These are diamonds," she said, her eyes glistening. "Eighteen carats." She pulled back her sweater so I could get a better view of the necklace.

"Did Gottlieb give you that?"

"I'm not saying. An admirer like you. And if you buy me something this nice, I'll personally come down to your room to thank you for it."

"Is this what Gottlieb does? He pays you for sex—"

"Shhh!" she hushed me. "Who said anything about sex? Now get out of here and let me do my work."

The phone rang and she answered it, dropping into a conversation with one of her girlfriends. As she spoke she held the telephone receiver clamped under her chin so she could continue with her "work," which consisted of filing her nails into stiletto points. I started down the hall toward my room, hoping in some foolish way that Julietta would follow me, even though it was ten o'clock in the morning. But when I turned around I saw Gottlieb lolling in front of her desk, exactly as I'd been doing a few minutes before—smiling as I'd been smiling, gesturing as I'd been gesturing, like a monstrous reflection that had finally been released from the agony of the mirrors to ape my steps. And Julietta was laughing, chatting merrily, just as she'd been doing with me a moment earlier. My fingers tightened around the knife in my pocket and my vision clouded. I ran to my room and slammed the door behind me.

It was during our next session that I finally understood how far away Nicole was from being able to function in the real world. She took a seat across from my desk as she always did, and after a friendly greeting I sat quietly waiting for her to begin the conversation. Admittedly I was distracted by my own problems and I might have been a little less warm and forthcoming than usual.

"God is a comedian performing for an audience that refuses to laugh," she said solemnly.

Neither the tone nor the content of what she said surprised me. In our last session she had cried hysterically when we talked about the death of her brother, and so I took her solemnity at face value.

She held her stern expression as long as she could and then burst out laughing. "Rousseau said that," she giggled. "Not me."

I was not amused.

"You're one of the people who refuses to laugh," she teased.

I managed a weak smile. "You think of life as a comedy?"

"No, not a comedy, exactly. But somewhere there's an intelligence at work—probably not God or the Devil, just some indifferent cosmic scribe writing and rewriting the book of the world in a thousand different plots and a thousand different styles. And I'm one of the very, very minor characters."

"The book of the world," I nodded. Accustomed to her habit of seeing the world in literary terms, I assumed I could safely indulge her in this metaphor. I had no idea that I was following her right down the rabbit hole. "What kind of book is that? A mystery? A tragedy?"

"True Crime. That's what Miss Whipple would have called it."

"Does that imply that the entire world is based on crime?"

"Not everything fits into that category. For example, if you asked me about what's been going on around here lately, I'd have to classify it as Post-Modern Neo-Gothic Horror."

"Horror?"

"Sure." Reaching in her jeans pocket, she pulled out a crumpled piece of writing paper which she then ironed flat on her knee. "Would you like to hear a synopsis?"

I suppressed a thrill of expectation mixed with dread. This was the first time she'd offered to share any of her writing with me. "Sure. Go ahead."

"'A beautiful opera singer hangs herself on the eve of her debut at the Met. Seven years later the opera she was rehearsing—Offenbach's *Tales of Hoffmann*—begins to take over the lives of her two schizophrenic children, the doctors who treat them and everyone else who crosses their paths, until all are enmeshed in a world of deception and delusion, of madness and ultimately of evil and death. Onto this shadowy stage steps Nicole P., a graduate student who discovers that she too has been assigned a role in the drama. What strange destiny is being worked out in their lives?'"

She stared at me as if she expected an answer. "I don't believe in stories taking over people's lives," I said.

"You believe in madness, don't you? What is madness but a story breaking through from the other side?"

It was time to pull Nicole away from literary fantasy and back to her own life and emotions. "Obviously you feel very close to Hunter," I said. "You want to help him, to save him, probably because of what happened to your brother and what you—"

"Hunter isn't the only character in the story," she interrupted. "There's Antonia, who can't speak but could sing if her father and her doctors would let her. There's Peter Bartolli and his otherworldly daughter who dances around the Institute like a sex-crazed wind-up doll."

"Let's not go into that."

"And there's you, Dr. Ned Hoffmann, who must struggle with his ill-fated loves—artiste, ingénue and *courtisane*—whoever they may turn out to be."

I rose to my feet, ready to end the session if she pursued her usual trick of turning the spotlight on me.

"And of course there's me."

"Yes," I agreed, a little embarrassed to have reacted so abruptly. I sat back down. "And what's your role in the story?"

"I stumbled into all this blindly—against my will, in fact—when I was brought to the Institute in the middle of a mental breakdown that I can hardly remember. It's obvious now that I'm here to play the role of Nicklausse, the faithful handmaiden of the other characters' self-destruction. I know what's going on, even if they don't. I'm a Cassandra who can foresee what's about to happen to them but I can't prevent it because no one will listen to me."

She seemed to have finished, but her words hung in the air like a half-finished cadence, impatient for resolution. "Even if I knew who the killer was, no one would listen to me."

That was my last session with Nicole before I left for Venice—in fact the last time I saw her until this morning when she finally succeeded in tracking me down. We had an awkward moment when I tried to escort her out of my office.

A few steps from the door she suddenly stopped and pointed at an empty spot on the wall. "What became of the mirror that used to hang there?"

I tried to keep her moving towards the door. "Well, that's all the time we have for today. I'm sure that next week—"

"It's already happened, hasn't it? She's stolen your reflection."

I held the door open and nudged her out into the hall. "Actually, our next session won't be for two weeks. Next week I'll be on vacation."

"You're going to Venice, aren't you?"

"Don't be ridiculous!"

"You're following her to Venice."

"Please!" I whispered. "Keep your voice down. People will think you're crazy."

It was ridiculous, perhaps, but true. I was leaving for Venice on Sunday, flying Air France to Paris and then connecting to Venice on Alitalia. I had told Dr. Palmer about a psychiatric conference and I suppose that even in my own mind I imagined that my trip had a professional purpose. But I'd made a point to reserve my room at the same hotel where Gottlieb had booked his "Romantic Getaway Vacation For Two." In the meantime my headaches and nightmares grew more frequent and intense. Every night I had the same dream: a woman hanging from the ceiling, her hands motionless at her side. I touch her and she sways slightly, rotating towards me. In a mirror on the wall I can see her face: she is bloated, unrecognizable—it's not Mrs. Paterson, but someone else. There's another figure in the mirror, standing beside her, touching her, spinning her around. Is that me? No, I tell myself, it couldn't be—Julietta has stolen my reflection. It must be someone else.

It was the last time Dubin and Nicole discussed the murders—and by this time there was no doubt in Nicole's mind that what they were talking about were murders. Four o'clock in the morning, Nicole in a playful mood, Dubin a little vulnerable. They'd split a bottle of chardonnay and for the first time Nicole felt that their relationship could turn in an amorous direction. He wasn't the kind of man she usually found attractive, but that was probably a good thing, given her track record with men she found attractive. A little too old and careworn, he was, and far too cynical. And the resemblance to Edgar Allan Poe would definitely count as a negative on those long winter evenings when you didn't want your life to read like a horror story. Then there was this matter of his being some kind of criminal—a blackmailer, Frank Lynch had told her. Blackmailers generally aren't the right sort of people, and Dubin was definitely cynical enough to be one. But what about all the kindness he'd shown her? And the sense of honor he tried so hard to conceal behind his cynicism?

They sat side by side on the couch, almost touching. The night's conversation had seemingly run its course. Playfully, perversely, she decided that it was time for a test.

"If this were a detective story," she said, "we'd consider all the possibilities. No one would be beyond suspicion, even ourselves.

Especially ourselves, if we were using the tools of post-modernist critical theory."

Dubin seemed more bored than curious. "What are you talking about?"

"For example," she asked, "how do I know you're not the murderer?" In spite of her playful smile she made it clear that she was waiting for an answer.

"Are you serious?"

"I've heard that you're a blackmailer."

"Who told you that?"

"Never mind who told me. Is it true?"

"Absolutely not."

"Naturally if you were a blackmailer you'd deny it."

Dubin shifted around to face her, trying to see if this was just one of her pranks. She looked away.

"All right," he said evenly. "Just for the sake of argument, assume I am a blackmailer. What I've been focusing on is the death of Maria Morgan. So I couldn't very well be the one who killed her, could I? Or the others, for that matter. I'd have to be blackmailing myself."

"Stranger things have happened," Nicole said. "In literature and probably in life as well. Maybe, for you, blackmail is an elaborate form of denial and defense, a game of cat and mouse between yourself and the rest of the world. Or maybe it's an indirect form of confession—don't criminals really want to get caught?—or just a convoluted way of returning to the scene of the crime."

He ventured a smile. "This is really very funny."

"Or maybe on the subconscious level you imagine that you can expiate your sins by exacting blood money from someone else for the crime you committed."

"I'd prefer to stay on the conscious level, if you don't mind." He was still smiling but he sounded annoyed. "My subconscious isn't someplace you'd want to go."

"In that case the whole thing would appear to be even more cunning and diabolical. You could be trying to pin the blame on someone who isn't guilty by blackmailing them for your crimes. If they pay you, that would look like an admission of guilt and then you could say what you said a few minutes ago—that you couldn't possibly be guilty of murder and blackmail at the same time."

"I didn't even know I was a suspect."

Nicole laughed. "The killer is always the last person you'd suspect, isn't it? If you're the detective, that would be yourself."

Dubin's smile had faded. "It's getting light," he said, standing up to leave. "I'd better be going."

Nicole sat on the edge of her bed, lighting matches one after the other and letting them drop to the floor as they started to singe her fingers. She felt bad about driving Dubin away, yet grateful for his absence. This was the most difficult part of her day and she needed to face it alone. In a few minutes she would fall asleep, and while she slept a new chapter would open in the book of the world. We're like fictional characters, she thought, highly complicated ink blobs which through natural selection have come to believe that we are different. Memories, dreams, personalities—these are the tales we tell ourselves to create a character we can identify with.

The search for Hunter Morgan spread like a slow-burning fire through the wooded backcountry that hangs like a shadow just beyond the bright lights of Megalopolis. Within a week there had been sightings from Maine to Florida, along with reports of strangled livestock and satanic inscriptions on barns and chicken coops. Avery Morgan moved his army of volunteers upstate, fanning desperately through the misty bare mountains before their hopes would vanish under winter's first snow. Frank Lynch stuck closer to home, in radio contact with the volunteers, digesting the intelligence that came in from all directions—none of which, in his opinion, was worth the time of day. By the end of the week, he would have no choice but to ask the state police to bring in their dogs. Sniffers, they called them. They could smell anything, even a dead body that no one wanted them to find.

Lynch sat in the cruiser with Tom Wozniak in front of the Seven Eleven, listening to the country music station as they drank coffee out of huge styrofoam cups. "Researching, then disappearing," he mused. "Researching, then disappearing. Quite a job description, isn't it?"

"You talking about Dubin?"

Lynch nodded slowly. "He's not a writer and he's not a detective. But he suddenly shows up and starts asking a lot of questions about Maria Morgan and how she died, then he drives away in his BMW. What does that sound like to you?"

"Blackmail?" Wozniak was incredulous. "After all this time?"

"If you've been covering up a crime for seven years, a little blackmail is just a cost of doing business. Of course Dubin wouldn't be blackmailing you unless you had enough money to make it worth his while."

Wozniak took a long sip of coffee as he thought about the implications of what Lynch had said. "You think Avery Morgan killed his wife?"

"Not necessarily. There's such a thing as a psychiatric coverup. If you have enough money and someone in your family commits a little indiscretion like killing another member of the family, you can always get your doctor to dump so many anti-psychotic drugs into the killer that it actually makes them psychotic. Then you can lock them up and avoid the whole criminal process. No prosecution, no trial, no guilty plea, no publicity."

"Then it's the kid? You think the kid killed his mother?"

Lynch smiled maliciously. "The same little psycho we've spent the last week trying to flush out of the woods. He killed the nurse and the librarian too. For all we know this whole disappearing act is a fake and they've got him stashed around here somewhere until they can spirit him out of the country. Or maybe he's already out of the country."

"And how does Dubin fit in?"

"Dubin got onto him somehow. Or onto the coverup, more likely. That's where the money is—the coverup. And who would that be? Avery Morgan and his wife and the doctors at the Institute."

As Nicole rolled into the parking lot she saw Dr. Ned Hoffmann hurrying out the front door with a suitcase in his hand, so preoccupied that he didn't seem to notice her waving to him as she parked her car. The Institute looked grim in the late November drizzle and there was something almost desperate in the way he threw himself and his suitcase into his car and drove away. She was tempted to follow him but it occurred to her that his absence might make it easier to carry out her plan. When she pushed open the heavy front door she was relieved not to be greeted by the snippy Julietta. In Julietta's place sat a fat blond woman she had never seen before. She strolled past the desk and down the carpeted hall.

"Can I help you?" the woman called after her.

"Oh!"—Nicole laughed and shot a reassuring glance over her shoulder—" I work here."

She stepped quickly around the corner and up a flight of stairs before the receptionist could say another word. At the end of the upstairs hallway she found Hunter's room unlocked. Someone had straightened it up but nothing seemed to have been removed. His books and magazines were still there, his compact disks stacked in neat piles along the walls. There were no old fashioned records, not surprisingly since his equipment didn't include a turntable. He did have a TV and a video player and a collection of videos, which Nicole was about to ignore until the title of one of them caught her eye. It was *The Tales of Hoffmann*, directed by Michael Powell—the same beautiful, surrealistic version of the opera she had enjoyed so much when she checked it out of the library. What a strange coincidence! she thought. But videos were not what she'd come here for—she was interested in records. And there was one other place she needed to look: the patient lounge, where she remembered a turntable and a collection of long-playing records that no one listened to anymore.

Back in the hallway, she eluded the stares of a sour-faced nurse and slipped downstairs to the patient lounge, which fortunately was not in use. This cavernous room—where she'd spent much of her time with Hunter when she was here as a patient—was really more like a library than a lounge. The walls were lined with books, which no one but Hunter ever read. There was a TV and a stereo and of course there was the grand piano where three months earlier he'd given the surprise performance that was still reverberating inside and outside of the Institute. Behind the stereo stood several shelves of old fashioned records. Nicole picked through them one by one until she found what she was looking for: *Piano Music of Robert Schumann*, played by Alicia de Larrocha. The record, according to Dubin, that had disappeared from Maria Morgan's studio after her death. Nicole squinted at it in the dim light. Was it the very same record that Maria Morgan had in her studio—or just another copy? No, she realized, this was not just another copy—it had come from the library and it was seven years overdue. The due date stamped on the return slip was in the month Maria Morgan died.

Nicole could hardly believe her own good luck. She ran over to the stereo and started to put the record on. But then she realized there was no way she could play it here—the forces of law and order, alerted by the receptionist and the sour-faced nurse, would soon be on her trail. She slipped the record into her backpack and hurried back out to the car, smiling a warm good-bye to the receptionist as she passed.

She could think of only one other place with a turntable—the music listening room at the library. She dreaded going there, repelled by memories of Miss Whipple and her gruesome death, but now that she had the record she could think of nothing else. If Miss Whipple were still alive she would have known how the record fit into the mystery, and in fact—Nicole realized with a start—maybe that was one of the reasons Miss Whipple was no longer alive.

The morning drizzle had thickened into a misty rain, and the cars had their headlights on, beaming their way through the downpour like visitors from another world. The library parking lot was almost empty and Nicole found a spot near the entrance. She was hoping to get in and out quickly with the record in her backpack, and without seeing anyone she knew. But as she stepped into the library she came face to face with Peter Bartolli, who was hurrying out the door with an armful of books clutched in front of him. They greeted each other with the quizzical smiles of people trying to remember how they were acquainted, but something in Bartolli's dark eyes told Nicole that he knew exactly who she was. "I met you here once before," she said.

"Yes," he nodded. "I remember. You asked me about *The Tales of Hoffmann*."

She smiled and started to walk away but Bartolli stood where he was, watching her expectantly. "You know Hunter Morgan, don't you?" she asked, turning back around.

He bowed slightly in his old world manner. "I worked with him for years when I was at the Institute."

"He's not a killer."

"I know that."

She lowered her voice. "Every night—I say every night but it's really during the day, that's when I sleep—I have the same dream. Hunter comes to my apartment and plays the piano, even though I don't have a piano. He plays the same piece he played at the Institute, Schumann's Kreisleriana. He plays until he comes to the same place in the music where he always stops and then he runs away."

"And then what happens?"

"I stand there calling after him, but he doesn't turn around. He just runs farther and farther away. And I keep chasing him until I wake up."

"You want to help him."

"I want to help him but all I can do is dream about him."

Bartolli glanced around to make sure no one was listening. "Dreaming is no idle occupation," he smiled, reaching out and clutching her wrist in his thin hand. "It's the way you build your world."

For a moment Nicole felt herself transfixed by Bartolli's fathomless eyes. She pulled away and he dropped two of his books. As he stooped to pick them up she murmured a quick good-bye and made her escape, glancing over her shoulder in time to see him shuffle out the door.

The new librarian—her name was Margot and she was from a neighboring town—escorted Nicole to the music listening room and showed her how to operate the old-fashioned record player. After Margot left, she pulled the record she'd found at the Institute out of her backpack, set it on the turntable and sat back to listen to the music. It was the same Kreisleriana she'd heard Hunter perform several times, both at the Institute and in her dreams, a skittish, disconcerting piece that made you conscious of your breathing. The music was building toward some kind of climax when suddenly—just at the point where Hunter always stopped playing—the needle hit a scratch and bounced back. It bounced back again and again, repeating the same annoying notes, until Nicole lifted it off the record. The scratch began right at the point where Hunter stopped playing and continued all the way to the end.

Obviously this was how Hunter had learned to play the piano. And the mystery of why he always stopped where he did had been solved. He stopped when he came to the end of the music.

But why did he always run away?

25

I come now to the part of the story I'd been hoping I would never have to tell. By the time Julietta and Gottlieb flew off to Venice for their "Getaway Vacation for Two," my symptoms had reached the tipping point: unbearable anxiety, sleeplessness, a growing sense of not knowing who I was—and finally the sensation, at all hours, that there was a radio playing in the next room in a language I couldn't understand. Someone or something was trying to send me a message, or to send a message through me to someone else— as if indeed, as Nicole had warned, I had been taken over by some external force. Should I have tried to get help from Dr. Neuberger? Should I feel guilty for what I did? We all do exactly what we have to do, no more, no less, especially when it comes to the basic instincts. Apeneck Gottlieb deserved no better than he got, though Julietta herself probably deserved better. She was an innocent, in spite of her sluttish ways. And Nicole—well, for obvious reasons I'll say as little as possible about Nicole. All I can say is that I wish none of it ever happened.

I arrived in Venice on a Thursday morning after a long, uncomfortable flight and scarcely two hours of sleep. It was raining, as it always is at that time of year, and the airport was shrouded in fog. I had booked a room in the same luxurious hotel where the "Getaway Vacation for Two" was unfolding in all its unsavory splendor, with a choice location on the Grand Canal, and quickly confirmed that "Dr. and Mrs. Gottlieb" were registered as guests. The mere knowledge that Julietta was in the hotel put me in a state of excitement that made it hard to think coherently. And the prospect of a confrontation with Gottlieb—especially one where I would have the advantage of surprise and embarrassment—triggered a sensation of anxious anticipation. Of course I'd brought my knife along on the trip, though without any intention of using it. I removed it from my suitcase, wrapped it in a handkerchief and stuck it in my jacket pocket. In retrospect that was a reckless and unnecessary thing to do. But at the time all I could think about was how large and obnoxious Gottlieb was and how angry he would be to find me there.

That first day I spent the better part of the afternoon sitting in the lobby behind a newspaper which I could raise in front of my face if either of them made an appearance. It was a gilded, high-ceilinged room in the style of a baroque palazzo, and the guests who tramped in and out had the bored, predatory look of habitual tourists, weary with the ennui of exhausted itineraries. After nearly two hours I spotted my quarry: Gottlieb, unshaven, characteristically oafish in a baseball cap and a windbreaker half-covering a New York Mets T-shirt; and Julietta, sensuous and faux baroque like everything else in the room, parading the spoils of what must have been an expensive shopping spree at his expense—a low-cut dress, a slinky raincoat, a pair of black leather boots laced up to her knees, and a necklace that sparkled like a string of diamonds. Without glancing in my direction, they joined a group gathering on the terrace, where a motor launch stood ready to take them on an excursion. When the boat had puttered a safe distance away I asked the ticket taker where it was going.

"San Marco," he said, offering me a ticket for the next vaporetto.

The vast piazza of San Marco was teeming with tourists and I knew I would never find Julietta and Gottlieb in that throng. Wandering past the campanile and the Doge's Palace, I bought a pastry from a street vendor and made my way to the enormous domed basilica. As I entered the church I was plunged into darkness, as if I had stepped into a vast, cavernous underworld, echoing with the muffled cruelty of time. High above my head, like sunlight playing on the ocean's surface, shimmered a mosaic of the Last Judgment. Its reflection lighted my way as my eyes adjusted to the darkness, along with the hundreds of tiny candles burning in the chapels that lined the church's perimeter. There was St. Mark, there St. Peter—and there, suddenly, was Gottlieb, still wearing his Mets cap, stalking around the nave pretending to look up at the mosaics as he ogled the women. Where was Julietta? I raced through the shadows until I found her in the Chapel of the Madonna, kneeling in prayer—her head bowed, her hands clasped in front of her, her lips moving slightly, the light from the votive candles flickering on her painted face.

It was touching, but also a little shocking, to see her in that position. I felt a thrill of sexual excitement tinged with jealousy and violence. I wanted to throw her down on the marble floor and ravish her mercilessly, but at the same time I wanted to kneel down and pray beside her, I wanted to sense her warmth and feel her murmuring breath and touch her spirit. Her promiscuous past, her flirtations with other men, the obscenities she whispered in Gottlieb's ear—those I could deal with. But this, this excited my jealousy and lust beyond anything I'd ever felt before. She was suddenly more desirable than I could have imagined, more desirable than any woman could ever be. I knew I would do anything to have her.

He wouldn't be able to come over that night. That was the message Dubin had left for Nicole on her answering machine. She panicked when she heard it, pushing the "Repeat" button again and again as if she expected the message to change if she listened to it the right number of times. He offered no explanation for not coming, and that troubled her. Obviously it was something she'd said or done the night before. Was it because she'd playfully mentioned him as a possible suspect in the killings? No, he couldn't have taken that seriously. More likely it was because she'd unmasked him as a blackmailer. Only a blackmailer would try to argue, even hypothetically, that he was above suspicion because he couldn't be blackmailing someone for his own crime. Obviously

Dubin was a troubled man, cynical yet tormented by guilt, and she was angry with herself for scaring him away.

Without Dubin, she sat in the dim light and followed the dark tangle of her own thoughts into the deepest part of the night. She listened to the cypresses scratching the eaves in the moaning wind, the rodents scrubbing and scrambling behind the walls, the leaky faucet tormenting the bathroom sink—and strained, amidst all this, to hear a footstep on the stairs, the slow creak of an intruder who would take her out of the web of fear and despair that encircled her. Just before dawn she imagined herself in the listening room at the library, putting a record on the turntable. The music of Schumann's Kreisleriana rattled through the little room, then came the sudden halt, the scratched record insisting on its imperfection over and over again. Hunter fled from the listening the room and Miss Whipple burst in, frowning as she bent over to lift the needle off the record. Nicole ran out to the front desk and found Julietta sitting there, knitting a tiny blue sweater.

Nicole jolted awake and sat thinking about her dream. It was incoherent, of course; it was a dream—all the more reason to think it had a meaning. But what about real life? Does anyone think real life must have a meaning?

She reached for her notebook and started writing. She became more and more agitated as she wrote, as if she was on the brink of a discovery she did not want to make, a momentous and inevitable discovery, like the knowledge of good and evil, that would make the space where she lived uninhabitable. Everything that had been weighing on her mind—her dissertation, the murders, the search for Hunter, her relationships with Dubin and Dr. Hoffmann—gave way to the temptation to follow her thoughts wherever they led:

> Freud imagined a dream censor, shielding us during sleep from the unwelcome attentions of the unconscious. But instead of a dream censor, maybe what we have is a reality censor that operates while we're awake, filtering out the essential incoherence of the world so we can survive in our dreamlike state for another day.

She laid down her pen and cradled her head in her flat hands. Tears welled up in her eyes as she read over what she had written. "No," she said, shaking her head. She picked up her pen and drew a giant "X" across the page, canceling what she had written while leaving it legible for future reference. Then she printed in bold letters at the bottom: "KEEP FROM GOING CRAZY."

When the sun rose she took a shower and put on fresh clothes. She boiled some water for tea and toasted an English muffin. When she was done eating she washed the dishes and put them away. "Follow him," she told herself. "Find him. Don't let him destroy himself."

She packed a small valise, carried it down the stairs and put it in her car. Then she came back upstairs. Before she locked the door, she poured a generous supply of dry food for the landlady's cat and filled two bowls with fresh water. Almost as an afterthought, she wrote Dubin a little note and left it tacked to the door.

The next morning I rose early and slipped down to the lobby, where I learned from a solemn but accommodating room clerk that Signora Gottlieb (that was what he called Julietta) was already at the pool. This being Italy, I did not have to make excuses to the room clerk for pursuing another man's wife. He could probably see the desperate gleam in my eye, imprinted there since I'd seen Julietta kneeling in the Chapel of the Madonna in those black leather boots laced to her knees.

She had come to the pool alone, decorated by a tiny blue bathing suit. I hid behind my newspaper as she swam laps with surprising gracefulness. On her lounge chair she had left her sandals, her towel and, of all things, a book. The book was *Cujo*, by Stephen King, and when I picked it up her room key—it was the old fashioned metal kind, not one of those plastic cards that most hotels use nowadays—jangled onto the floor. I reached for the key and thought about sticking it in my pocket. But at the last minute I slid the key back under the book and shuffled back to my room. How much trouble and anguish I could have avoided by keeping that key!

A desperate plan began to take shape in my mind. I slipped out into the fog and made my way through a maze of narrow passageways and bridges to the train station, where I rented a car and stashed it in the parking lot. On my way back to the hotel I bought a dozen long-stemmed roses and left them for Julietta at the front desk, with a note that read, "5:00 o'clock in the bar. An admirer."

At five o'clock I waited in a dim corner booth. A few minutes later she sidled up to the bar and perched beside an older man who acted as if he'd been expecting her. He looked rich and charming and sinister, with a reptilian smile, a high, broad forehead and a shock of graying hair combed straight back like Count Dracula's. The two of them flirted shamelessly as he ordered her a drink, stroked the back of her hand and lit her cigarette with a flame that he seemed to pull out of the air. I sat quietly sipping my wine as he droned on in words I couldn't quite hear or understand, and after about twenty minutes he pulled out a necklace of glittering jewels, which he fastened lovingly around her neck. She seemed delighted with the gift but disturbed by the words that accompanied it. After a brief argument she suddenly stood up and hurried away without a backward glance. "*A più tardi*," the man called after her. "Later. At the Casino!"

What a coincidence! I thought, downing the last of my wine. The Casino was exactly where I planned to spend the evening.

Nicole's sudden disappearance left Dubin feeling more guilty and depressed than ever. Two women were dead because of him and he desperately wanted to stop this nightmare before it got worse. And now it seemed as though Nicole had been swept up in it and lost to the night. It was her playing on his guilt—pretending, as if it were a joke, that he was one of the suspects in the murders—that made him angry and frightened and kept him away that night. He'd left her a noncommittal phone message and stayed home drinking by himself until he fell asleep. He wondered whether guilt could reach backwards in time, drawing in all the causes and effects that swirled around an event. If he was responsible for the deaths of Mrs. Paterson and the librarian—as he knew he was—then wasn't he also somehow implicated in the death of Maria Morgan? Where had he been on the night she died? He couldn't answer that question, though he could cite the date. That was the year of his breakdown and there wasn't much he could remember. He couldn't even be sure whether or not he'd been to Egdon before or even to the Institute. When he woke up he wanted to see Nicole. He wanted to tell her how he felt and see if she had any wacky theories that could explain it. He drank a cup of black coffee and drove over to her apartment but she was gone. All he found was her note: "There's something I have to do. Back in a few days. P.S. Hunter took the record. I found it at the Institute."

At the bottom of the stairs Dubin came face to face with Peter Bartolli, who jumped back from the door like a rabbit and stood eyeing him warily as if he expected him to pounce.

"Is Nicole at home?" Bartolli asked. "I wanted to see how she was doing."

"She's gone away for a few days. I don't know where."

"Out searching for Hunter?"

"I don't know," Dubin repeated, though he'd made the same assumption.

Bartolli stayed put, as if he expected Dubin to step aside and let him pass. Dubin stepped toward his car and Bartolli still didn't move.

"Did I pass the test?" Bartolli asked.

"What test?"

"To be able to buy the Offenbach manuscript?"

Dubin had dreaded this moment. "I'm afraid that doesn't matter anymore. The owner has decided to sell it to someone else."

Bartolli took the news calmly. "I'm sure I can change her mind. Would you like to come back out to my house to discuss it? I can make it worth your while."

"Too late. It's already been sold."

"Nothing's ever final, though, is it? Why don't you stop by and we can discuss it?"

Dubin shrugged and continued toward his car. "The manuscript has been sold."

"Please come anyway." Bartolli followed him out to the street and stood behind him as he unlocked his car. "You'd enjoy seeing the rest of my collections. I've got a number of interesting manuscripts, including the autograph score of Boito's *Mefistofile*, dozens of ritual masks from Polynesia, and of course my collection of kaleidoscopes."

"Kaleidoscopes?"

"Yes. I collect kaleidoscopes from all over the world."

Dubin smiled for the first time and took a deep breath to keep from showing his excitement. "That's something I am interested in," he said evenly. "I'd like to come out and see them."

They arranged to have lunch the next afternoon. Bartolli hinted that there was something else, in addition to the Offenbach manuscript and his collecting interests, that he wanted to discuss with Dubin. "As you know," he added for no apparent reason, "I'm a practicing psychiatrist."

Dubin climbed into his car and Bartolli smiled down at him through the open window. "I've often said that a psychiatrist is a kind of detective," Bartolli said. "But a cynic might say we're more like blackmailers than detectives."

Dubin felt a little chill run through him as he returned the smile. "Really? Why is that?"

"What does a psychiatrist do? He gets you to tell him something you're ashamed of and then makes you pay him large sums of money to keep it to yourself."

They both laughed. "But a psychiatrist can never tell anyone what he found out," Dubin said.

"Neither can a blackmailer, Mr. Dubin.   As soon as a blackmailer reveals the secret, it's not a secret anymore. So, like a psychiatrist, he makes you pay an amount you can just barely afford—not all at once, but on a regular basis—for an indefinite period of time stretching far into the future. And you pay it, hoping that someday, if you're lucky, your tormentor will go away and you can get on with your life."

Dubin started the car and raced the engine, forcing Bartolli back from the window. "Then being a psychiatrist must be a dangerous profession."

"Oh, it is, Mr. Dubin. It's a very dangerous profession. Almost as dangerous as being a blackmailer."

26

It was nearly ten o'clock by the time Julietta and Gottlieb, arm in arm, swayed across the terrace to board the gondola that would carry them to the Casino. They were dressed to kill, Julietta in a black evening gown, Gottlieb stuffed into his white tie and tails like a penguin on an eating binge. Together they moved in stately pomp down to the boat landing, without so much as a glance at the desolate figure huddled beneath his umbrella on the windy terrace. Having fortified myself with an entire bottle of wine, I caught the next vaporetto toward the Casino. And I wondered as I watched the boat's lights carve their way through the fog: Did Gottlieb realize that a rival waited for him at the Casino? That in that playground of desire, where money is the soul of a soulless world, his fate would be decided?

My reverie was interrupted by a familiar voice behind me.

"Dr. Hoffmann! Do you know where she's leading you?"

I spun around and came face to face with Nicole. Beautiful, bedeviled Nicole, who in another lifetime I might have made my own. "Nicole," I stammered. "What are you doing here?"

"I followed you," she said. "That day you left the Institute with your suitcase. I figured out where you were going and followed you."

"You should go back," I said, trying to sound professional. "There's no reason for you to be here. We can talk again at your next session." I clung to the rail as the wake from another vaporetto lifted the boat and made me stagger.

"You've been drinking."

"It's the boat."

"No, it's you. You can hardly stand up."

We found a pair of seats across from each other near the back of the boat. Nicole pleaded with me to give up my quest for Julietta.

"Does Dr. Gottlieb know you're here?"

"Not yet," I smiled, enjoying the prospect of a confrontation at the Casino.

"Don't let him see you, then. You'll lose your job if they find out you followed her here."

It was touching, as Nicole almost always is. She was caring, persuasive and absolutely right, as I must have known even then. But she was, after all, a mental patient. I wasn't about to have her directing my life.

The Casino was a gloomy, fantastic structure overhanging the canal. When our boat stopped I jumped off without looking back to see if Nicole was behind me and hurried through a series of narrow alleyways to the entrance. A large crowd stood milling on a terrace that extended over the Grand Canal. "Richard Wagner died in this palazzo in 1883," I heard a man telling his wife. And it was as if Wagner's worst nightmares had been left behind as guests of the Casino—overstuffed blondes who looked like they might be named Brünnhilde, crazed Dutchmen, vixens and valkyries, even a dwarf, all dressed like characters in a 1930s musical. They circulated around the foyer and the terrace and up the stairs to the gaming rooms, ignoring each other in a dozen languages.

At the top of the stairs I was greeted by Julietta's sinister admirer, who held out his spindly hand and welcomed me as if he owned the palazzo. "Dr. Hoffmann," he crooned in his syrupy voice. "Very pleased that you could be here tonight."

I must have shown my alarm. "How did you know my name?"

"Oh, I know all Julietta's friends," he replied, smiling his lizard smile.

I walked away without asking his name and sidled over to the bar, where I ordered a double scotch. My eyes ranged over the crowd, hoping for a glimpse of Gottlieb. I was done playing hide and seek.

Suddenly Julietta appeared at my side. "Hi, Ned!"

"Julietta!" I bolted down my scotch. "Funny meeting you here."

She giggled. "You came all the way to Venice to see me. I kind of like that."

I could hardly believe what I was hearing. I turned and met her dark glistening eyes. "I'm crazy about you," I murmured.

Her smile was as bright as the jewels on her necklace. "You've got to help me get rid of Gottlieb," she said. "He won't leave me alone."

I slammed my glass down on the bar and lurched into the crowd like the drunk that I was. "Where is that swine?" I bellowed. "He'd better stay the hell away from you!"

"No, it's not that simple," she frowned, pulling me back. "He's got the key to my room. They only gave us one. He's got it dangling on a chain around his fat neck. It's like a symbol of his power. He thinks he owns me."

"I'll get it back for you."

She leaned forward and whispered in my ear. "Whoever has that key, that's who I'll be spending the night with."

I plunged into the crowd and into the gaming room. There was a tug on my sleeve and I turned to find Nicole dogging my steps. "Don't go in there," she pleaded. "Please don't go in there!"

I shook her off and ran my eyes over the crowd to a long bar with an enormous mirror behind it that multiplied the room and everything in it. I quickly found Gottlieb, hunched over the craps table with a fevered look on his face. The harsh light streaming down from overhead seemed to pass through him without casting a shadow on the table.

"Gottlieb!" I called out.

"What the hell?"

"I want that key."

He stopped playing and stared at me incredulously. "Hoffmann, I don't know what the hell you're doing here but as you can see I'm busy with something. So chill out until I'm done here and I'll talk to you later."

"No. I want that key now."

"What key?"

"The key to Julietta's room."

"That's my room. Are you crazy?"

Two security guards had swooped in when we raised our voices and shoved their way between us. "Gentlemen," one of them said, "we must ask you to come with us, please."

"Come on!" Gottlieb protested. "I'm in the middle of a game here."

One of the guards grabbed his arm and marched him across the room and down the stairs. The other one glared at me and I followed without resisting. They took us to what must have been a side door, away from both the main entrance and the Grand Canal, and shoved us out into a narrow, dimly-lit alleyway.

Gottlieb lurched toward me with his fists raised. "Hoffmann, this really pisses me off! You really piss me off!"

"I want that key!" I jumped on his neck like a pit bull and tore his collar open as he staggered backwards. There was a gold chain around his neck and I tried to get my fingers around it. He pushed me away and ran into the shadows trying to escape, but I caught up with him at the edge of a small canal. The place was deserted except for a boy of about twelve who sat on a balcony playing the mandolin.

Gottlieb dodged away and leaped onto an arching footbridge. I threw my arms around his neck and pulled him down onto the parapet, tugging at the gold chain until I had the room key in my grasp. Cursing and gasping for breath, he wrapped his hamlike hands around my throat and choked me while he tried to roll me over the parapet into the canal.

I panicked. I panicked because I knew Gottlieb was either going to strangle me or drown me if I couldn't get away from him. I was fighting for my life. I yanked my hands away from his throat but he still didn't stop choking me. I couldn't breathe, I couldn't even beg for my life. Somehow I managed to get one hand into my jacket pocket and pulled out my knife.

I jammed it into his lower back, which was the only spot I could reach. Hot blood spurted out all over my hand. He cried out and released his grip, staring at me with the astonished look of the dead. I pulled the key off the chain and rolled him into the canal.

A sardonic voice sang out from the darkness beyond the end of the bridge. "And so the fool beloved of God rejoins his shadow."

Julietta's sinister admirer stepped into the light, puffing a cigarette. The man was everywhere, a collector of souls come to claim his trophy. And there too, I realized, stood Julietta, smiling triumphantly. The boy with the mandolin had stopped playing; he stood watching from the balcony.

"Julietta!" I said, moving toward her. "I've got the key."

She pulled back and clutched the old man's arm. Her smile twisted into a sneer.

"*Polizia!*" the man cried out. "Help! Police! Murder!" He flicked his cigarette onto the spot in the canal where Gottlieb had gone down.

I heard a muffled sound behind me. It was Nicole, sobbing as she crouched on the pavement to wipe the blood off my knife. Her movements seemed to be in slow motion.

"Help! Police!"

The keening of sirens circled in from all sides as police boats sped toward the canal. The old man stepped over and snatched the key out of my hand, slipping it into his breast pocket with a contemptuous smile. Then he led Julietta down a flight of stone steps to a landing beneath the bridge, where a gondola waited to carry them away. I watched in stunned silence as they climbed into the boat, laughing and chattering as if nothing had happened.

Laughing! They were laughing at me for stupidly walking into their trap! I leaped down the steps and into the gondola before they could pull away and threw myself on Julietta, choking off her laughter with my hands clenched around her bare white throat. She struggled violently as the old man and the gondolier beat me from behind and tried to pull me off, but I lowered my head and held on until the screaming stopped and her body went limp. In a frenzy I fought off the two men and jumped back on the landing.

Nicole stood on the footbridge holding the knife. "Give me that!" I demanded. I thought about throwing the knife into the canal but instead dropped it back into my pocket. "Now get out of here!"

She was still sobbing. "Where are you going?"

"Never mind where I'm going! And don't follow me!"

"You killed him in self defense!" she moaned, as if she hadn't noticed what I did to Julietta. "If you run away—"

"No! I was trying to kill him."

I pushed her out of my way and ran back up the alleyway toward the Casino. The sirens suddenly wailed louder as the police boats began to arrive. I stepped on the vaporetto and in a few minutes found myself strolling toward the parking lot near the train station. A tiny car sped past me with lights flashing. It skidded to a halt and five or six policemen tumbled out, one after another, like mimes in a circus. By this time I should have been feeling guilt or remorse or, at the very least, fear. But all I could think about was the absurdity of the whole thing. They were coming after me in a clown car.

27

When the snow started he knew he had to move on. Search parties were still combing the area and with snow on the ground they would soon track him down. He found an icy creek and waded upstream into mountain country, dodging the road that switchbacked over the stream until it turned downhill, leaving him on the shoulder of a thickly forested ridge. As he climbed higher the creek became an icicled ravine, leading nowhere. He scrabbled to the rim and found shelter from the snow under a craggy outcrop near the top of the ridge.

The next morning he crawled out of his lair into the bright sunlight and explored the ridge summit. A hundred yards down the other side he found another road and a small hotel that looked like a Swiss chalet. He planted himself behind a huge pine tree and studied the hotel carefully. Was this the type of place Nicole would come to? he wondered. If he watched it long enough, would he find her there?

At night, lying in his rocky hideaway, he closed his eyes and had the sensation that he was back at the Institute watching a movie. The movie stopped when he opened his eyes and started again when he closed them. He could hear his own voice as the slightly pompous narrator. Living at the Institute, ironically, was taking its toll on my mental health. The isolated setting, the hushed, padded corridors, the inexorable routine of endless days and boring nights... He was talking to Nicole, giving her an elaborate explanation for everything he had done in his life. The atmosphere of suspension and futility that permeated the place—all of these, week after week, made it difficult for me to maintain a sense of reality...

When he woke up he was shivering with cold. Where was Nicole? She would understand, she would grasp his meaning, if only he could find her, if only she would listen. He closed his eyes and there she was, wading toward him through the fresh snow. She tried to hold me in place with her fierce emerald eyes....

He stood up and looked down at the ravine. You could scream all you wanted in there and no one would hear you. The world was white and quiet, muffled in the silence of fresh snow. The fresh snow, it seemed to him, made everything permissible.

28

Dubin stood in Peter Bartolli's living room examining his collection of grotesque wooden masks, which filled three of the walls and continued around the corner into the dining room. "Most of these are Polynesian," Bartolli explained. "Eighteenth and nineteenth century, before the Christian missionaries stamped out the native religion. I show them to new patients to give them an idea of what they can expect to find in the unconscious."

The masks stared at Dubin knowingly, as if the secret purpose of his visit was obvious. He was there for one reason alone: to investigate the possible connection between Bartolli and the kaleidoscope found in Maria Morgan's studio after she died.

Bartolli seemed surprisingly eager to cooperate. He approached a closed wooden cabinet that occupied a short wall between two windows. "Let me show you my kaleidoscopes." Pulling a key from his pocket, he unlocked the cabinet and opened its doors to reveal a collection of metallic instruments in various shapes and sizes, most of which Dubin would never have recognized as kaleidoscopes. "They come from all over the world," he said, "and every one has its own story to tell." He handed Dubin a brass tube that looked like a trumpet with a crank on one side, carved with images of multi-limbed Indian gods. "Here. Try looking through this."

Dubin peered inside and saw a colorful erotic scene that started to dissolve as soon as he raised it to the light. He turned the crank but that only chased the images farther away.

"Our world is a transitory one," Bartolli explained, smiling pleasantly. "If you keep turning the crank you'll pass through every combination of color and shape in the world of appearances until eventually you come back to where you started. It might take four billion years but you will come back."

"I'll have to take your word for it." Dubin handed the instrument back to Bartolli, who slipped it back into its place. "There was a kaleidoscope in Maria Morgan's studio when she died."

"Yes," Bartolli replied without looking up. "I gave it to her."

"Is it one of these?"

"No. It was hers. I don't know what became of it after she died."

"It disappeared from the studio."

Bartolli hesitated, then shook his head and said, "That's a shame. It was a very lovely piece from southeastern Iran." He snapped the cabinet shut and walked away.

In the dining room Dubin took his seat amidst the curious stares of Polynesian witch doctors while Bartolli brought the food in from the kitchen. He served a *salade niçoise* garnished with cold grilled tuna, ripe olives and anchovies, along with three kinds of cheese and a plate of fresh berries. There was a red wine and a white wine, both Italian and both very good.

They ate quietly for a few minutes before either spoke again. "Have you met Antonia Morgan?" Bartolli asked unexpectedly.

"I don't think so. Isn't she...?"

"Schizophrenic? Yes, that's her official diagnosis, though I've never accepted it."

"What is she then?"

"I don't know if we have a word for it. Freud probably would have called it hysteria. A couple of hundred years ago they would have said she was mad. I'd describe it as a severe personality disorder, similar to her mother's, but much more debilitating—and aggravated by the drugs that have been prescribed to treat it."

"Similar to her mother's?" Dubin could hardly believe what he'd just heard. "I thought Maria Morgan was being treated for depression."

"A family euphemism, I'm afraid." Bartolli smiled bashfully, as if to acknowledge his own complicity in the deception. "Maria Morgan was a borderline schizophrenic. Most of the time she managed to stay on this side of the border, but there were times when she couldn't resist the lure of the other side."

"Like Antonia?"

Bartolli nodded. "Antonia bears an uncanny resemblance to her mother. In outward appearance that's not unusual in a daughter. But what's so striking about Antonia is her voice. She has her mother's voice."

"I've heard that Antonia never speaks."

"She doesn't speak but sometimes she sings. And when she sings it's with the voice of an angel—her mother's voice." Bartolli opened a large bottle of sparking water, which he poured into their glasses. "You know, that was how Maria Morgan coped with her illness—by singing. That's what allowed her to live a fairly normal life."

"Has singing helped Antonia?"

Bartolli's smile hardened. "Unfortunately she suffers from severe asthma. She was on the verge of a breakthrough when I was forced to leave the Institute. Since then, she hasn't made any progress at all. Even now, if I were given a chance, I think I could help her."

"How?"

"By completing the course of treatment she was on when I left. By putting her in touch with a world where the voice of an angel wouldn't sound out of place."

Dubin lowered his eyes, wondering whether Bartolli was straying again into the strange territory they had visited on their tour of the puppet theater.

Bartolli offered more salad, more bread, more wine. "I said the resemblance between Antonia's voice and her mother's is uncanny," he resumed when Dubin's plate and glass had been refilled. "Do you know what that means?"

"I know what uncanny means."

"Do you, really?" He raised his eyebrows as if this claim were absurd.

"It means supernatural, fantastic—"

"What we call uncanny isn't just what's fantastic or supernatural. What's uncanny is when irrational forces seem to be intruding unexpectedly into everyday life—at a time when we've stopped believing in them. Dolls seem to wink at us, chance patterns repeat themselves wherever we turn, the most familiar objects seem unaccountably strange. And all of a sudden—"

Bartolli broke off and for a moment it seemed that he would not finish the sentence.

"All of a sudden what?"

"All of a sudden we're not sure we can believe our eyes. When we peek into the crevices of our workaday world, a whole different universe seems to be peering out at us."

Dubin hesitated. "A whole different universe?"

"You can call it the fourth dimension," Bartolli said, "or the collective unconscious, if you prefer. You can get there through drugs, dreams, madness—and above all, through music. Madness is just a one-way ticket to the same place music can take you to and bring you back from."

"I've got to be going," Dubin said, tossing his napkin on the table.

"Don't you see? It's through music that I hope to bring Antonia back from the clutch of madness. And I need you to help me."

I had parked my rental car in a long-term lot near the train station. Luckily the lot was still open and I was able to complete my escape before they closed the roads out of Venice. So this was how I would end my Getaway Vacation—fleeing with Julietta's blood on my hands rather than lose her to a man old enough to be her father. Where had I seen that man before? It seemed that all my life I'd been hounded by some hostile force, some nemesis—

usually an older man—that blocked and thwarted every love I aspired to. Not the same man, of course, but with more than a coincidental resemblance among them. If I had been watching a movie, I would have said that the roles of my tormentors were all played by the same actor, in various clever disguises that made him look completely different—young or old, fat or thin, bearded or bald—but always recognizably the same man. You could see it in the eyes, like a family resemblance. And as I pictured the eyes of Julietta's treacherous lover I suddenly recognized the man I saw hidden there. *If he but blench, I know my course. Murder will speak.*

I drove up toward the Dolomites, as they call the Alps in that country. It's a region where they speak German as much as Italian and the bare peaks loom over your head like the pipes of a monstrous organ reaching into the clouds. In a few hours the police would trace the car and I would have no choice but to abandon it. But before I could construct my plan I had a shock. Stopped at a light in a small town, I spotted Nicole in the rearview mirror, sitting behind me in what appeared to be a Volvo. She must have been following me every minute since I fled the scene of the crime. For some reason I feared her more than the police. On my way out of town I jogged onto a dirt road that led up a steep mountainside, and as luck would have it a truck turned in behind me. The truck blocked the Volvo from following close behind, and I was able to speed up and disappear down a side road. The side road continued uphill only about a mile before it dead-ended at a scenic overlook. Looking down, I could see the Volvo winding its way up toward me. In a panic I eased my car to the edge of the embankment and jumped out just before it went over the edge into a thicket of hemlocks. Then, without looking back, I bolted down a narrow path into the forest.

There was a light dusting of snow on the mountainside, and so my escape route was impossible to conceal. I knew Nicole would follow, and although she seemed intent on saving me I perceived her as a threat. After all, besides the old man and the gondolier—I had all but forgotten about the boy with the mandolin—she was the only witness to my crimes.

'The clutch of madness'— it was that phrase more than anything that had held Dubin in his seat across the table from Peter Bartolli. To bring Antonia back from the clutch of madness.   Bartolli hurried into the kitchen and returned with a pot of coffee and an assortment of pastries. The man was bizarre, possibly in the clutch of madness himself, and Dubin found himself at once fascinated and repelled. The more he saw of Bartolli the more unlikely it became that he'd been Maria Morgan's secret lover. No sign of an unprofessional attachment to her, or hostility to Avery Morgan, or a dog named Nero. The kaleidoscope collection, which inspired this awkward visit, had proved inconclusive, but one fact of crucial importance had come to light: Maria Morgan had suffered from the same mental disorder as her children. Did Bartolli try to rescue her from the world of madness in the same way as he was now proposing to rescue Antonia?

"Why did you give Maria Morgan a kaleidoscope?" Dubin asked.

"I often give little gifts to my patients."

"Why a kaleidoscope?"

"A kaleidoscope is a particularly appropriate gift for someone with Maria's illness."

"Was it part of her therapy?"

Bartolli took a sip of his coffee and smiled. "Try to imagine life as a schizophrenic. It's like living in a kaleidoscope, constantly bedazzled by the endless cycles of transformation that the rest us perceive, if at all, only as a momentary intuition."

"Aren't you talking about psychotic delusions?"

"'Delusions' or 'perceptions,' I don't know which. There's a part of the universe—probably the largest part—that lies beyond our ability to give it a name."

Bartolli set down his coffee cup and leaned forward intently. "Please don't misunderstand me. I don't think schizophrenia is normal or desirable—in fact, I've devoted a large part of my life to combating it. But in order to treat its victims you have to understand them on their own terms. So to answer your question: yes, it was part of her therapy. A kaleidoscope can be another route of passage into the unconscious. I was hoping that for Maria it might have been a window of escape."

"Might have been?"

"Had she lived."

Dubin remembered what he had said about Antonia. "Did she try to sing her way out?"

"She tried, yes." Bartolli averted his eyes. "She tried."

For a few minutes they nibbled on their pastries in silence. Then Bartolli finally came to the point. "I asked you here today because I need your help."

"I told you the Offenbach manuscript has been sold."

"You never had that manuscript," Bartolli frowned, shaking his head. "I've spoken with Stephen Witz and Casimir Ostrovsky." He waved the whole subject aside with a dismissive gesture. "It's of no importance."

Dubin watched Bartolli carefully. "I'd better be going. Thanks again for the lunch."

"Please stay a moment." Bartolli tilted his head to the side and smiled like an imploring child. "It's not about the manuscript. I want to talk to you about Antonia."

"I don't even know Antonia."

"I think I can help her."

"What does that have to do with me?"

"I'm trying to get her father to bring her to me for treatment."

"And?"

"And I need you to help me persuade him to do that."

"What makes you think I have any influence on Avery Morgan?"

Bartolli smiled wanly. "I know about you, Mr. Dubin. I know... what you are."

"What are you talking about?"

"To be blunt, I know you're a blackmailer. And I'm quite sure that at the moment you're blackmailing Avery Morgan."

Dubin drained his coffee cup and pushed his chair back to stand up. "I don't know Avery Morgan either."

"I've seen your car at his house several times."

"How do you know I'm not just sleeping with his wife?"

"That's probably true too, knowing his wife. Is she the one who's paying you?"

Dubin stood up and started for the door. "I'll see you around."

"All I'm asking," Bartolli said, following him, "is that you try to persuade Avery Morgan to take Antonia out of the Institute for a few hours and bring her here for treatment."

"What kind of treatment?"

"Hypnotic regression. To put her in touch with the unconscious so she can escape from it. Avery and Susan can stay in the room the whole time to make sure nothing bad happens. I'm sure you can persuade them to do that."

Dubin had reached the foyer. He turned to face Bartolli. "Even if I were a blackmailer, why should I do this?"

"Because you're not an ordinary blackmailer."

"Really? What kind of blackmailer am I?"

"An honest one, I think."

Dubin let himself laugh. "It's been a long time since anyone accused me of that. Who have you been talking to?" Without waiting for an answer he turned toward the door, but Bartolli reached out and held it shut.

"I understand," Bartolli smiled. "Whatever you've got on Morgan, you don't want to squander it helping me. But you must understand, this is for Antonia, not for me. If we can get through to Antonia—if we can coax her away from the demon who's seized control of her mind just for a few minutes—I think we can save her, and at the same time find the secret you've been searching for."

Dubin nudged Bartolli aside and reached for the doorknob, but the black cat had slipped unnoticed between himself and the door, blocking him from opening it.

"Nero!" Bartolli whispered, stooping down to pick up his pet. "Leave Mr. Dubin alone."

29

It was cold sleeping in the forest but not nearly so cold as the bottom of the canal where I'd sent Jeff Gottlieb. The police had followed me from Venice, of course. Two or three times a day they swarmed over the mountainside in a show of force, but since they never strayed more than fifty feet from their cars it was absurdly easy to keep out of their sight. Nicole was the one I was worried about. She spent her days searching for me in the forest, returning at night to a small chalet-like hotel just below the crest of the ridge. I watched her every minute, tracking her footprints in the snow. Did she know I was following her? Sometimes I caught her glancing over her shoulder as if she knew I was there. When she drove to town I climbed to the top of the ridge and watched the Volvo wind its way down into the valley until it disappeared. Then I waited, in a culvert or behind a tree, until I could hear the car groaning its way back up the mountainside to the hotel.

On that last night I watched her park the Volvo and trudge wearily into the hotel lobby. I knew how long it would be before the lights in her room flashed on and how long before they'd snap off again. Behind the curtains my mind's eye saw everything that happened in between. Let her sleep, I thought, wishing I could sleep as soundly in my frigid hiding place as she in her bed. Before sunrise, after my breakfast of stale crusts I'd stolen the day before, I crept down and pressed my face against her window, angling for a glimpse inside through a crack in the curtains. I tried to be careful but I must have made a noise or cast a shadow—all at once the curtains swung open and for a full thirty seconds Nicole and I stared at each other in astonishment, the glass frosting between us until I slipped back down off the balcony and disappeared into the woods.

She followed me to a spot I knew well, the narrow ravine that ended with a sheer rock wall encrusted with ice. You could scream all you wanted in there and no one would hear you, and when you got to the wall you had no choice but to turn around and go back. I hurried into the cul de sac, leaving a trail in the fresh snow, and then doubled back to hide behind a tree about fifty feet up the trail. She plodded past and when she came to the wall she turned around and saw me standing in the path. Neither of us said anything. The world was white and quiet, muffled in the silence of fresh snow. The fresh snow, it seemed to me, made everything permissible.

"I found you," she finally said.

"Unfortunately for you."

She glanced around at the frozen wall and realized that she was trapped. "What do you mean?"

"I murdered Gottlieb and you saw me do it."

"You didn't murder Dr. Gottlieb."

"You shouldn't have followed me here." I moved toward her, swishing the snow as I went. I still had my knife in my pocket, but I didn't think I'd need to use it. I could do what I had to do with my bare hands. It would be better that way.

She tried to hold me in place with her fierce emerald eyes. I glanced away and took another step forward, my hands raised in front of me. I was close enough now that I could see the snowflakes melting on her white skin. The two ends of her woolen scarf dangled within my reach.

"Hunter!" she shouted in my face. "Don't do this! Stop!"

I stood still and squinted into her eyes. "Hunter? Why did you call me Hunter?"

"Because that's your name."

Was this some kind of a trick? I felt queasy, heavy, as if I needed to sit down. "No, you're wrong about that," I said. "My name is Hoffmann. I'm Dr. Ned Hoffmann. Hunter is a patient of mine at the Institute."

"No." She shook her head. "You're Hunter Morgan." She stepped forward and wrapped her arms around me. "You're Hunter Morgan and I'm taking you home."

Nicole dug her fingernails into her thigh, to remind herself, for the thousandth time that afternoon, that she wasn't dreaming.

Dr. Klein reached across the table to turn off the tape recorder as soon as it was clear that Hunter had come to the end of his narration. "Is there anything else you'd like to tell us?" he asked, fingers poised over the controls. Hunter stared down at the tile floor as though he were deaf.

Dr. Klein was Chief of Psychiatry at the small community hospital in the mountains where Nicole had brought Hunter that morning after she found him in the woods. He nodded to an orderly, who touched Hunter's arm and led him out of the room. "Almost five hours," Dr. Klein said. "Let me wind these tapes back to the beginning to make sure we got all of it."

Dr. Ned Hoffmann mustered a reassuring smile for Nicole, who'd been sitting between him and Hunter throughout the session. They had started at noon and now it was almost five o'clock. Everything Hunter said had been recorded on tape. Before trying to talk to him, Dr. Klein had called in Dr. Hoffmann, who had previously informed him that he was in the area searching for Hunter. It was Dr. Hoffmann who decided that Nicole should also be present since she was responsible for finding Hunter and bringing him in.

They sat in stunned silence for almost five hours as Hunter told his tangled tale. Now Ned and Nicole waited as Dr. Klein rewound the first tape back to the beginning. He pushed the "Play" button and they heard Hunter's voice:

"All right, Dr. Klein, you can turn that thing on now. I'm ready to tell my story. But first you have to understand, I'm not who you think I am."

"Okay," Dr. Klein said on the tape. "We're listening."

And Hunter began to talk:

"Late last summer, after less than two months at the Palmer Institute, I witnessed an extraordinary performance. One of my patients, Hunter Morgan (that was not his real name), sat down at the piano in the patient lounge and started playing like a virtuoso. Hunter was a twenty-one year old schizophrenic who had lived in the Institute for the past seven years, and as far as anyone could remember he'd never touched the piano before. The piece he played was classical music—that was about all I could tell—and it sounded fiendishly difficult, a whirlwind of chords and notes strung together in a jarring rhythm that seemed the perfect analog of a mind spinning out of control...."

Dr. Klein clicked the tape recorder off and shook his head. There was more, almost five hours more: Hunter as his own psychiatrist, Hunter as Nicole's psychiatrist, Hunter as the lover of the mechanical Olympia and the voluptuous Julietta, finally as the crazed murderer of Gottlieb and Julietta herself on a Venetian canal—all of this a gargantuan fabrication that swept in all the movies he'd ever seen, all the books he'd ever read and everyone and everything he'd encountered in his cloistered life at the Institute. It was like an elaborate novel in which the narrator turns out to be a different character than the one he purports to be. Did Hunter Morgan really think he was Ned Hoffmann? Dr. Klein wondered. And had he actually experienced these events in some hallucinatory fashion during his week in the wilderness? Or was it only in the recollection that they had burst into existence?

Dr. Klein fixed his eyes on Ned. "I gather that he thinks he's you, Dr. Hoffmann."

Ned Hoffmann nodded warily. "Hunter has a number of different personalities."

"And one of them is you?"

"Evidently. I never realized it before. It leaves me feeling a little uncomfortable, to say the least."

"Understandably."

Multiple personality disorder, Nicole thought. A delusional parallel world, and she'd been dreamed into it. Luckily her doctor, the real Dr. Ned Hoffmann, was sitting beside her.

"Hunter's version of my life is a little too convincing," Ned smiled. "Frankly, it seems more lifelike than the one I've been living."

Dr. Klein turned to Nicole and asked, "Is there any truth to the story?"

"Absolutely not," Ned interrupted. "It's a classic confabulation—with a few realistic details, of course."

Dr. Klein peered over the tops of his glasses. "Such as?"

"Well, there really is a receptionist named Julietta."

"And your relationship with her?"

"He made all that up. I didn't do any of those things."

"The violence in Venice?"

"A complete fantasy."

Dr. Klein posed his questions almost hypothetically, as if he were talking to one of his patients. "Then Julietta is safe? And the other physician—Dr. Gottlieb?"

"He seemed in good health when I called him this morning." Ned glared back at Dr. Klein in triumph, his color rising. "And so was Julietta, who answered the phone. They do sleep together, as you might as well know, since everyone else does. But as far as I know neither of them has ever been to Venice."

Ned glanced at Nicole as if for confirmation, but she was in no condition to talk after listening to Hunter's narration. The last part was no fantasy—she had followed Hunter into the ravine that morning and the encounter he described was accurate to the last detail. But it was only in the retelling that she understood what had really happened.

"And neither have I, by the way," Ned added.

Dr. Klein nodded and smiled, and then he stood up. "As I'm sure you understand, I'll have to confirm all this with the Institute before I can turn the patient back over to you."

III. Antonia

30

The day they found Hunter, the temperature dropped below freezing and there was snow in the air. Dubin woke up with a savage hangover from drinking half a bottle of Jack Daniel's in a desperate effort to get some sleep. After his last visit to Peter Bartolli he'd spent three sleepless nights in an agony of excitement and dread. He knew he'd found the killer—when he heard Bartolli call his black cat 'Nero' it was like the last cylinder of an intricate combination lock falling into place. But now what was he going to do with him? Better to be a blackmailer, he realized, than the lowliest of detectives. A blackmailer doesn't have to prove anything; it's just a matter of preying on the victim's conscience and fear of exposure. But that wouldn't work with Bartolli. He had to prove that Bartolli was guilty, or trick him into revealing himself—and in the meantime keep him from hurting Antonia, who seemed to be marked as his next victim. He'd never even considered Bartolli's request that he persuade Avery Morgan to bring Antonia to him for treatment. The man had killed three women and there was no telling where he would stop.

Dubin wondered if Avery Morgan would listen to him. He picked up the phone and dialed, assuming for some reason— probably because he and Susan had been avoiding each other since Hunter's disappearance—that Avery or the au pair would answer. He thought about hanging up when he realized it was Susan.

"I need to talk to you," he said in a low voice. "It's—"

"Did you hear the news? They found Hunter this morning."

"Where?"

"Upstate somewhere, hiding in the woods. That Irish girl he met at the Institute is the one who found him."

"Nicole?"

Dubin had blurted his question a little too eagerly. "Yes," Susan said after an awkward pause. "I think that's her name. Do you know her?"

"I've spoken with her."

"Well"—she seemed to be choosing her words deliberately— "Hunter must have stayed in touch with her somehow because she went up there and found him and brought him to the local hospital. Apparently he's OK. Dr. Hoffmann's up there with him now. Frank Lynch is driving up to bring them back."

"Why are they sending Lynch?" Dubin asked, though he knew the answer.

"The police don't want to lose sight of him. They think—well, you know what they think."

Susan was called away from the phone by the au pair, who was taking the children to the movies. "I have a busy schedule today," she said. "If you want to talk to me you're going to have to come over here and stand in line."

He took his time getting there, stopping for a breakfast of eggs and pancakes at a diner along the highway. Which Susan would it be today? he wondered. The loyal wife standing by her man in his time of crisis? Or the jaded equestrienne pining for a roll in the hay? He rehearsed his lines and braced himself with three cups of coffee but he still wasn't prepared for the scene that ensued. Susan rushed out to meet him in the driveway with a raw, tormented look on her face, as if she'd awoken in the middle of a nightmare.

"What's the matter?"

"It's Antonia. He's taken Antonia."

"Who's taken her? Where?"

She gripped his hands and pulled him into the barn. It was Peter Bartolli, she explained. One of the physicians at the Institute had called a little while earlier with the news. No one knew how it happened—Dr. Hoffmann was upstate with Hunter, Dr. Palmer was traveling home from Washington, Dr. Gottlieb had been put on probation after being caught in bed with the receptionist—but somehow Bartolli had spirited Antonia away from the Institute and driven off with her in his car.

"Damn it!" Dubin shouted. "I shouldn't have let this happen."

"No, nobody could—"

"You don't understand. I should have seen this coming. Bartolli tried to get me to talk you and Avery into bringing her to him for some crackpot therapy. That's what I wanted to see you about."

"We wouldn't have agreed to it anyway."

He followed her past the horse stalls into the apartment in the back of the barn where they had played their little game of cat and mouse. All that seemed far in the past now, like an ancient ritual whose meaning had been forgotten. The couch was cluttered with papers, magazines, odd bits of clothing. They sat across from each other at the table she used as a desk. She flicked a wisp of hair away from her hollow eyes and tried to smile. "I don't know what to do," she said. "I don't think I can take this."

The phone rang and she answered it. The acting director of the Institute had evidently received a call from Bartolli and was able to provide some new information. "It's just as you thought," she told Dubin when she hung up. "Bartolli claims Antonia isn't in any danger. He just wants to put her under hypnosis and he's willing to have us there when he does it—at his house at eight o'clock tonight."

Susan made some coffee while Dubin leafed through a stack of newspaper clippings about the search for Hunter. That search had ended and now Hunter would be charged with two murders unless Dubin acted quickly to expose the real murderer. Had Bartolli made a fatal mistake with his abduction of Antonia? The little soiree he'd planned for that evening—if Dubin could find a way to manipulate it—might be his undoing. And what was he to make of Susan? Something hung in the air between them like a winter fog. When she poured his coffee he studied her weary eyes. Her summer tan had faded and she looked blotchy and bruised, far away even from her own emotions.

"How well do you know Peter Bartolli?" he asked her.

"I haven't seen much of him in the past few years," she answered. "He's been sort of weird since he left the Institute."

"'Sort of weird' doesn't begin to do him justice."

"Eccentric, for sure."

"More like stark raving mad. He's got a puppet theater set up for mass executions in his basement and he thinks schizophrenics are travelers to a parallel universe." Dubin took a sip of his coffee and waited until she sat back down to face him. "Did you know Bartolli was Maria Morgan's lover?"

"No," she blushed. "I mean, I always suspected it, but I wasn't sure."

Maybe he was your lover too, Dubin thought. "I think he killed her."

She seemed more curious than surprised. "Why?"

"Jealousy, most likely."

"No, I mean what makes you think he killed her?"

"I found a letter he wrote a few days before she died. Evidently your husband knew about their affair and was trying to stop it, and Bartolli was threatening to do something drastic if he got in the way."

She looked down at her coffee, avoiding the obvious question.

Dubin supplied it for her. "How do I know the killer wasn't your husband? Remember the three items that were missing from the studio? I think the person who killed her was the one who went back to the studio after Frank Lynch had completed his inventory and removed those three items. One of them, the record, turned up at the Institute. Could Hunter have taken it there?"

"No. I was here when they came for him. He didn't take anything with him but a few clothes. Neither did Antonia."

"They can be ruled out then. And it's safe to assume that Avery didn't sneak those items out of his own barn and stash them at the Institute. That leaves the jealous lover. He admits to giving her the kaleidoscope. He denies taking it back, but there are dozens just like it in his house. One of them was probably hers."

Susan lowered her head and began to cry. Was it because Avery was innocent or Bartolli was guilty? Dubin had no way of knowing and he decided he didn't care. He came around the table and leaned down to put his arm around her as she cried. It was a position he couldn't maintain for very long, and after a few minutes he sat down on the couch. She nestled beside him, wiping her tears on his shirt.

"I can't stand this much longer," she said. "This has got to end."

"It's going to end soon."

She turned and kissed him on the mouth. It was not a chaste kiss but it was not a sensuous one either, more a request than a demand. He answered it with a gentle kiss on the cheek, tasting the salt of her tears, and held her as she started crying again. Yes she was a cynic but he didn't want to take advantage of her cynicism, even at the price of his own. He would have felt diminished, as if he'd been paying for sex, or being paid for it. And he kept thinking about Nicole—even though he'd never touched Nicole—and how he would owe her an explanation. Susan seemed to understand all this without his saying anything. They both knew it was a moment that would pass and never happen again.

When she had finished crying he stood her up and wiped her face with a damp washcloth. She stood in front of the mirror staring into her own vacant eyes. "Does this mean you're not blackmailing me any more?" The old ironic tone was back in her voice.

"I never was," he said. "I'm a detective, remember?"

"I almost forgot." She rustled through the papers on her desk until she found her checkbook. "Don't you still need a client?"

"Not really. Ever since those two women were killed, I've been self-employed."

"You must have expenses."

"I sort of enjoy being my own boss."

She tossed the checkbook on the table. "I have to tell Avery something. I can't tell him you're helping out with Antonia because you wouldn't sleep with me."

"No," he said, pulling on his jacket. "Don't tell him that."

He smiled ambiguously and headed for the door. She followed him past the horse stalls and out into the driveway.

"Avery's going to be home soon." There was a note of panic in her voice. "He'll go ballistic when I tell him about Antonia. He'll jump back in his car and drive over there to get Antonia, even if he has to kill Peter to do it."

"Make him wait until tonight. Tell him to humor Bartolli, let him think you're playing into his hands. Antonia will be all right."

Dubin climbed into his car and started the engine. She tapped on the window and he rolled it down so he could hear her. "Will you come with us tonight?"

"Give me a call when you're ready to go."

She leaned closer. "Promise me something."

"I never make promises."

"Promise me you'll see this through. For Hunter's sake, and Antonia's—and mine."

"I never make promises," Dubin repeated. "Even if I intend to keep them."

31

Ned Hoffmann and Nicole filed out of Dr. Klein's office in stunned silence, followed by a security guard who had been summoned to escort them along with Hunter to a locked waiting area. There they were to remain for two hours until Frank Lynch arrived to drive them all back to the Institute. For liability reasons, Dr. Klein would release Hunter only to the police. Ned was reluctant to let either Hunter or Nicole out of his sight.

"Why did you tell Dr. Klein that Hunter's story was all a fantasy?" Nicole asked Ned as they padded down the hall. "You know there was a lot of truth in it. His piano playing, the two deaths, your rivalry with Dr. Gottlieb—"

"Keep quiet!" Ned whispered, pulling her along by the elbow. "Dr. Klein doesn't need to know about any of that."

The waiting area adjoined the emergency room and seemed to have been designed for mental patients. There was nothing in it but plastic chairs and a few old magazines—and no way out without the blessing of the security guard, who parked himself by the door reading a newspaper. Ned and Nicole took seats near the door and wrestled with their private thoughts. Hunter sat in the corner as far away from the others as possible and started flipping through magazines at a furious pace as if he expected to find encoded messages stuck between their pages.

Nicole thought about the tale Hunter had told and was astonished at the breadth of his genius. He had memorized and internalized *Hamlet* along with every other book at the Institute. He had deconstructed her thesis topic and demolished whole schools of philosophy and literary theory in the process. He had taught himself to play the piano by listening to a record and turned all the people around him into characters in *The Tales of Hoffmann* by watching a video. She was one of those people, one of those characters—of course she'd told him about her childhood traumas and her work with Dr. Hoffmann and the agony of writing her thesis, so it wasn't surprising that these elements had found their way into his story. But it was humbling to realize that many of the words he put in her mouth were more insightful than anything she'd actually thought of on her own.

"I feel like one of those authors I've been writing about," she said to Ned Hoffmann in a low voice, "meeting myself in someone else's story."

"Scary, isn't it?"

Ned stood up and wandered off in search of coffee, avoiding Hunter's eyes, which were aimed at him across the top of the magazine. He felt exhausted, shaken, exposed. When he passed a mirror in the hall he instinctively looked away: he couldn't bear to see the shambling, unkempt figure he'd become after ten days of scouring the wilderness for this delusional young man who, in his own wild imaginings, had turned into himself. He ached with a sense of repugnance and fear that no patient had ever aroused in him before. He felt that Hunter had captured his personality or something even deeper than his personality. In that five-hour narration, Hunter had displayed all of Ned Hoffmann's favorite gestures and facial tics; he even spoke in a simulation of Ned's voice. He wasn't just pretending to be Ned Hoffmann: he *was* Ned Hoffmann, and no one knew that better than Ned himself. It was as if Hunter had observed Ned from within and molded his delusions out of Ned's deepest secrets. His meanest impulses, his weirdest fantasies, his most shameful self-deceptions—they were all there in living color: the affair with Peter Bartolli's daughter "Olympia" (that wasn't her real name, of course, but she really was like a wind-up doll and Hunter had been diabolically clever in describing how she lured Ned with sex and then dropped him when she realized he couldn't help her father), the fascination with Julietta, the jealous resentment of Gottlieb, even the fantasy that Nicole was in love with him. But Hunter had taken this admittedly embarrassing material and distorted it beyond all recognition. Ned wasn't insane and he wasn't the monster depicted in Hunter's story—he'd never been to Venice, never stabbed or strangled anyone, never actually said or done anything the least bit unprofessional or malicious. He'd never stalked Julietta or had those crazy conversations with Olympia or Nicole or Dr. Palmer; in fact none of his secret fantasies would have come to light if Hunter hadn't worked them into his delusions. And how did Hunter find out about them? Did he spy on Ned? Gossip with the staff? Or was his own illness so finely tuned that he could detect the merest whiff of mental derangement in others?

Over an hour had passed in the hospital waiting room. Hunter had devoured every magazine—back issues of *People*, *Newsweek* and various medical journals—while Nicole drifted in and out of sleep. The security guard had made slow progress with his newspaper, as if he were studying an ancient text.

Ned touched Nicole's arm to wake her up. "Remember when you tried to warn me that the opera plot was taking over everybody's life?"

"I didn't really say that."

"No, of course not. He said you said it. He had you saying it in his story."

"Right."

"You didn't really say it."

"No. But it was a clever thing to have said, wasn't it? So I won't deny that I would have said it, if I had really been me."

The security guard looked up from his newspaper. "You folks patients at the Institute?"

They all laughed, except Hunter. It was a few minutes before Ned dared to continue, and then he lowered his voice to keep the guard from overhearing. "What happens in the next act?"

"What do you mean?"

"Assume that you—I mean your other self, the Nicole in Hunter's story—were correct that the opera plot was taking over. What would happen next?"

Nicole grinned and darted her eyes toward the guard. "Are you serious? Or are you just—"

"Assume for the moment that I'm serious," Ned whispered. "Near the beginning of the story he said he'd become obsessed with three women—an artist, an ingénue, and a nymphomaniac— each of whom brought him a step closer to ruin."

"I remember him saying that."

"Obviously the nymphomaniac was Julietta. And the artist—"

"That would be Olympia, the dancer."

"Right. Which leaves the ingénue. What the hell is an ingénue, by the way?"

"It's an innocent young girl. Invariably a virgin."

"That's what I thought. Don't you see? He's talking about Antonia. She's next."

"Next? What do you mean?"

"I don't know."

Nicole's face had been drained of all its color. "I do," she whispered. She glanced up at the guard, who was still engrossed in deciphering his newspaper. "Let me tell you what happens in the next act."

"Your daughter is like an enchanted princess who has fallen under a spell. I know the magic that can wake her from her seven year sleep."

Peter Bartolli stood on the stage in his underground theater, fixing his fierce eyes on Avery Morgan. Antonia sat beside him in a folding chair facing the audience, her eyes wide but unseeing. Her father, who had just arrived with Susan Morgan and Dr. Palmer, seemed momentarily transfixed by Bartolli's imperious gaze.

"Don't do anything sudden," Dr. Palmer told Avery Morgan in a whisper that everyone could hear. "You and Susan have a seat. Let me handle this."

Dubin watched from the doorway. He had followed the Morgans and Dr. Palmer in his own car after meeting them at the Institute. At Bartolli's house they found a note on the door inviting them to proceed to the basement. The theater was dark except for a spotlight on the stage and a half-dozen candles flickering from a candelabra on the grand piano. Over the stage hung a photograph of Maria Morgan. Dubin wondered if it was the one Bartolli had taken from her studio.

"It's not the kiss of a prince that will break the spell," Bartolli continued, "but the charm of music, which speaks directly to the soul. And not just any music, but the voice of one of the finest sopranos who ever lived."

"Peter," Dr. Palmer said in an even voice, "I hope you're not—"

"The voice that more than one critic called the voice of an angel. The voice of Antonia's mother, Maria Morgan."

Avery Morgan glared at Bartolli with a fury he made no effort to suppress. "I won't stand for this."

Dr. Palmer clamped a hand on Morgan's arm and pulled him back from the stage. "Sit down, Avery."

Avery and Susan dropped into seats in the front row and Dr. Palmer sat beside them. "What are you getting at, Peter?" he asked wearily.

Bartolli seemed eager for an opportunity to explain. "As you know, Antonia hasn't spoken more than a few words since her mother died," he said. "But on rare occasions she's been known to sing, in a hauntingly beautiful soprano voice that comes as a shock to anyone who ever heard Maria Morgan."

"She has severe asthma," Avery Morgan argued. "She shouldn't be allowed to sing."

"The asthma began at the time her mother died. It's a symptom of the same illness that made her stop talking. She believes that when she sings it's really her mother singing through her—that by singing she can, in effect, bring her mother back to life."

Dr. Palmer shook his head. "Voice projection is a common delusion in schizophrenia."

"That's true," Bartolli agreed. "And like any delusion it can be used therapeutically. The patient must be allowed to experience the personality that's speaking through her—"

Avery Morgan interrupted: "You're going to make her sing?"

"If she wants to. She will only get better if she can bring her unconscious memories to the surface."

Dr. Palmer stood up and took a step toward the stage. "Peter, let's put a stop to this right now. Any prolonged singing could trigger a serious asthma attack. You're jeopardizing her health and all the progress we've made with her."

"There's been no progress. This is the only way to help her."

"Please. I insist that you let us take her back to the Institute."

"I'm going to proceed as planned." The candlelight flickered defiantly in Bartolli's cavernous eyes. "You mustn't interfere or interrupt while she's under hypnosis. It could have the most serious consequences."

Dr. Palmer sat back down and whispered something to Avery Morgan, probably to confirm the dangers of disturbing a patient under hypnosis. Bartolli pushed some buttons on the sound equipment at the back of the stage and disappeared momentarily behind the puppet theater, which was still concealed beneath its canvas cover. Susan glanced over her shoulder at Dubin, silently pleading with him to stop this train wreck before it was too late, but her goal—and her husband's and Dr. Palmer's—was only to protect Antonia. Dubin was there to catch a murderer, and before he could spring the trap he had to allow Bartolli to set it. He couldn't see very far into that twisted mind, nor did he aspire to. But he had a hunch that the performance they were about to witness, played out before a hand-picked audience of the injured and the frightened and the guilt-ridden, was Bartolli's symbolic way of returning to the scene of his crime. And why did the killer return to the scene of the crime? It was a ritual of triumph from which he imagined he would once again escape unscathed.

Dr. Palmer was the first to break the silence. "I'm almost afraid to ask what you're going to ask her to sing."

"A few highlights from *The Tales of Hoffmann*, of course."

Avery Morgan growled, "That's the opera Maria was rehearsing when she died."

"Yes," Bartolli agreed, "but it will be quite different from anything you've heard before. What you are about to see is *Hoffmann* as it was meant to be performed."

32

Frank Lynch arrived at the hospital before Nicole could tell Ned Hoffmann about the last act of *The Tales of Hoffmann*. He strode into the waiting room murmuring into his cell phone and shook hands with the security guard without ending the conversation. Then he stepped toward Ned Hoffmann, paying no more attention to Hunter or Nicole than he paid to the pictures on the wall. "Listen," he said, "I just found out something you need to know. Our friend Dr. Bartolli has pulled one of his famous stunts. He took Antonia out of the Institute and has her over at his house, where he says he's going to give her some kind of hypnosis therapy."

"How did that happen?"

"I don't know. Apparently nobody was watching."

"Are they bringing her back?"

"They're afraid to do anything sudden, in case she's in distress or already under hypnosis. Bartolli wants everybody to come over at eight o'clock tonight."

"Everybody?"

Lynch leaned closer. "You and Dr. Palmer, and Avery and Susan Morgan. And Hunter too."

"Hunter?"

"He wants Hunter there."

Ned agreed to leave his car at the hospital so he could return in the police cruiser with Lynch and the two patients. He sat in the back seat bouncing between Hunter and Nicole as Lynch piloted the cruiser over winding mountain roads. "Could you slow down a little?" Ned called through the barrier that separated the driver from the back seat. "There's—"

"No, keep going!" Nicole interrupted, pulling Ned back. It was the first time she'd spoken since Lynch arrived. "Don't slow down. We've got to get there as fast as we can."

"What do you mean? There's plenty of time to get there by eight o'clock."

"You don't understand," she said, turning back to face Ned. "You still don't know what happens to Antonia."

"I must apologize for my lack of operatic resources," Peter Bartolli said. He stood beside his puppet theater, wearing a dark smile that looked anything but apologetic. "Not having live singers at my disposal, we'll have to make do with these marionettes."

Dubin was the only one in the audience who knew what to expect when Bartolli raised the curtain—a row of hooded figures that dangled over the stage like corpses on a scaffold. The others gasped when they saw the figures and they gasped again when Bartolli removed the hoods from two of them. The first was obviously Antonia, who sat behind Bartolli staring fixedly over the audience as if to confirm the resemblance, and the second was her mother. The other characters remained faceless under their hoods.

"Hoffmann's three loves are Antonia, Olympia and Giulietta." Bartolli jiggled the hooded figure of a woman in a gaudy dress, which swung back and forth helplessly a few times before coming to rest. "All are fated to die untimely and gruesome deaths."

He pushed the other marionettes aside and grabbed a tall hooded figure in a long blue coat, raising its arms menacingly toward the three females. "Thanks to our hero. Let's call him Hoffmann."

He reached behind Antonia and pushed some buttons on the audio equipment. "Olympia is the first to die." A high female voice began to sing a lilting, jagged tune that didn't sound quite human. "This is her famous aria from the second act, 'La Chanson d'Olympie.' She's an automaton, of course. A beautiful, lifelike doll. Everybody knows that except Hoffmann, who thinks he loves her." From behind the stage he pulled the strings and Olympia danced her mechanical dance, skittering impossibly across the proscenium as the Hoffmann figure stood motionless. Then the music slowed, like a clock running down. There came a mechanical winding sound and the high, angular singing began again.

"The voice you hear is Maria Morgan's," Bartolli said through the little hatch above the stage. "You all know that, I'm sure. But here's something you don't know. Here's how she dies."

Suddenly the Hoffmann figure sprang to life, hurtling toward Olympia and wrapping his enormous arms around her neck, strangling her, until the singing stopped. Then he stood with her limp body dangling from his arms and hung his head in regret. "The murderer, of course, claims to love poor Olympia even after he realizes that she's only a doll, even after he's destroyed her. But still he must cover up his crime." Hoffmann pulled down a noose and fastened it around Olympia's lifeless corpse, which he hoisted up and out of sight as if her death were a suicide.

"Do you want to see his face?" Bartolli's hand appeared over the puppets as he reached down and started to remove the hood. "No, on second thought, let's leave the hood on. We'll need it again in a few minutes for the execution."

Frank Lynch navigated relentlessly over the dips and curves of the mountain roads. In the back seat Hunter swayed in silence, staring into the darkness.

Ned Hoffmann held Nicole's hand, trying to calm her fear. "I almost forgot," he said. "You were going to tell me what happens in the next act."

"The Antonia act," Nicole said weakly. "It's about a young woman named Antonia whose mother was a famous opera singer. She has her mother's voice, but she's ill with consumption and her father has forbidden her to sing."

"So far it sounds familiar."

Nicole nodded and went on. "She's fallen under the spell of a sinister figure named Dr. Miracle, who urges her to sing in spite of her illness. Just as her lover Hoffmann rushes in to save her, she collapses in the arms of Dr. Miracle. She has sung herself to death."

"Who's Dr. Miracle? Is he the Devil?"

"He's Hoffmann's nemesis, the same fiend who's dogged him every step of the way and spoiled the three loves of his life. He's the false father who shattered Olympia and he's Dappertutto, the collector of souls, who tricked Hoffmann into killing his rival and then drifted off in the gondola with Giulietta."

"Then do you think—"

"To answer your question—yes, he's the Devil. That's exactly who he is."

Several minutes passed before Ned spoke again. "You're worried about Antonia," he said.

"Yes, of course. I'm afraid she's the next victim."

"I think we can rule out Hunter's notion that reality has somehow been captured by the plot of an opera. You agree, don't you?"

"Of course. But Hunter's story mirrored both the opera and reality so closely that the connections couldn't be coincidental." She glanced at Hunter, hoping for confirmation, but he kept staring out the window as if she were speaking a different language.

"What significance could they have?"

"Isn't it possible that Hunter has been trying to tell us something?"

"Of course he has. Any patient—"

"Something specific, I mean. Not just the kind of psychological fluff you'd be expecting from a patient, but clues to the mystery."

Ned looked past her trying to catch Hunter's attention. "What mystery?"

"The mystery of who killed his mother. And the other women."

Frank Lynch jammed on the brakes as he brought the car a little too sharply around a curve, propelling Ned forward and almost into the barrier.

"The piano playing was real, wasn't it?" Nicole went on. "I think he was trying to tell us something. And in the past life regression—"

"That didn't really happen."

"No, I know that. But all the more reason to try and figure out what it meant. It ended with Olympia's two 'fathers' tearing her apart as they struggled over who would control her. If that isn't symbolic, was is it?" She turned to Hunter, hoping vainly that he would give her argument some support.

"Maybe it was just a scene from an opera."

"Sometimes a good cigar is just a good cigar. Is that it?"

"Something like that. Or the opposite, actually. Sometimes a tale full of sound and fury really signifies nothing."

"I think you're wrong," Nicole said, shaking her head. She laid her hand on Hunter's knee, and although he kept staring out the window he didn't try to pull it away. "This was not a tale told by an idiot."

Peter Bartolli's guests had watched in horror as Olympia's strangulation had been played out on the puppet stage, and Dubin wondered how much they could endure. Bartolli came down from his perch and again stood beside the stage. "Of course the murderer isn't punished until the very end of the story," he said. "Before that he has to dispose of his two other loves, the innocent Antonia and the lustful Giulietta. Antonia comes first."

He set the Antonia puppet in center stage and hoisted the hooded Hoffmann back down. "Again we'll use the recording of Maria Morgan, this time singing the role of Antonia. But we'll also have something even better. Something very special. The real Antonia."

He whispered Antonia's name and coaxed her forward until she stood beside him, terrified in her hypnotic trance. "Antonia," he said gently, "I want you to look behind you. Do you see that picture on the wall? That's your mother, isn't it? Now turn back around, because in a minute she's going to start singing and she's going to need your help."

Antonia faced the audience while Bartolli adjusted the recording equipment. When Maria Morgan's voice rose from the speakers—and even to Dubin it seemed to be coming from the picture on the wall—Antonia began to sing. She sang without hesitation, as if she'd known this aria all her life. As Bartolli predicted, she sang with the voice of an angel: her voice merged with her mother's and any difference between the two became imperceptible. And as she sang, the hypnotic veil lifted from her eyes and genuine emotion, genuine communication played across her face for the first time in many years. She was able to reach out to each member of the audience—to Dubin, Dr. Palmer, Susan and especially her father, who seemed deeply moved, almost hypnotized, by this otherworldly duet. For Avery Morgan, Dubin realized, it must have been as if both his wife and his daughter had come back from the dead.

As the music rose in volume and pitch, Antonia sang with mounting intensity, gasping for breath as she modulated into higher and higher keys. Her face was flushed and she tottered on her feet, staggering backwards into Bartolli's arms. Still he urged her on, and for a few more minutes she stood singing urgently, desperately, until it seemed that her heart would burst.

The audience sat transfixed, immobilized by the terrible beauty of the catastrophe that was unfolding before them.

Suddenly the spell was broken. A crashing noise, shouting voices, tramping feet—and Frank Lynch and Hunter Morgan clattered through the door, followed by Ned and Nicole. The music continued, but for a few seconds the audience forgot about Antonia.

The sight of Hunter—the fugitive son, madman and murderer—was almost too much for Avery and Susan Morgan after what they'd experienced that night. They both burst into tears and rushed over to embrace him. He pushed them away and lurched desperately toward the stage, restrained only by Frank Lynch's heavy grip.

Ned dodged past them and hurried towards Antonia. When she saw him she stumbled backwards, losing her place in the music.

"Don't frighten her!" Bartolli warned. "She's under hypnosis."

"You can stop singing now, Antonia," Ned murmured, ignoring Bartolli. "That's enough singing for now."

Nicole darted onto the stage and clicked off the audio system and suddenly the orchestra and the voice of Maria Morgan stopped. Antonia sang a few more notes, staring in desperate confusion like a lost child. When she ran out of notes she started choking and crying and gasping for breath, and then she collapsed in Ned's arms. He sat her down in the first row of seats and held an asthma inhaler in front of her face until she could breathe again.

Bartolli remained alone on the stage, his face contorted in anger. He must have known that whatever he'd hoped to accomplish with this bizarre performance was now lost; he would never be allowed another minute with Antonia. Dubin doubted if she had been in any real danger, otherwise Dr. Palmer would have intervened. He'd been humoring his brother, Dubin realized, not appreciating how dangerous he could be. That would change in a few minutes, as soon as all the commotion around Antonia's singing and Hunter's arrival had died down. The time had come to confront the murderer, and to expose him.

Dubin stepped toward the stage and addressed Bartolli in a voice that everyone in the room could hear. "You've shown us how Hoffmann's first love died. The beautiful toy Olympia. How she was strangled, how her body was hoisted up to the ceiling to make it look like suicide."

"That's correct," Bartolli said, glaring back suspiciously.

"And that's how Maria Morgan died, isn't it?"

The room was alive with silence as all conversation, all movement ceased.

"Yes, I believe it was," Bartolli mumbled.

"You could be right," Dubin said, smiling. He couldn't resist a glance at the audience as he said this, fastening his gaze on Nicole, who stared back with a troubled expression that seemed to warn of impending danger. "Things might have happened as you depicted in your puppet show. In Maria Morgan's studio there are still signs of a violent struggle, a struggle her murderer tried to conceal. And those signs tell a story of their own."

"What story is that?"

"The turntable was knocked onto the floor, and the record on it was scratched when it fell. A few days later that record disappeared, along with a couple of other items: a photograph of the victim, and a kaleidoscope. The record was never returned to the library; instead it turned up at the Institute, where you happened to work. You took it there, didn't you? And the other things that were removed from the studio?"

"I have no idea what you're talking about. A record? I don't have any record."

"I saw the kaleidoscope when I was here before."

"I have dozens of kaleidoscopes. I collect them."

"You have a cat named Nero."

"Yes." Bartolli squinted back at Dubin with a look of puzzlement. "Is my cat somehow implicated in this?"

"A man with a pet named Nero wrote a love letter to Maria Morgan a couple of days before she died. I have the letter."

"I was in Geneva when she died, attending—"

"You were Maria Morgan's lover, weren't you?"

He shook his head. "You really don't understand what's going on here, do you?"

"Don't deny it. It's obvious from the letter."

There came a muffled cry and the voice of Avery Morgan, which had always sounded so colorless and thin, rumbled through the room like the growl of some enormous beast. "You?" he bellowed. "You... were the one she was having the affair with?"

Bartolli winced uncomfortably. "Yes, I was her lover. But I didn't kill her."

"You killed her," Dubin said.

"I was at a conference in Geneva. And I can prove it."

There was something new in Dubin's manner, an air of moral certainty that had been submerged in years of cynicism and self-indulgence. "You went to her studio and strangled her just as your Hoffmann strangled Olympia," he said, suppressing a triumphant smile, "and then you strung her up from the ceiling like a marionette to make it look like suicide. And seven years later, in an attempt to cover up your crime, you did the same thing to Mrs. Paterson and Francine Whipple."

Bartolli looked away, shaking his head.

Dubin turned to Frank Lynch, who, along with the others, seemed as immobilized as the puppets hanging on the stage. "This man should be arrested and charged with murder."

Lynch reached for his cell phone to call for support.

"No," Nicole said, rising hesitantly. "He didn't kill her."

Ten pairs of eyes bore in on her like a swarm of hornets. "I'm sure he didn't kill Maria Morgan or the other women," she said. Her voice was dry with stage fright; she tried to smile but found that her face would not obey. "And I know who did."

33

Lurching over the mountain roads beside Hunter and Ned Hoffmann in the desperate hope of arriving in time to save Antonia, Nicole had suddenly realized that she herself was the key to the mystery.

Yes, Hunter had been trying to tell them something and it was through her that he was communicating. She was the only person who could grasp his meaning and draw the necessary conclusions. And she could do that by using the critical tools she used in her work and applying them to his fictional creation as she would to any other text. Where Hunter's narration was false as fact, it was true as fiction. She asked herself: what was the hidden thread that ran through his dreams and hallucinations and bound them all together? She thought back to his account of her final session with Dr. Hoffmann before he set off for Venice in his mad pursuit of Julietta. Hunter had cast her in the role of Nicklausse, the faithful servant who followed Hoffmann from one disastrous affair to another and could always see through his delusions. In that guise she'd told Ned she knew who the killer was but no one would listen to her. That was her destiny, she realized, a Cassandra, an unheeded seer of the truth. And to fulfill it she would have to unlock the unconscious—whose unconscious? hers or Hunter's? or did it make any difference?—the only way she knew how: she must not only read the book of the world but deconstruct its text with all the ingenuity at her disposal.

How could she make sense of Hunter's story? It all began with his playing the piano: the Kreisleriana, Schumann's portrait of the deranged composer who found in music and madness his gateway to the spirit world. "To find God he first had to find the Devil," Dr. Palmer had told Ned Hoffmann in the story; and the same might have been said of Nicole, expelled from school and family—in an earlier age she would have been burned at the stake—for not believing in the Devil. Her true crime lay in seeing her father for what he was. Like Hamlet she feigned madness in self-defense—is that what Hunter had done? When he'd imagined another life for himself it was as his psychiatrist, the ultimate father figure. In that persona he imagined that he'd followed Julietta to Venice and murdered her under the eye of Dappertutto, the collector of souls. Who was Dappertutto? Who was Hoffmann? Ask one who was there: the boy on the balcony with the mandolin. Ask the boy—who was the murderer?

Suddenly Nicole saw herself not from the inside, the way people normally do, even in dreams, but objectively, as if she were a character in a story. She was standing off to one side watching herself and the others in the room: Bartolli still on the stage with Antonia tottering blankly beside him, being comforted by Ned Hoffmann; Avery and Susan Morgan, both looking angry and distraught, with Dr. Palmer frowning beside them; Frank Lynch grimacing through his broken teeth as he clamped a tight grip on Hunter's arm and kept an eye on Bartolli; and Dubin, frozen and expressionless after Nicole's foiling of his brilliant denouement. This could be dangerous, she realized. She was violating the rules of dreaming: you can't dream yourself outside of your own mind. You might have multiple personalities—who doesn't, in the course of a lifetime?—but there's only one you. It's the eye behind the camera. When you become so dissociated that you start seeing yourself from outside your own skin, you're sailing close to the edge. That's what happened to Hunter, and that's what had been happening to her since she was fourteen, when she knew her father had killed her brother but she couldn't bring herself to say anything. She had never mentioned it to anyone before she told Hunter and that was only because she thought he was crazy. Why? Was the whole world a conspiracy to keep you from telling the truth about the Devil? Everyone knows who it is but they will lock you up and throw away the key if you tell the truth. Now she saw

Hunter staring fiercely ahead, past her, past his father and Bartolli, past the walls to another world.

Time stood still and in its infinite imagination lighted every corner of her life, as if this were her last moment on earth. And suddenly she was back on the inside of her skin and she knew who the killer was. *If he but blench, I know my course. Murder will speak.*

Nicole stepped toward Hunter and gently touched his hand. "Hunter, would you play the piano for us?"

Hunter seemed to favor that idea in his savage, brooding way. Without a word, he lurched toward the piano, restrained only by Frank Lynch's tight grip on his arm. The others—Avery and Susan Morgan, Bartolli, Dr. Palmer, even Dubin—glared back at Nicole as if she had made an outrageous suggestion.

"It's all right," said Ned Hoffmann. "He won't do anything."

"It's important," Nicole told Frank Lynch. "It's important that you let him play."

Finally Hunter was allowed to sit down at the piano, with Lynch crouching beside him on a small folding chair like a heavily-armed page turner. After a pause he raised his hands and set them to skittering across the keys in a fantastical whirlwind of notes which, Dubin thought, must have resembled the jagged inner landscape of his mind.

"Hunter is playing the only piece he knows," Nicole explained. "The Kreisleriana of Robert Schumann. If it sounds a little crazy that's because it's Schumann's portrait of a fictional madman created by the poet Hoffmann—the same Hoffmann who was later fictionalized as the alcoholic hero of *The Tales of Hoffmann*. Schumann was driven toward what Hoffmann called the spirit world, that parallel universe of absolute truth and beauty that can be entered most easily through drugs, music and madness. Schumann chose music but he ended up with madness. And this piece provides a chilling glimpse into his future."

Dubin had been watching Avery and Susan Morgan, who sat frowning and whispering with Dr. Palmer. "Nicole," Dr. Palmer said in his most soothing voice, as if he were humoring a child, "this is a very interesting perspective on music history which I'm sure everyone would enjoy hearing on some other occasion. But Hunter is exhausted after his ordeal and he shouldn't stay up late playing the piano. And Dr. Bartolli"—he hesitated as he pondered a diplomatic way to address the accusation Dubin had made against his brother—"has some business to discuss with the police. Why don't you schedule an appointment with Dr. Hoffmann for next week and you can talk about it then?"

"This isn't just an irrelevant excursion into music history," Nicole replied confidently, to show how she felt about being patronized. "Maria Morgan had a recording of Kreisleriana in her studio when she was rehearsing her role in *The Tales of Hoffmann*. She was trying to do something rarely attempted in modern times: to play all three of Hoffmann's loves. She would be Olympia the wind-up doll, Antonia the innocent young girl, Giulietta the deceitful courtesan. For a woman who was under treatment for schizophrenia this was a dangerous undertaking. It required her to have three selves. And for the men in her life—since there was more than one—she could not be all three. She could only be the treacherous courtesan. And so the question is as Dr. Bartolli posed it: Who was Hoffmann?"

With these last words Hunter's playing seemed to reach a climax, as the volume rose and his fingers scurried furiously over the keys. He pounded a few inconclusive chords, and then just as abruptly his agitation cooled and he wandered off into another, less violent episode.

"Maria Morgan took her work very seriously," Nicole went on, "and she liked to steep herself in the background of whatever she was working on. That's probably why she checked this recording out of the library. What we do know is that this was the music she was listening to in the last moments of her life. This piece, this

Kreisleriana—the one that Hunter suddenly started playing a few weeks ago—is the music she was listening to right up to the end."

Avery Morgan leaned forward, his face dark, the growling beast still lurking in his voice. "How do we know that?"

"There's a big scratch in the record that starts about two-thirds of the way through the Kreisleriana. So when you play the record, the music comes to a sudden stop, right at the point where the turntable toppled to the floor. That was the moment when Maria Morgan died. And that's the place where Hunter always stops playing, at the exact place where his mother died. We'll be there in a couple of minutes."

"But Dubin said the record was missing from the studio."

"That's right. It was missing. But I found it."

The dynamics of the music had risen again as it surged toward another climax. Antonia listened with her eyes wide, her breath quickening, her color fading as if Hunter's frenetic hands had whirled her back into a hypnotic state. If Nicole was right about the record, then he was mapping the last moments of their mother's life. Every note he played pushed them another step closer to the catastrophe. Wasn't there some way to stop the music, some way to turn back?

"Stop!" Avery Morgan sputtered. "Please stop!"

"No," Nicole pressed on. "Let me sketch out the scene. Maria Morgan in her studio, listening to this music as she struggles with her three conflicting roles. Maybe it arouses a self-destructive impulse in her as it did for its composer. How could she play all three of Hoffmann's loves? How could she be an innocent young girl and a treacherous prostitute at the same time? If she was Giulietta, then who was her jealous lover? Who was the man who, though she despised him, couldn't bear the thought of sharing her with two other men? He's there with her in the studio; an argument breaks out. And then something terrible happens— maybe it's this demonic music, this glimpse into the spirit world that scrapes a little too deeply into the unconscious and triggers it off; maybe it's a fit of jealous rage; we'll never know. In any case, the man attacks, savagely strangling her, knocking the turntable off its stand, stopping the music dead; and then, in the cold light of his guilty conscience, he ties a nylon cord around her neck and hoists her up on the light fixture and lets her drop again to make it look like suicide. He thinks no one is watching but he doesn't know about the loft at the other end of the studio. There are two eyewitnesses in the studio."

"And they're both extremely ill," Dr. Palmer said, rising slowly. "I insist that this performance stop right now."

And then, as if the universe took its cues from Dr. Palmer, the performance stopped. It stopped as Nicole had told them it would: when Hunter, tracing the fossil record of his mother's death struggle, arrived at the point in the music where the scratch had always blocked his way. He lifted his hands from the keyboard, as he always did, in the middle of a dissonant phrase. The deed was done, and there was nothing more he or anyone else could do about it. He dropped his hands to his lap and sat with his head hanging, breathing heavily.

"Did anyone even ask the eyewitnesses?" Nicole asked.

"This is absurd," Dr. Palmer objected. "They don't know what they saw."

Bartolli turned to face Avery Morgan. "I was Maria's lover," he said, "but I had a rival. Two rivals, in fact. One was you, Avery, but you weren't much of an impediment. You were only her husband."

"Who was the other one?" Avery demanded.

"The other one—"

Bartolli turned his eyes toward Dr. Palmer and a look of infinite sadness spread across his face. "The other one was my brother."

Before anyone knew what was happening, Hunter leaped up from the piano and threw himself on Dr. Palmer. He would have choked him to death if Dubin and Lynch hadn't pulled him off and dragged him across the room, clawing and biting like the madman he was.

Dr. Palmer said nothing, but the terror in his eyes told them everything they needed to know. He slipped on his coat and hurried out the door.

Antonia staggered after him, rubbing her eyes. She looked as if she were waking from a dream.

Epilogue

It seems only right that I should finish this tale, since my name, my voice, even my profoundest hopes and fears, have been appropriated to its telling. As the real Ned Hoffmann, I think I have a right to be heard. Ugly rumors have swirled around the Institute, especially since I was named Acting Director, and only a policy of candor and transparency can lay them to rest. If this were a mystery novel, I would have the opportunity—perhaps even the obligation—to tie up all the loose ends and explain the discoveries and deductions that brought the murderer to justice, or he would have saved me the trouble by issuing a full confession before blowing his brains out. But in real life the denouement is never so neat or conclusive. Miles Palmer has not confessed his crimes and in fact has retained a firm of shameless lawyers to proclaim his innocence. They may be correct in their assessment that the eyewitness accounts of twin schizophrenics will not stand up in court (despite the dramatic improvement Hunter and Antonia have shown in the weeks since Palmer was arrested). But for the slow-burning fury of Frank Lynch, who risked everything to keep the killer of Maria Morgan from slipping through his hands a second time, Palmer might never have seen the inside of a prison cell. Lynch followed him out the door that night and arrested him before he had a chance to return to the Institute and destroy the crucial evidence: the publicity photo, the kaleidoscope—both in a locked desk drawer; a note from the librarian, Miss Whipple, warning him that a blackmailer named Dubin was trying to reach Mrs. Paterson; and a packet of love letters from Maria Morgan, dated from shortly after she became his patient until the week before her death and culminating in the revelation that she had decided to leave her husband and marry Peter Bartolli. Further investigations of a more forensic nature—DNA tests and the like—are continuing and likely to be even more persuasive.

At the Institute, things are almost back to normal. Poor Jeff Gottlieb was terminated after being caught *in flagrante* with Julietta, who had the audacity to file a sexual harassment charge against the Institute. I like Jeff—he's not nearly as bad as Hunter portrayed him—and I hope he lands on his feet. With both Palmer and Gottlieb out of the picture, I am the only serious candidate for Director other than Dr. Neuberger (a staff psychiatrist who also treated Hunter before I arrived). Peter Bartolli would like to come back, but that is a change I intend to resist. The twins, as I've said, are doing amazingly well. Antonia chatters incessantly and she seems to be edging closer and closer to reality. Hunter swings between poles of depression and exhilaration, as he always has, but his speech is coherent and his memory is like a steel trap. He can describe in exhaustive detail not only his mother's murder but everything that happened since, including the way Palmer set him up for the deaths of Mrs. Paterson and Miss Whipple (after battering and strangling Mrs. Paterson, he roused Hunter and dropped him off in the mountains, taking care to use the same methods two days later when he murdered the poor librarian). From the moment Hunter found the old recording of Kreisleriana in the patient lounge—where Palmer had apparently left it—and began, note by note, second by second, to reconstruct his memory of the hour his mother died, to the dramatic epiphany in Peter Bartolli's basement theater when he finally broke through the years of fear and guilt to confront his memory of who the killer really was, and continuing since then as he has struggled to replace those years of drug-induced oblivion with something approximating reality—his recovery has been one of the most remarkable in the annals of psychiatry. I expect that in a few months he will be able to leave the Institute and begin a new life on his own.

As for me, in the past weeks I've spent many hours alone in my room trying to make sense of my life as seen through the lens of Hunter's tape-recorded narration. In the transcript, which I've read half a dozen times, his voice is so convincingly my own that even for me the events of that period have become impossible to unscramble completely. To anyone having the same problem I will say only this: If you think something happened because Hunter said it did, you should think very carefully about what happened to the people in his story when they weren't in his story—that is, when they were living in the third person, as it were. That's when they were real—and I include myself among them. Yet still I can't help thinking about Hunter's imagined history of my three "loves": Olympia, Julietta, and Antonia—three women I scarcely knew but will surely never forget. Antonia I loved in her innocence, in her very inability to connect with this miserable world. At the opposite pole stood Julietta, sensual, worldly, the embodiment of everything Antonia could never be; in fact I knew her only in my fantasies, which (I'm embarrassed to admit) Hunter captured with a certain degree of accuracy. Somewhere in the middle was Olympia, the artiste—both of this world and not of this world, ultimately incomprehensible, as if she were under the control of powers beyond my imagination. I loved them all, each in her own way; but they were impossible loves, mad loves, because each of them was absolute and therefore incomplete. And the more I thought about it, the closer I came to understanding the message Hunter was trying to send me, a message I had been doing everything in my power to resist: that all three of my loves were really the same woman. And that woman was Nicole.

I confessed this to Nicole one afternoon in a gloomy corridor in the county courthouse, where we waited for some proceedings against Palmer to grind on in a nearby courtroom. Unfortunately she was standing next to Dubin, a man I have come to despise not least because he and Nicole will soon be living together in New York. I've tried to counsel her against this relationship—a newly-reformed blackmailer hardly seems an improvement over the abusive Richard—but she remains adamantly loyal. "Of course all your loves were the same," she said. "Even to Hunter it was obvious that you were in love with me."

"It's ironic, isn't it?" I murmured, sidling closer as Dubin seemed to be distracted by some disturbance in the corridor. "I'm the one who's crazy. Or at the very least a fool. How am I going to get on with my life?"

"Divine is the art of forgetting," she smiled.

"I'd suggest you take up heavy drinking," Dubin said without turning around. "It can work wonders."

Just then Peter Bartolli emerged from the courtroom and huddled toward us with his overcoat hunched around his shoulders. He seemed a diminished figure, unsure in his movements and hesitant in his approach, with the indelible stamp of sadness in his dark, distant eyes. "Miles has pleaded not guilty," he reported.

"That's no surprise," Dubin said.

"I wonder"—Bartolli glanced sharply at Dubin, then let his gaze drift into the gloom of the empty corridor—"how the rest of us would plead if we were asked."

"What do you mean?"

"I know how I would plead. Miles has always been insanely jealous of me—I should have known that I was playing with fire carrying on an affair with his mistress. But at the time I had no inkling of what had really happened to Maria. It was only years later, when he ran me out of the Institute on a flimsy pretext after I started making progress with Antonia, that I began to suspect the truth."

"Were you the one who asked the librarian for her news clippings about Maria Morgan's death?"

"Yes; and then last year I foolishly set the stage for the whole tragedy to unfold again. I gave Hunter that video of *The Tales of Hoffmann* and sent my daughter to perform her interpretive dance, acting out the murder as I envisioned it taking place. I thought that by reviving unconscious memories I could not only cure Hunter and Antonia but expose the truth—and isn't that always a good thing?"

"Then when you started this…," Nicole hesitated.

"I had no idea what I was setting in motion," Bartolli completed her thought. "Even at the end I was groping in the dark: I had no inkling of the mad operatic fantasy Hunter would relate about my daughter and Julietta when Dr. Klein sat him in front of the tape recorder—and no expectation that my own desperate plan for Antonia would be the last act of that bizarre melodrama. Above all I had no idea how evil my brother really was. And for that reason I would plead guilty."

"Then the priests were right," Nicole said. "Denial of the Devil is a mortal sin, worse than denying God."

"Possibly," Bartolli agreed. "Because God forgives and the Devil doesn't."

"That's what Hoffmann was guilty of, isn't it?" Nicole said, and before I could protest she must have noticed the sickened look on my face. "I mean Hoffmann the poet," she laughed. "Not you, Ned."

Just a coincidence, I'm sure; nevertheless she seemed to be aiming her explanation at me. "Hoffmann was a Romantic," she said. "He believed in the spirit world and his whole purpose in life was to find a way into that world, through music, dreams, drugs— or madness, if that was what it took. He imagined that the spirit world was not only real, but fundamentally beautiful and good. What he didn't realize, or couldn't acknowledge, was that evil can be unlocked as easily as goodness and beauty—only more suddenly, more powerfully, more irrevocably. He and the other Romantics unlocked an evil force that couldn't be controlled, a hundred-year nightmare culminating in two world wars, the Holocaust and the other horrors of the modern age."

"You sound like the other Nicole," I said weakly, trying to change the subject. "The one in Hunter's story."

"No, I'm done with that Nicole. Among other vanities, I've given up the notion that there's some true plot that events have to follow. If you search for what's not there, you can be sure you'll never find it."

"Is that how you solved the mystery?"

"No," she said, moving closer to Dubin. "I solved the mystery by seeing what was in front of my face. There's nothing harder than seeing what's in plain view." She brushed her hand across Dubin's cheek, smoothing his moustache with her fingertips. "Isn't that right, Mr. Poe?"

That was the last time I saw Nicole. The next week it was Valentine's Day and she sent me a nice card from New York, with a little note diplomatically omitting any mention of Dubin. She reassured me that she was doing well and thanked me for the many hours I had spent with her. "You made me see myself as a character in my own story," she wrote. "I'll see you there for a long time to come, gently guiding me in the right direction, especially when someone else is trying to be the narrator of my life. In his own way Hunter did the same thing for you, and I hope you can benefit from it as I did. Here's a little poem I wish I could claim for my own (actually it's by William Blake):

> The rules of dreaming
> Are simple and few:
> True is false, and false is true;
> Forgotten fire lights
> Each moment's seeming,
> And all that happens
> Happens to you.

The End

AUTHOR'S NOTE AND ACKNOWLEDGEMENTS

I've dreamed of writing about *The Tales of Hoffmann* ever since I watched the Michael Powell/Emeric Pressburger film starring Moira Shearer and Robert Rounseville (the first of many performances I've seen of this beautiful work). My interest in the opera led to a study of E.T.A. Hoffmann, a writer known in the English-speaking world almost entirely through derivative works (*The Tales of Hoffmann*, *The Nutcracker*, Kreisleriana, *Coppélia*, Freud's essay on "The Uncanny") and the stream of influence that traces back to him (Schumann, Poe, Baudelaire, Dumas, Offenbach, Dostoevsky). Unconsciously standing knee-deep in that stream of influence, I recalled an image (Hoffmannesque, without my knowing it) which had occurred to me as an idea for a story: a patient in a mental hospital who sits down and flawlessly plays a difficult piece on the piano (it would have to be Kreisleriana), without the benefit of any musical training or experience. Where did that music come from? Where does any music come from? Does it come from a higher, spiritual world (as Hoffmann and his Romantic contemporaries might have asked in the early nineteenth century)? Or from deep in the unconscious (as Freud and other realists might have asked fifty years later)?

Such were the speculations that led me to *The Rules of Dreaming*. I got off to a bad start by reading Hoffmann's amazing but flawed novel, *Die Elixiere des Teufels* (translated as *The Devil's Elixirs* by Ronald Taylor and recently reissued by OneWorld Classics; also available in a translation by Ian Sumter published by Grosvenor House and in an old and not very accurate translation entitled *The Devil's Elixir* republished by BiblioBazaar), with its incoherent plot involving madness, murder and multiple identities. Better to stick with the Offenbach opera, with its incoherent plot involving—madness, murder and multiple identities! From there it was a small step to psychiatry, blackmail, puppetry, sexual obsession, past life regression, and the nature of evil.

Offenbach's *Les Contes d'Hoffmann* has a fascinating history, much of which has come to light in recent years as new manuscripts have been discovered and published, by Michael Kaye, Fritz Oeser and others, resulting in innovative interpretations and a good deal of controversy.

A DVD recording of the Powell/Pressburger movie is available with an intriguing commentary by Martin Scorsese, whose film making has been influenced by a lifelong fascination with the opera and this film. Also well worth watching is the 1995 Opéra de Lyon production/adaptation based on the Michael Kaye edition, conducted by Kent Nagano and released on DVD under the title *Des Contes d'Hoffmann*. In this version, Hoffmann is an inmate in an insane asylum.

I am greatly indebted to Heather Hadlock's outstanding monograph, *Mad Loves: Women and Music in Offenbach's Les Contes d'Hoffmann* (Princeton University Press, 2000), which contains a wealth of information and insights about the opera and its history.

Many of Hoffmann's most characteristic stories are included in *The Best Tales of Hoffmann*, edited with an excellent introduction by E. F. Bleiler (Dover Publications, 1967). Another collection in English is *Tales of Hoffmann*, selected and translated with an introduction by R.J. Hollingdale (Penguin Books, 1982).

Freud's classic essay, "The Uncanny," is included in the collection entitled *The Uncanny*, translated by David McLintock (Penguin Books, 2003).

Bruce Hartman lives with his wife in Philadelphia. His previous novel, *Perfectly Healthy Man Drops Dead*, was published by Salvo Press in 2008. Special thanks to Martha, Jack, Tom, Kelly and Isabel for helping pull this project through.

19499603R00174

Made in the USA
Charleston, SC
27 May 2013